Critics rave about *Colette*

"There is probably no other body of works which captures the full experience of womanhood as inclusively and incisively...To read Colette today is to find ourselves mirrored in an immediacy that is almost fifty years old."
  —*San Francisco Review of Books*

"Colette is entirely at home with the physical, with touch, sight, feel, and smell."
  —*The New Statesman*

"The greatest of French women writers!"
  —*Mademoiselle*

"Colette has a special ability to write...about love and sex with a combination of the sensuous and a sense of fun...well disciplined elegance, clarity and forcefulness...one of the notable women writers of her time anywhere."
  —*San Francisco Chronicle*

"Colette was an innovator, as well as a master, of the art of fiction."
  —*The New York Times*

Chéri

and

The Last of Chéri

....

Chéri

and

The Last of Chéri

....

COLETTE

WINGS BOOKS

New York · Avenel, New Jersey

This 1995 edition is published by Wings Books,
distributed by Random House Value Publishing, Inc.,
40 Engelhard Avenue, Avenel, New Jersey 07001,
by arrangement with Farrar, Straus and Giroux, Inc.

Random House
New York · Toronto · London · Sydney · Auckland

Book design by Kathryn W. Plosica

Printed and bound in the United States of America

Library of Congress Cataloging-in-Publication Data

Colette, 1873–1954.
    [Chéri. English]
    Chéri ; and, The last of Chéri / Colette.
        p.   cm.
    ISBN 0-517-12260-X
    1. Man-woman relationships—France—Fiction.   2. Middle-aged
women—France—Fiction.   3. Young men—France—Fiction.   I. Colette,
1873–1954. Fin de Chéri. English.   II. Title.   III. Title: Last of Chéri.
PQ2605.O28C513   1995
843'.912—dc20   94-30318
                                                                  CIP

8 7 6 5 4 3 2 1

CONTENTS

Chéri

"Give it me, Léa, give me your pearl necklace! Do you hear me, Léa? Give me your pearls!"

No answer came from the huge brass-bedecked wrought-iron bedstead that glimmered in the shadows like a coat of mail.

"Why won't you let me have your necklace? It looks every bit as well on me as on you—even better!"

At the snap of the clasp, ripples spread over the lace frilled sheets, and from their midst rose two magnificent thin-wristed arms, lifting on high two lovely lazy hands.

"Leave it alone, Chéri! You've been playing long enough with that necklace."

"It amuses me. . . . Are you frightened I'll steal it?"

He was capering about in front of the sun-drenched rosy pink curtains—a graceful demon, black against a glowing furnace; but when he pranced back towards the bed, he turned white again from top to toe, in his white silk pyjamas and white Moorish slippers.

"I'm not frightened," the soft, deep voice answered from the bed. "But you'll wear out the thread. Those pearls are heavy."

"They certainly are," Chéri said with due respect. "Whoever gave you this lot never meant to make light of you!"

He was standing in front of a pier-glass framed in the space between two windows, gazing at the reflection of a very youthful, very good-looking young man, neither too short nor too tall, hair with the blue sheen of a blackbird's plumage. He un-buttoned his pyjamas, displaying a hard, darkish chest, curved like a shield; and the whites of his dark eyes, his teeth, and the pearls of the necklace gleamed on the over-all rosy glow of the room.

"Take off that necklace!" The female voice was insistent. "Do you hear what I say?"

The young man, motionless in front of his image, laughed softly to himself: "Yes, yes, I heard you. I know so well you're terrified I'll make off with it!"

"No, I'm not. But if I did offer it to you, you're quite capable of taking it."

He ran to the bed and bounded into it. "You bet I am! I rise above the conventions. Personally, I think it's idiotic for a man to allow a woman to give him a single pearl for a tie-pin, or two for a pair of studs, and then to consider himself beyond the pale if she gives him fifty. . . ."

"Forty-nine."

"Forty-nine—as if I hadn't counted! I dare you to say they don't look well on me! Or that I'm ugly!"

Léa sat up in bed. "No, I won't say that. For one thing, because you'd never believe me. But can't you learn to laugh without crinkling up your nose like that? I suppose you won't be happy till you've wrinkles all up the side of your nose!"

He stopped laughing at once, let the skin on his forehead relax, and drew in the fold under his chin like a coquettish old woman. They looked at each other in open hostility—she, lean-ing on her elbow in a flurry of frills and lace; he, sitting side-saddle on the edge of the bed. He was thinking 'Who's she to talk of any wrinkles I may have one day?' and she 'Why is he so ugly when he laughs?—he who's the very picture of beauty!' She thought for a moment, then finished aloud: "It's because you look so ill-natured when you're joking. You never laugh except unkindly—*at* people, and that makes you ugly. You're often ugly."

"That's not true!" Chéri exclaimed, crossly.

Anger knitted his eyebrows close above his nose, magnified his eyes, glittering with insolence behind a palisade of lashes, and parted the chaste bow of his disdainful mouth. Léa smiled to see him as she loved him best: rebellious only to become submissive, enchained lightly but powerless to free himself. She put a hand on his young head, which impatiently shook off the yoke. Like someone quieting an animal, she murmured, "There, there! What is it? What is it, then?"

He fell upon her big beautiful shoulder, nuzzling and butting his way into his favourite resting-place with eyes already shut, seeking his customary long morning sleep in the protection of her arms. But Léa pushed him away. "None of that now, Chéri! You're having luncheon with our national Harpy, and it's already twenty to twelve!"

"Not really? I'm lunching at the old girl's? You too?"

Lazily Léa settled deeper into the bed.

"Not me, I'm off duty. I'll go for coffee at half-past two, or tea at six, or for a cigarette at a quarter to eight. Don't worry; she'll always see enough of me. And besides, I've not been asked."

Chéri's sulky face lit up with malice.

"I know, I know why! We're going to have high society. We're going to have the fair Marie-Laure, and that poisonous child of hers."

Léa brought her big blue wandering eyes to rest.

"Oh, really! The little girl's charming. Less so than her mother, but charming. Now take off that necklace, once and for all."

"Pity," Chéri sighed, as he undid the clasp. "It would look so well in the trousseau."

Léa raised herself on her elbow: "What trousseau?"

"Mine," Chéri said with ludicrous self-importance. "*My* trousseau, full of *my* jewels, for *my* marriage!"

He bounded in the air, executed a perfect *entrechat-six*,

returned to earth, butted his way through the door-curtains, and disappeared, shouting: "My bath, Rose! And quick about it! I'm lunching at the old girl's!"

'That's that,' Léa thought. 'We'll have a lake in the bath-room and eight towels floating in it, and razor scrapings in the basin. If only I had two bathrooms!'

But, as on former occasions, she soon saw that this would mean getting rid of a wardrobe and lopping off a corner of her dressing-room, and so concluded, as on former occasions: 'I shall simply have to put up with it till Chéri gets married.'

She lay down again on her back and noticed that Chéri, undressing the night before, had thrown his socks on the man-telpiece, his pants on the writing-table, his tie round the neck of her portrait bust. She could not help smiling at this hasty mas-culine disorder, and half closed her large tranquil eyes. Their blue was as beautiful as ever, and so were the thick chestnut lashes.

At the age of forty-nine, Léonie Vallon, called Léa de Lonval, was nearing the end of a successful career as a richly kept courtesan. She was a good creature, and life had spared her the more flattering catastrophes and exalted sufferings. She made a secret of the date of her birth; but willingly admitted—with a look of voluptuous condescension for Chéri's special benefit—that she was approaching the age when she could in-dulge in a few creature comforts. She liked order, fine linen, wines in their prime, and carefully planned meals at home. From an idolised young blonde she had become a rich middle-aged *demi-mondaine* without ever attracting any outrageous pub-licity. Not that she went in for any pretences. Her friends re-membered a Four-in-Hand Meet at Auteuil, about 1895, when the sub-editor of *Gil Blas* had addressed her as "dear artist" and she had answered: "Artist! Oh come, my good friend, my lovers must have been telling tales. . . ."

Her contemporaries were jealous of her imperturbable good health, and the younger women, whose figures were padded out in front and behind after the fashion of 1912, scoffed at her opulent bust. Young and old alike envied her the possession of Chéri.

"Though, good heavens!" Léa used to say, "there's no reason why they should. They're welcome to him! I don't keep him on a lead. He goes out by himself."

But in this she was not altogether speaking the truth, for she was proud of a liaison—sometimes, in her weakness for the truth, referring to it as "an adoption"—that had lasted six years.

'Trousseau,' Léa said over again. 'Marriage for Chéri! It's not possible, it's not . . . human . . . you can't give an innocent girl to Chéri! Why, it would be throwing a doe to the hounds! People don't know what Chéri is!'

As if telling the beads of a rosary, she ran her fingers over the necklace which Chéri had tossed on the bed. She put it away at night now because, with his passion for fine pearls and his fondness for playing with them in the morning, he would have noticed too often that her throat had thickened and was not nearly so white, with the muscles under its skin growing slack. She fastened the pearls round her neck without getting up, and took a hand-mirror from the bedside-table.

'I look like a gardener's wife,' was her unflattering comment, 'a market-gardener's wife. A market-gardener's wife in Normandy, off to the potato-fields wearing a pearl necklace. I might as well stick an ostrich feather in my nose—and that's being polite!'

She shrugged her shoulders, severely critical of everything she no longer loved in herself: the vivid complexion, healthy, a little too ruddy—an open-air complexion, well suited to emphasise the pure intensity of her eyes, with their varying shades of blue. Her proud nose still won her approval. "Marie-Antoinette's nose!" Chéri's mother was in the habit of saying, without ever forgetting to add: "and in another two years, our Léa will have a chin like Louis Seize'." Her mouth, with its even row of teeth, seldom opened in a peal of laughter; but she smiled often,

a smile that set off to perfection the lazy flutter of her large eyes
—a smile a hundred times lauded, sung, and photographed—a
deep, confiding smile one never tired of watching.

As for her body—"Everyone knows," Léa would say, "that
a well-made body lasts a long time." She could still afford to
show her body, pink and white, endowed with the long legs and
straight back of a naiad on an Italian fountain; the dimpled hips,
the high-slung breasts, "would last," Léa used to say, "till well
after Chéri's wedding."

She got out of bed, and, slipping into a wrap, went to draw
back the long curtains. The noonday sun poured into the gay,
rosy, over-decorated room. Its luxury dated: double lace curtains, rose-bud watered silk on the walls, gilded woodwork, and
antique furniture upholstered in modern silks. Léa refused to
give up either this cosy room or its bed, a massive and indestructible masterpiece of wrought iron and brass, grim to the
eye and cruel to the shins.

"Come, come!" Chéri's mother protested, "it's not as bad
as all that. Personally, I like this room. It belongs to a period. It
has a style of its own. It suggests La Païva."

The remembrance of this dig made Léa smile as she pinned
up her hair. She hurriedly powdered her face on hearing two
doors slam, and the thud of a male foot colliding with some
delicate piece of furniture. Chéri came back into the room in
shirt and trousers, his ears white with talcum powder. He was in
an aggressive mood.

"Where's my tie-pin? What a wretched hole this is! Have
they taken to pinching the jewellery?"

"Marcel must have stuck it in his tie to go to the market,"
Léa gravely replied.

Chéri, who had little or no sense of humour, was brought
up short by the little quip like an ant by a lump of coal. He
stopped his angry pacing up and down, and found nothing better to say than: "Charming! and what about my boots?"

"Your what?"

"The calf, of course!"

Léa smiled up at him from her dressing-table, too affectionately. "You said it, not I," she murmured in caressing tones.

"The day when a woman loves me for my brains," he retorted, "I shall be done for. Meanwhile I must have my pin and my boots."

"What for? You don't wear a tie-pin with a lounge suit, and you've got one pair on already."

Chéri stamped his foot. "I've had enough of this! There's nobody here to look after me, and I'm sick of it all."

Léa put down her comb. "Very well, say goodbye to it all for good!"

He shrugged his shoulders, like a young tough. "You wouldn't like it if I did!"

"Be off with you! I hate guests who complain of the cooking and leave bits and pieces all over the place and cream-cheese sticking to the mirrors. Go back to your sainted mother, my child, and stay there."

Unable to meet Léa's gaze, he lowered his eyes, and broke out into schoolboy protests. "Soon I shan't be allowed to open my mouth! Anyhow, you'll let me have your motor to go to Neuilly?"

"No."

"Why not?"

"Because I'm going out in it myself at two, and because the chauffeur is having his dinner."

"Where are you going at two?"

"To say my prayers. But if you need three francs for a taxi . . . Idiot," she added tenderly. "At two I'll probably come to your lady mother's for coffee. Does that satisfy you?"

He tossed his head like a young buck. "You bite my head off, you won't give me anything I ask for; they hide my things away, they . . ."

"Will you never learn to dress yourself?"

She took the tie from Chéri's hands and tied it for him.

"There! And that frightful purple tie. . . . However, it's just the thing for the fair Marie-Laure and family. . . . And

you wanted to wear a pearl on top of all that! You little dago.
. . . Why not earrings into the bargain?"

His defences were down. Blissful, languid, irresolute, supine, he surrendered again to a lazy happiness and closed his
eyes. . . .

"Nounoune darling . . ." he murmured.

She brushed the hair off his ears, combed a straighter part-
ing in the bluish locks of his black hair, dabbed a little scent on
his temples, and gave him a quick kiss, unable to resist the
tempting mouth so close to her own.

Chéri opened his eyes, and his lips, then stretched out his
hands.

She moved away. "No. It's a quarter to one! Be off now,
and don't let me see you again!"

"Never?"

"Never," she laughed back at him with uncontrollable tenderness.

Left to herself, she smiled proudly, and a sharp little sigh of
defeated desire escaped her as she listened to Chéri's footsteps
crossing the courtyard. She saw him open and close the gates,
drift away on his winged feet, only to encounter the adoring
glances of three shop-girls walking along arm in arm.

"Lawks! He's too good to be true! Let's touch him to see if
he's real!"

But Chéri took it all for granted and did not even turn
round.

"My bath, Rose! Tell the manicurist she can go, it's far too late now. My blue coat and skirt—the new one—the blue hat with the white under brim, and the little shoes with the straps . . . No, wait . . ."

Léa, with one leg across the other, rubbed her ankle and shook her head.

"No, the blue kid laced boots. My legs are a little swollen to-day. It's the heat."

Her elderly maid, butterfly-capped, raised understanding eyes to Léa. "It's . . . it's the heat," she repeated obediently, shrugging her shoulders as much as to say: "We know . . . Nothing lasts for ever. . . ."

With Chéri out of the house, Léa became herself again, very much alive, cheerful, and on the spot. Within an hour, she had been given her bath, followed by a spirit-rub scented with sandal-wood, and was ready dressed, hatted, and shod. While the curling-tongs were heating, she found time to run through the butler's book and send for Emile, the footman, and call his attention to the blue haze on one of the looking-glasses. She ran an experienced eye—rarely taken in—over everything in the room, and lunched in solitary bliss, with a smile for the dry Vouvray and for the June strawberries, served, with their stalks, on a plate of Rubelles enamel as green as a tree-frog after rain. Someone in the past who appreciated good food must have chosen the huge Louis Seize looking-glasses and the English furniture of the same period, for this rectangular dining-room:

light, airy side-boards, high pedestalled dumb-waiters, spindly yet strong Sheraton chairs, in a dark wood with delicate swags. The looking-glasses and the massive silver caught the full light of day, with a touch of green reflected from the trees in the Avenue Bugeaud. Léa, as she ate, examined a fork for any suspicion of pink cleaning-powder left in the chasing, and half-closed one eye the better to judge the quality of the polish on the dark wood. Standing behind her, the butler watched this performance nervously.

"Marcel!" Léa said, "for the last week or so, the wax on your floors has been smeary."

"Does Madame think so?"

"Madame does think so. Add a little turpentine while you're melting it in a double saucepan; it's quite easy to do again. You brought up the Vouvray a little too soon. Close the shutters as soon as you've cleared the table; we're in for a heat-wave."

"Very good, Madame. Will Monsieur Ch—Monsieur Peloux be dining?"

"Probably. . . . No *crème-surprise* to-night. We'll just have a strawberry water ice. Coffee in the boudoir."

As she rose from the table, straight and tall, the shape of her legs visible under a dress that moulded her hips, she had ample time to note the "Madame is beautiful" in the butler's discreet glance, and this did not displease her.

"Beautiful," Léa whispered on her way up to the boudoir. "No. . . . No longer. I have now to wear something white near my face, and very pale pink underclothes and tea-gowns. Beautiful! Pish. . . . I hardly need to be that any longer."

All the same, she allowed herself no siesta in the painted silk boudoir, when she had finished with coffee and the newspapers. And it was with battle written on her face that she gave her chauffeur the order: "To Madame Peloux's."

The tree-lined road through the Bois, dry beneath the young, already wind-faded June foliage—the toll-gate—Neuilly—

Boulevard d'Inkermann—'How many times have I come this way?' Léa wondered. She began to count, then tired of counting and softened her step on the gravel outside Madame Peloux's house to overhear any sounds coming from it.

'They're in the garden-room,' she concluded.

She had put on more powder before approaching the house and tightened the fine-meshed, misty blue veil under her chin. Her answer to the manservant's formal request to pass through the house was: "No; I'd rather go round by the garden."

A real garden—almost a park—completely surrounded the vast white villa, typical of the outer suburbs of Paris. Madame Peloux's villa had been called "a country residence" in the days when Neuilly was still on the outskirts of Paris. This was apparent from the stables, converted into garages, the other offices with their kennels and wash-houses, not to mention the size of the billiard-room, entrance hall and dining-room.

"This is a handsome investment of Madame Peloux's," her female devotees never tired of repeating—the old toadies who, in exchange for a dinner or a glass of brandy, came there to take a hand against her at bezique or poker. And they added: "But then, where has Madame Peloux not got money invested?"

Walking along in the shade of the acacia trees, between trellised roses and huge clumps of rhododendrons in full blaze, Léa could hear the murmur of voices, and, rising above it, Madame Peloux's shrill nasal trumpet notes and Chéri's dry cackle.

'That child's got an ugly laugh,' she thought. She paused a moment to listen more attentively to a new feminine note; weak, pleasing, quickly drowned by the redoubtable trumpeting. 'That must be the girl,' she said to herself, and a few quick steps brought her to the garden-room with its glass front, from which Madame Peloux burst out with a "Here comes our beautiful friend!"

A little round barrel of a woman, Madame Peloux—in reality Mademoiselle Peloux—had been a ballet-dancer from her tenth to her sixteenth year. Occasionally Léa would search for some trace in Madame Peloux that might recall the once chubby little fair-haired Eros, or the later dimpled nymph, and found nothing except the big implacable eyes, the delicate aggressive nose, and a still coquettish way of standing with her feet in 'the fifth position', like the members of the *corps de ballet*.

Chéri, coming to life in the depths of a rocking-chair, kissed Léa's hand with involuntary grace and ruined his gesture by exclaiming: "Hang it all! you've put on a veil again, and I loathe veils."

"Will you leave her alone!" Madame Peloux interposed. "You must never ask a woman why she is wearing a veil. We'll never be able to do anything with him," she said to Léa affectionately.

Two women had risen to their feet in the golden shade of a straw blind. One, in mauve, rather coldly offered her hand to Léa, who looked her over from head to foot.

"Goodness, how lovely you are, Marie-Laure! you're perfection itself!"

Marie-Laure deigned to smile. She was a red-haired young woman with brown eyes, whose physical presence alone was enough to take your breath away. She drew attention, almost coquettishly, to the other young woman, by saying: "But would you have recognised my daughter Edmée?"

Léa held out a hand which the girl was reluctant to shake.

"I should have known you, my child, but a schoolgirl alters so quickly, and Marie-Laure alters only to become always more disconcertingly lovely. Are you quite finished with school now?"

"I should hope so, I should hope so," exclaimed Madame Peloux. "You can't go on for ever, hiding her under a bushel, such a miracle of grace and charm, and she's nineteen already!"

"Eighteen," said Marie-Laure, sweetly.

"Eighteen, eighteen! . . . Yes of course, eighteen! Léa, you remember? This child was just making her first Communion the year that Chéri ran away from school, surely you remember? Yes, yes, you did, you little good-for-nothing, you ran away and Léa and I were driven nearly out of our wits!"

"I remember perfectly," Léa said, and she exchanged an imperceptible little nod with Marie-Laure—something corresponding to the *'touché'* of a punctilious fencer.

"You must get her married soon, you must get her married soon!" pursued Madame Peloux, who never failed to repeat a basic truth at least twice. "We'll all come to the wedding."

She brandished her little arms in the air, and the young girl glanced at her with ingenuous alarm.

'She's just the daughter for Marie-Laure,' thought Léa, gazing at her more closely. 'She has all her mother's dazzling qualities, but in a quieter key: fluffy, ash-brown hair, that looks as if it were powdered; frightened, secretive eyes, and a mouth she avoids opening even to speak or smile. . . . Exactly what Marie-Laure needs as a foil—but how she must hate her!'

Madame Peloux insinuated a maternal smile between Léa and the young girl: "You ought to have seen how well these two young people were getting on together in the garden!"

She pointed to where Chéri stood smoking a cigarette on the other side of the glass partition, his cigarette-holder clenched between his teeth, and his head tilted back to avoid the smoke. The three women looked at the young man who—forehead held at an angle, eyes half-shut, feet together, motionless —looked for all the world like a winged figure hovering dreamily in the air. Léa did not fail to observe the expression of fright and subjugation in the girl's eyes, and she took pleasure in making her tremble by touching her on the arm. Edmée quivered from head to foot, withdrew her arm, and whispered almost savagely, "What?"

"Nothing," Léa replied, "I dropped my glove."

"Come along, Edmée!" Marie-Laure called, negligently.

Silent and docile, the girl walked towards Madame Peloux, who flapped her wings: "Leaving already? Surely not? We must meet again soon, we must meet again soon!"

"It's late," Marie-Laure said, "and you'll be expecting any number of people as it's Sunday afternoon. The child is not accustomed to company."

"Of course not, of course not," Madame Peloux said tenderly. "She's had such a sheltered existence . . . such a lonely life!"

Marie-Laure smiled, and Léa gave her a look as much as to say, "That's one for you!"

"But we'll call again soon."

"Thursday, Thursday! Léa, you'll come to luncheon on Thursday?"

"I'll be here," Léa answered.

Chéri had rejoined Edmée at the entrance to the room and stood beside her, disdaining all conversation. He heard Léa's promise, and turned round: "Splendid, then we can go for a run in the motor."

"Yes, yes, just the thing for you young people," Madame Peloux insisted, touched by his proposal. "Edmée can sit in front next to Chéri, at the wheel, and the rest of us will go at the back. Youth at the helm, youth at the helm! Chéri, my love, will you ask for Marie-Laure's motor?"

Her small stumpy feet kept slipping on the gravel, but she managed to take her two visitors to the corner of the path, where she handed them over to Chéri. On her return, she found that Léa had taken off her hat and was smoking a cigarette.

"Aren't they sweet, those two!" Madame Peloux gasped. "Don't you think so, Léa?"

"Delicious," Léa breathed out in the same puff as her cigarette smoke. "But really, that Marie-Laure!"

"What's Marie-Laure been up to?" asked Chéri, as he rejoined them.

"How lovely she is!"

"Ah! Ah!" Madame Peloux began in formal assent. "That's true, that's true. She has been really lovely."

Chéri and Léa caught each other's eye and laughed.

"Has been?", Léa emphasized the past tense. "But she's the picture of youth. Not a single wrinkle! And she can wear the palest mauve, such a foul colour! I loathe it and it loathes me."

Madame Peloux raised her big pitiless eyes and thin nose from her brandy-glass.

"The picture of youth, the picture of youth!" yapped Madame Peloux. "Pardon me, pardon me! Marie-Laure had Edmée in 1895, no . . . '94. She'd just run away with a singing-teacher, leaving Khalil Bey flat, though he'd given her the famous pink diamond which . . . No, no! Wait! . . . That must have been the year before!"

The trumpet notes were shrill and off key. Léa put a hand over her ear, and Chéri declared, with some feeling: "Everything would be heavenly on an afternoon like this, if only we could be spared my mother's voice!"

She looked at her son with no sign of anger, accustomed to his insolence. Dignified, feet dangling, she settled herself back in a basket chair too high for her short legs. In one hand she warmed her glass of brandy. Léa, rocking herself gently to and fro, glanced occasionally at Chéri, who lay sprawled on a cool cane settee, coat unbuttoned, a cigarette dying between his lips, a lock of hair over one eyebrow. 'He's a handsome young blackguard,' she thought admiringly.

There they remained, peacefully side by side, making no effort to talk or be sociable, happy after their own fashion. Years of close familiarity rendered silence congenial, and Chéri slipped back into his lethargy, Léa into her calm. As the afternoon became hotter, Madame Peloux pulled her narrow skirt up to her knees, displaying her tight little sailor's calves, and Chéri ripped off his tie—reproved by Léa in an audible "Tch, tch."

"Oh! leave the child alone," Madame Peloux protested, as from the depths of a dream. "It's much too hot! Would you care for a kimono, Léa?"

"No, thank you. I'm perfectly comfortable."

Their unbuttoned siestas disgusted her. Never once had her

17

young lover caught her untidily dressed, or with her blouse undone, or in her bedroom slippers during the day. "Naked, if need be," she would say, "but squalid, never!"

She picked up her picture paper again, but did not read it. 'These Pelouxs—mother and son alike!' she thought dreamily. 'They've only to sit themselves down at a good meal or in the heart of the countryside and—snap!—the mother whisks off her stays and the son his waistcoat. They behave like publicans out on a holiday, the pair of them.' She cast a vindictive eye on one of the publicans in question, and saw that he had fallen asleep, his eyelashes spread against his pallid cheeks, his mouth closed. His upper lip, lit from below, reflected two silver pinpoints of light at the twin curves of its delicious Cupid's bow, and Léa was forced to admit that he looked far more like a sleeping god than a licensed victualler.

Without moving from her chair, she gently plucked the lighted cigarette from between Chéri's fingers and put it in the ash-tray. The hand of the sleeper relaxed and the tapering fingers, tipped with cruel nails, drooped like wilting flowers: a hand not strictly feminine, yet a trifle prettier than one could have wished; a hand she had kissed a hundred times—not in slavish devotion—but kissed for the pleasure of it, for its scent.

From behind her paper, she glanced at Madame Peloux. Was she asleep too? Léa always liked to remain awake while mother and son dozed, allowing her a quiet hour's self-communing in the dappled sunlight of a broiling afternoon. But Madame Peloux was not asleep. She was sitting bolt upright in her wickerwork chair, like a Buddha staring into space, and sipping her *fine-champagne* with the absorption of an alcoholic baby.

'Why doesn't she go to sleep?' Léa wondered. 'It's Sunday. She's lunched well. She's expecting her sponging old cronies to drop in for her five o'clock tea. By rights she ought to be having a snooze. If she's not snoozing, it's because she's up to some devilment or other.'

They had known each other for twenty-five years. Theirs

was the hostile intimacy of light women, enriched and then cast aside by one man, ruined by another: the tetchy affection of rivals stalking one another's first wrinkle or white hair. Theirs was the friendship of two practical women of the world, both adepts at the money game; but one of them a miser, and the other a sybarite. These bonds count. Rather late in their day, a stronger bond had come to link them more closely: Chéri.

Léa could remember Chéri as a little boy—a marvel of beauty with long curls. When quite small he was known as Fred, and had not yet been nicknamed Chéri.

Sometimes forgotten and sometimes adored, Chéri grew up among wan housemaids and tall sardonic men-servants. Although his birth had mysteriously brought wealth to the house, no "Fräulein", no "Miss" was ever to be seen at Chéri's side; and his mother had preserved him, to the accompaniment of piercing shrieks, from "these ghouls".

"Charlotte Peloux, you belong to another age." The speaker was the moribund, mummified, but indestructible Baron de Berthellemy. "Charlotte Peloux, in you I salute the only light woman who ever had the courage to bring up her son as the son of a tart! You belong to another age! You never read, you never travel, you make a point of knowing your neighbour's business, and you abandon your child to the tender mercies of the servants. How perfect! How absolutely About![1] . . . Or, better still, how like a novel by Gustav Droz. . . . And to think that you've never heard of either! . . ."

Chéri had enjoyed the full freedom of a profligate upbringing. When barely able to lisp, he was quick to pick up all the backstairs gossip. He shared in the clandestine suppers of the kitchen. His ablutions varied between milky immersions in his mother's orris-root baths and scanty cat-licks with the corner of

[1] Edmond About (*Roman d'un brave homme*, etc.) and Gustav Droz (*Monsieur, Madame et Bébé*, etc.) light popular novelists of the last half of the nineteenth century, some of whose books appeared in English translation. (*Papa, Mamma and Baby*, illustrated by Morin 1887.)

a towel. He suffered from indigestion after a surfeit of sweets, or from pangs of hunger when no one remembered to give him his supper. He was wretchedly bored at every Battle of Flowers, where Charlotte Peloux would exhibit him—half-naked and catching cold—sitting on drenched roses; but it so happened, when he was twelve, that he had a glorious adventure in an illicit gambling-den, when an American woman allowed him to play with a fistful of louis d'or, and called him 'a little masterpiece'. At about the same time, Madame Peloux imposed a tutor on her son—an Abbé, whom she packed off at the end of ten months "because," she confessed, "whenever I caught sight of that black robe trailing along the passages, it made me think I was housing a female relation: and God knows there are few things more depressing than having a poor relation to stay!"

At the age of fourteen, Chéri had a taste of school. He didn't believe in it. He broke prison and ran away. Madame Peloux not only found the energy to incarcerate him a second time, but also, when faced with her son's tears and insults, took to her heels with hands over her ears screaming, "I can't bear the sight of it! I can't bear the sight of it!" So sincere were her cries that she actually fled from Paris, in the company of a man who was young but far from scrupulous. Two years later she came back, alone. It was the last time she succumbed to an amorous impulse.

She found, on her return, that Chéri had shot up too fast; that his cheeks were hollow and his eyes black-ringed; that he dressed like a stable-lad and spoke with a worse accent than ever. She beat her breast, and snatched him back from the boarding school. He utterly refused to work; demanded horses, carriages, jewels; insisted on a substantial monthly allowance; and, when his mother began to beat her breast and shriek like a pea-hen, he put a stop to her cries by saying: "Madame Peloux, ma'am, don't carry on so. My venerable mother, if no one except me drags you down into the gutter, you're likely to die a comfortable death in your downy bed; I don't altogether fancy a trustee for my estate. Your cash is mine. Let me go my own way! Men friends cost next to nothing—a dinner and a bottle of champagne. As for the fair sex, surely Ma'me Peloux, seeing that I take after you, you can trust me not to treat 'em to more than a trinket—if that!"

He pirouetted about while she shed tears and proclaimed herself the happiest of mothers. When Chéri began buying motor-cars, she trembled once more; but he simply advised her: "Keep an eye on the petrol, Ma'me Peloux, if you please!" and sold his horses. He was not above checking the two chauffeurs' books. His calculations were quick and accurate, and the figures he jotted down on slips of paper—dashed off rapidly, round and regular—were in marked contrast to his rather slow and childish handwriting.

At seventeen he was like a little old man, always fussing over his expenses: still good-looking—but skinny and short-winded. More than once Madame Peloux ran into him on the cellar steps, coming up from checking the bottles in the racks and bins.

"Would you believe it?" she said to Léa. "It's too wonderful."

"Much too wonderful," Léa answered, "he'll come to a bad end. Chéri! Show me your tongue!"

He put out his tongue, made a face, and showed other signs of disrespect. Léa took no notice. She was too intimate a friend, a sort of doting godmother, whom he called by her Christian name.

"Is it true," Léa enquired, "that you were seen last night at a bar, sitting on old Lili's knees?"

"Her knees!" scoffed Chéri. "She hasn't had any for ages. They foundered years ago."

"Isn't it true," Léa persisted with greater severity, "that she made you drink gin laced with pepper? You know gin is bad for the breath!"

On one occasion, Chéri, hurt, snapped back at Léa: "I can't

think why you bother me with all these questions. You must have seen what I was up to; you were tucked away in that cubby-hole at the back, with Patron your prize-fighter friend."

"That's perfectly correct," Léa answered, unmoved. "There's nothing of the dissipated schoolboy about Patron. He has other attractions, and a good deal more to recommend him than a perky little face and two black rings round his eyes."

That week Chéri had been out on the razzle in Montmartre and les Halles, consorting with ladies of the town who called him "poppet" and "my pet vice", but he had got no kick out of it: he suffered from migraines and a dry cough. Madame Peloux poured out her heart-breaking woes—"Life is nothing but a series of crosses for us mothers"—to her masseuse, to her stay-maker, Madame Ribot, to old Lili, to the Baron de Berthellemy, and thus passed painlessly from the state of being the happiest-of-parents to that of the martyr-mother.

A night in June, when Madame Peloux and Léa and Chéri were together in the garden-room at Neuilly, was to change the destinies of the young man and the middle-aged woman. Chéri's friends had gone off for the evening—little Baxter, a wholesale wine-merchant, and the Vicomte Desmond, a hanger-on of his, barely of age, difficult and arrogant—and so Chéri had returned to the maternal fold, and habit had drawn Léa there also.

For one more evening, in a whole sequence of such occasions, these two women, each suspicious of the other, found themselves together. They had known each other for twenty years; they shared a past made up of similarly dull evenings; they lacked other friends; and, in their later days, they had become mistrustful, self-indulgent, and cut off from the world, as women are who have lived only for love.

Both were staring in silence at Chéri, who never spoke. Madame Peloux lacked the strength to take her son's health in hand, but hated Léa a little more each time she bent her white neck and glowing cheeks over Chéri's pallid cheek and transparent ear. She would willingly have bled that healthy female neck, already wrinkled by the so-called lines of Venus, in order to give a touch of colour to her slim lily-green son: yet it never occurred to her to take her darling away to the country.

"Chéri, why are you drinking brandy?" Léa scolded.

"Out of politeness to Ma'me Peloux—who would otherwise be drinking alone," Chéri answered.

"What are you going to do to-morrow?"

"Dunno, and you?"

"I'm off to Normandy."

"With?"

"That's none of your business."

"With our friend Spéleïeff?"

"Don't be so stupid. That was over two months ago. You're behind the times. Spéleïeff's in Russia."

"Chéri, darling, what can you be thinking of?" sighed Madame Peloux. "Don't you remember going last month to the charming dinner given by Léa to celebrate the end of the affair? Léa, you've never let me have the recipe for those langoustines I enjoyed so much."

Chéri sat up, his eyes sparkling. "Yes, yes, langoustines, swimming in a creamy sauce! How I'd like some now!"

"You see," Madame Peloux said reproachfully, "he's got no appetite to speak of and yet he's asking for langoustines."

"Shut up!" Chéri snapped. "Léa, are you off to the shady woods with Patron?"

"Certainly not, my boy. Patron and I are merely friends. I'm going on my own."

"Nice to be so rich!" Chéri threw out.

"I'll take you with me, if you like: there'll be nothing to do but eat and drink and sleep. . . ."

"Where is this place of yours?" He had risen to his feet and was standing over her.

"You know Honfleur—the Côte de Grâce—don't you? Sit

down; you're green in the face. Now as you go down the Côte de Grâce, you know those farm gates where we always say, in passing, your mother and I . . ."

She turned round to where Madame Peloux was sitting. Madame Peloux had disappeared. The discretion with which she had faded away was something so unlike the normal Charlotte Peloux, that they looked at each other and laughed in surprise.

Chéri sat down close to Léa. "I'm tired," he said.

"You're ruining your health."

He drew himself up in his chair, with offended vanity. "Oh! I'm still in good enough fettle, you know."

"Good enough! For others perhaps . . . but not . . . not for me, I'd have you know."

"Too green?"

"The very word I was looking for. So why don't you come down to the country? No nonsense, of course. Ripe strawberries, fresh cream, cakes, grilled spring chicken . . . that's just what you need—and no women."

He let himself snuggle up to Léa's elbow and shut his eyes.

"No women . . . grand . . . Léa, tell me, you're my pal? You are? Then let's be off. Women indeed! I'm fed up with 'em. Women! I've seen all they've got to show."

These vulgarities were muttered in a drowsy voice. Léa listened to his soft tone, and felt his warm breath against her ear. He had taken hold of her long string of pearls and was rolling the larger ones between his fingers. She slipped her arm under his head and so accustomed was she to treating the boy in this way that, almost without thinking, she pulled him towards her and rocked him in her arms.

"How comfy I am!" he sighed. "You're a good pal. I'm so comfy."

Léa smiled, as though hearing praise she valued intensely. Chéri seemed to be ready to drop off to sleep. She looked very closely at his glistening, almost dewy, eyelashes sunk flat against the cheeks, and then at the cheeks themselves, hollowed by his joyless dissipation. His upper lip, shaved that morning, was already bluish, and the pink lampshades lent his mouth an artificial colour.

"No women!" Chéri exclaimed, as though dreaming. "Then . . . kiss me!"

Taken by surprise, Léa made no movement.

"Kiss me, I tell you!"

He rapped out his order, frowning, and Léa felt embarrassed by the rekindled gleam in his eyes. It was as if someone had switched on the light. She shrugged her shoulders and kissed the forehead so close to her lips. He drew his arms tighter around her neck, and pulled her down towards him.

She shook her head only at the very instant that their lips touched, then she remained absolutely motionless, and held her breath like someone listening. When he released his hold, she broke away from him, rose to her feet, took a deep breath, and put a hand up to tidy her unruffled hair. She turned to him, rather pale and with rueful eyes, and said, teasingly: "That was a bright idea!"

He lay far back in the rocking-chair, speechless, and scrutinized her with a suspicious, questioning gaze, so that she asked: "What is it?"

"Nothing," Chéri said. "I know what I wanted to know."

She blushed with humiliation, then skilfully defended herself.

"What do you know? That I like your mouth? My poor child, I've kissed uglier. What does that prove? D'you think I'm going to fling myself at your feet and cry, 'Take me!' You talk as if you've known only nice young girls! D'you imagine I'm going to lose my head because of a kiss?"

She grew calmer while speaking and wished to prove her self-control.

"Listen, child," she persisted, as she leaned over him, "d'you think a handsome mouth means anything to me?"

She smiled down at him, completely sure of herself, but unaware that there remained on her face a sort of very faint

quiver, an appealing sadness, and that her smile was like a rainbow after a sudden storm.

"I'm perfectly calm. Even if I were to kiss you again, or
even if we . . ." She stopped and pouted with scorn. "No, no, I
really can't see you and me doing that."

"Nor could you see us doing what we did just now," Chéri
said, taking time over his words. "And yet you don't mind doing
it, and not in a hurry, either. So now you're thinking of going
further, are you? *I* never suggested such a thing."

They faced each other like enemies. Léa was afraid to reveal
a desire she had not yet had time to develop or to disguise; she
resented this child, so suddenly cold and perhaps derisive.

"You're right," she conceded lightly. "Let's say no more
about it. Shall we say instead that I'm offering to put you out to
grass! And the food will be good . . . *my* food, in other
words."

"We'll see," Chéri answered. "Shall I bring the Renouhard
tourer?"

"Of course; you're not going to leave it behind with Charlotte."

"I'll pay for the petrol, but you'll feed the chauffeur."

Léa burst out laughing. "I'll feed the chauffeur! Ha! Ha!
There speaks the son of Madame Peloux! Get along with you!
You forget nothing. . . . I'm not usually inquisitive, but I
should love to eavesdrop when you're making up to a woman."

She sank into a chair and fanned herself. A sphinx-moth and
a number of long-legged mosquitoes hovered round the lamps;
scents of the countryside drifted in from the garden, now that
night had fallen. A sudden waft from an acacia burst in upon
them, so distinct, so active, that they both turned round, half
expecting to see it advancing towards them.

"It's the rose-acacia," Léa said.

"Yes," Chéri said. "But to-night it has sipped a draught of
orange-flower water."

She stared at him, in vague admiration, astonished that he
had hit upon such an idea. He was breathing in the scent in

helpless rapture, and she turned away, suddenly fearful lest he might call her; but he did call, and she went to him.

She went to kiss him, on an impulse of resentment and selfishness, and half thinking to chastise him. 'Just you wait, my boy. . . . It's all too true that you've a pretty mouth, and, this time, I'm going to take my fill because I want to—and then I'll leave you, I don't care what you may say. Now . . .'

Her kiss was such that they reeled apart, drunk, deaf, breathless, trembling as if they had just been fighting. She stood up again in front of him, but he did not move from the depths of his chair, and she taunted him under her breath, "Well? . . . Well?" and waited for an insult. Instead, he held out his arms, opened his vague beautiful hands, tilted his head back as if he had been struck, and let her see beneath each eyelash the glint of a shining tear. He babbled indeterminate words—a whole animal chant of desire, in which she could distinguish her name —"darling"—"I want you"—"I'll never leave you"—a song to which she listened, solicitous, leaning over him, as if unwittingly she had hurt him to the quick.

When Léa recalled their first summer in Normandy, she would sum it up impartially: "I've had other naughty little boys through my hands, more amusing than Chéri, more likeable, too, and more intelligent. But all the same, never one to touch him."

"It's funny," she confided to the old Baron de Berthellemy, towards the end of the summer of 1906, "but sometimes I think I'm in bed with a Chinee or an African."

"Have you ever had a Chinaman or a Negro?"

"Never."

"Well then?"

"I don't know. I can't explain. It's just an impression."

The impression had grown upon her slowly, also an astonishment she had not always been able to conceal. Her earliest memories of their idyll were abundantly rich, but only in pictures of delicious food, superb fruit, and the pleasure of taking pains over her country larder. She could still see Chéri—paler in the blazing sunlight—dragging along his exhausted body beneath the lime-tree tunnels in Normandy, or asleep on the sunwarmed paving beside a pond.

Léa used to rouse Chéri from sleep to cram him with strawberries and cream, frothy milk, and corn-fed chicken. With wide, vacant eyes, as though dazed, he would sit at dinner watching the mazy motions of the moths round the bowl of roses, and then look at his wrist-watch to see whether the time had come to go to bed: while Léa, disappointed but unresentful, pondered over the unfulfilled promises of the kiss at Neuilly and good-naturedly bided her time.

"I'll keep him cooped up in this fattening-pen till the end of August, if need be. Then, back in Paris again—ouf!—I'll pack him off to his precious studies."

She went to bed mercifully early, so that Chéri—after nuzzling against her till he had hollowed out a selfishly comfortable position—might get some sleep. Sometimes, when the lamp was out, she would watch a pool of moonlight shimmering over the polished floor, or listen, through the chorus of rustling aspens and shrilling crickets, unceasing by night or day, to the deep, retriever-like sighs that rose from Chéri's breast.

'Why can't I go to sleep? Is there something wrong with me?' she vaguely wondered. 'It's not this boy's head on my shoulder—I've held heavier. The weather's wonderful. I've ordered him a good plate of porridge for to-morrow. Already his ribs stick out less. Then why can't I go to sleep? Yes, of course, I remember. . . . I'm going to send for Patron, the boxer, to give the boy some training. We've plenty of time between us, Patron and I, to spring a surprise on Madame Peloux.'

She fell asleep, lying stretched out on her back between the cool sheets, the dark head of her naughty little boy resting on her left breast. She fell asleep, to be aroused sometimes—but all too rarely—by a waking desire of Chéri's towards the break of day.

Patron actually arrived after they had been two months in their country retreat, with his suitcase, his small pound-and-a-half dumb-bells, his black tights, his six-ounce gloves, and his leather boxing-boots, laced down to the toe. Patron, with his girlish voice, his long eyelashes, and his splendid tanned skin, as brown as the leather of his luggage—he hardly looked naked when he took off his shirt. And Chéri, by turns peevish, listless, or jealous of Patron's smooth strength, started the slow, oft-repeated movements. They were tiresome, but they did him good.

"One . . . sss . . . two . . . sss . . . I can't hear you breathing . . . three . . . sss. . . . Don't think I can't see you cheating there with your knee . . . sss. . . ."

An awning of lime foliage filtered the August sunlight. The bare bodies of instructor and pupil were dappled with purple reflections from the thick red carpet spread out upon the gravel. Léa watched the lessons with keen attention. Sometimes during the quarter of an hour's boxing, Chéri, drunk with new-found strength, lost all control and, red-faced with anger, attempted a foul blow. Rock-like, Patron stood up to his swings, and from the height of his Olympian glory let fall oracular words—words of wisdom that packed more weight than his proverbial punch.

"Steady on now! That left eye's wandering a bit! If I hadn't stopped myself in time, it would have had a nasty taste of the stitches on my right glove."

"I slipped," Chéri said, enraged.

"It's not a question of balance," Patron went on, "it's a question of morale. You'll never make a boxer."

"My mother won't let me, isn't that a pity?"

"Whether your mother lets you or not, you'll never make a boxer, because you've got a rotten temper. Rotten tempers and boxing don't go together. Aren't I right, Madame Léa?"

Léa smiled, and revelled in the warm sun, sitting still and watching the bouts between these two men, both young and both stripped. In her mind she kept comparing them. 'How handsome Patron is—as solid as a house! And the boy's shaping well. You don't find knees like his running about the streets every day of the week, or I'm no judge. His back, too, is . . . will be . . . marvellous. Where the devil did Mother Peloux drop her line to fish up a child like that? And the set of his head! quite a statue! But what a little beast he is! When he laughs, you'd swear it's a greyhound snarling!' She felt happy and maternal—bathed in quiet virtue. 'I'd willingly change him for anyone else,' she said to herself, with Chéri naked in the afternoon beside her under the lime-tree-bower, or with Chéri naked in the morning on her ermine rug, or Chéri naked in the evening on the edge of the warm fountain. 'Yes, handsome as he is, I'd willingly make a change, if it weren't a question of conscience!'

She confessed her indifference to Patron.

"And yet," Patron objected, "the lad's very nicely made. There's muscles on him now such as you don't see on our French lads; his are more like a coloured boy's—though he couldn't look any whiter, I must say. Nice little muscles they are, and not too showy. He'll never have biceps like melons."

"I should hope not, Patron! But then, you know, I didn't take him on for his boxing!"

"Of course not," Patron acquiesced, letting his long lashes droop, "there's—your feelings to be considered."

He was always embarrassed by Léa's unveiled allusions to sex, and by her smile—the insistence of the smiling eyes she brought to bear on him whenever she spoke of love.

"Of course," Patron tried another tack, "if he's not altogether satisfactory . . ."

Léa laughed: "Altogether! no . . . but I find being disinterested is its own reward. Just as you do, Patron."

"Oh! me . . ." He waited in fear and hope for the question that did not fail to follow.

"Always the same, Patron? You still won't give way an inch?"

"I won't give way, Madame Léa, and I've just had a letter from Liane by the midday post. She says she's all alone, that I've no good reasons for refusing, and that her two admirers have left her."

"Well?"

"Well, I don't believe it! I won't give way, because she won't give way. She's ashamed, she says, of a man who works for his living—specially when it pulls him out of bed so early every day for his training—a man who gives boxing lessons and teaches Swedish gymnastics. We've only got to meet, and the row starts all over again. 'Anyone'd think,' she shouts at me, 'that I'm not in a position to support the man I love!' That

31

shows very nice feelings, I don't say it doesn't, but it doesn't fit in with my ideas. Everyone's funny about something. It's just like you said, Madame Léa, it's all a question of conscience."

They were talking in low tones under the trees: he prudish and half naked; she dressed in white, the colour flaming in her cheeks. They were enjoying the pleasure of a friendly understanding: they shared the same taste for the simple things of life, good health and a sort of plebeian decency. And yet Léa would not have been shocked had Patron received handsome presents from a beautiful and expensive woman like Liane. "Fair exchange is no robbery." And she did her best to break down Patron's "funny feelings" by arguments based on homespun justice. These leisurely conversations always revealed their worship of the same twin deities—love and money, and would drift away from money and love to come back to Chéri and his deplorable upbringing, to his exceptional good looks ("harmless, after all," as Léa would say) and to his character ("virtually non-existent," as Léa would say). They had a taste for sharing confidences, and a dislike of new words or ideas, which they satisfied in these long talks. They were often disturbed by the preposterous apparition of Chéri, whom they thought either asleep or motoring down some baking hot road—Chéri, looming into sight, half naked, but equipped with an account book, a stylo behind his ear.

"Look at our Mister Adding-machine," Patron said admiringly. "All got up as a clerk in a bank."

"What can this mean?" Chéri shouted from afar. "Three hundred and twenty francs for petrol? Somebody must be swilling the stuff! We've been out four times in the last fortnight —and seventy-seven francs for oil!"

"The motor goes to the market every day," Léa replied. "And while we're on the subject, it appears your chauffeur had three helpings of the joint for his dinner. Don't you think that's stretching our agreement a bit far? . . . Whenever a bill sticks in your throat, you look just like your mother."

At a loss for an answer, he stood uncertain for a moment,

shifting from one slender foot to the other, poised with winged grace like a young Mercury. This always made Madame Peloux swoon with delight and yelp, "Me when I was eighteen! Winged feet! Winged feet!" He cast about for some insolent retort, his whole face a-quiver, his mouth half-open, his forehead jutting forward, in a tense attitude that showed off to advantage the peculiar and diabolic upward twist of his eyebrows.

"Don't bother to think of an answer," Léa said kindly. "I know you hate me. Come and kiss me. Handsome devil. Fallen angel. Silly goose. . . ."

He came, calmed by the softness of her voice, yet ruffled by her words. Seeing them together, Patron once again let the truth flower on his guileless lips.

"As far as first-rate bodies go, Monsieur Chéri, you have one all right. But whenever I look at it, Monsieur Chéri, I feel that if I was a woman I'd say to myself: 'I'll come back again in ten years' time'."

"You hear, Léa? He says in ten years' time," Chéri said insinuatingly, pushing away the head of his mistress as she leaned towards him. "What do you think of that?"

But she did not deign to listen. The young body owed to her its renewed vigour, and she began patting it all over, touching it anywhere and everywhere, on the cheek, on the leg, on the behind, with the irreverent pleasure of a nanny.

"What d'you get out of being spiteful?" Patron then asked.

Chéri allowed a savage, inscrutable gaze to sweep over every inch of the waiting Hercules before he answered. "I find it comforting. You wouldn't understand."

In fact, Léa herself understood precious little about Chéri after three months' intimacy. If she still talked to Patron, who now came only on Sundays, or to Berthellemy, who arrived without being invited but left again two hours later, about "sending Chéri back to his blessed studies", it was because the phrase had become a kind of habit, and as though to excuse herself for having kept him there so long. She kept on setting a limit to his stay, and then exceeding it. She was waiting.

33
.....

"The weather is so lovely. And then his trip to Paris last week tired him. And, besides, it's better for me to get thoroughly sick of him."

For the first time in her life, she waited in vain for what had never before failed her: complete trust on the part of her young lover, a self-surrender to confessions, candours, endless secrets —those hours in the depths of the night when, in almost filial gratitude, a young man unrestrainedly pours out his tears, his private likes and dislikes, on the kindly bosom of a mature and trusted friend.

'They've always told me everything in the past,' she thought obstinately. 'I've always known just what they were worth—what they were thinking and what they wanted. But this boy, this brat . . . No, that would really be the limit.'

He was now strong, proud of his nineteen years, gay at meals and impatient in bed; even so he gave away nothing but his body, and remained as mysterious as an odalisque. Tender? Yes, if an involuntary cry or an impulsive hug is an indication of tenderness. But the moment he spoke, he was "spiteful" again, careful to divulge nothing of his true self.

How often at dawn had Léa held him in her arms, a lover soothed, relaxed, with half-closed lids! Each morning his eyes and his mouth returned to life more beautiful, as though every waking, every embrace, had fashioned them anew! How often, at such moments, had she indulged her desire to master him, her sensual longing to hear his confession, and pressed her forehead against his, whispering, "Speak. Say something. Tell me . . ."

But no confession came from those curved lips, scarcely anything indeed but sulky or frenzied phrases woven round "Nounoune"—the name he had given her when a child and the one he now used in the throes of his pleasure, almost like a cry for help.

"Yes, I assure you, he might be a Chinee or an African," she declared to Anthime de Berthellemy, and added, "I can't tell you why." The impression was strong but confused, and she felt lazily incompetent to find words for the feeling that she and Chéri did not speak the same language.

It was the end of September when they returned to Paris. Chéri went straight to Neuilly, the very first evening, to "spring a surprise" on Madame Peloux. He brandished chairs, cracked nuts with his fist, leaped on to the billiard-table and played cowboy in the garden at the heels of the terrified watch-dogs.

"Ouf!" Léa sighed, as she entered her house in the Avenue Bugeaud, alone. "How wonderful—a bed to myself!"

But at ten o'clock the following night, she was sipping coffee and trying not to find the evening too long or the dining-room too large, when a nervous cry was forced from her lips. Chéri had suddenly appeared, framed in the doorway—Chéri, wafted on silent, winged feet.

He was not speaking or showing any sign of affection, but just running towards her.

"Are you mad?"

Shrugging his shoulders, disdaining all explanations, just running towards her. Never asking "Do you love me?", "Have you already forgotten me?". Running towards her.

A moment later they were lying in the middle of Léa's great brass-encumbered bed. Chéri pretended to be worn out and sleepy. This made it easier to grit his teeth and keep his eyes tight shut, suffering as he was from a furious attack of taciturnity. Yet, through his silence, she was listening as she lay beside him, listening with delight to the distant delicate vibration, to the imprisoned tumult thrumming within a body that sought to conceal its agony, its gratitude and love.

"Why didn't your mother tell me this herself at dinner last night?"

"She thought it better it should come from me."

"No!"

"That's what she said."

"And you?"

"What about me?"

"Do you think it better?"

Chéri raised uncertain eyes to Léa's. "Yes." He appeared to think it over a moment and repeated: "Yes, far better, in fact."

In order not to embarrass him, Léa looked away towards the window.

The August morning was dark with warm rain, which fell vertically on the already rusted foliage of the three plane-trees in the garden court.

"It might be autumn," she said, and sighed.

"What's the matter?" Chéri asked.

She looked at him in astonishment. "Nothing, I don't like the rain, that's all."

"Oh! All right, I thought . . ."

"What?"

"I thought something was wrong."

She could not help giving a frank laugh. "Wrong with me, because you're getting married? No, listen . . . you're . . . you're so funny."

She seldom laughed outright, and her merriment vexed

Chéri. He shrugged his shoulders and made the usual grimace while lighting a cigarette, jutting out his chin too far and protruding his lower lip.

"You oughtn't to smoke before luncheon," Léa said.

He made some impertinent retort she did not hear. She was listening to the sound of her own voice and its daily lectures, echoing away down the past five years. 'It's like the endless repetition in opposite looking-glasses,' she thought. Then, with a slight effort, she returned to reality and cheerfulness.

"It's lucky for me that there'll soon be someone else to stop you smoking on an empty stomach."

"Oh! *she* won't be allowed to have a say in anything," Chéri declared. "She's going to be my wife, isn't she? Let her kiss the sacred ground I tread on, and thank her lucky stars for the privilege. And that will be that."

He exaggerated the thrust of his chin, clenched his teeth on his cigarette-holder, parted his lips, and, as he stood there in his white silk pyjamas, succeeded only in looking like an Asiatic prince grown pale in the impenetrable obscurity of palaces.

Léa drew the folds of her pink dressing-gown closer about her—the pink she called "indispensable". She was lazily turning over ideas which she found tiresome, ideas that she decided to hurl, one by one, as missiles against Chéri's assumed composure.

"Well, why are you marrying the child?"

He put both elbows on the table and, unconsciously, assumed the composed features of his mother. "Well, you see, my dear girl . . ."

"Call me Madame or Léa. I'm neither your housemaid nor a pal of your own age."

She sat straight up in her armchair and clipped her words without raising her voice. He wanted to answer back. He looked defiantly at the beautiful face, a little pale under its powder, and at the frank blue light of her searching eyes. But he softened, and conceded, in a tone most unusual for him, "Nounoune, you asked me to explain. . . . It had to come to this in the end. And besides, there are big interests at stake."

"Whose?"

"Mine," he said without a smile. "The girl has a considerable fortune of her own."

"From her father?"

He rocked himself to and fro, his feet in the air. "Oh, how do I know? What a question! I suppose so. You'd hardly expect the fair Marie-Laure to draw fifteen hundred thousand out of her own bank account, would you? Fifteen hundred thousand, and some decent family jewels into the bargain."

"And how much have you?"

"Oh, I've more than that of my own," he said with pride.

"Then you don't need any more money?"

He shook his smooth head and it caught the light like blue watered silk. "Need . . . need . . . ? You know perfectly well we don't look at money in the same way. It's something on which we never see eye to eye."

"I'll do you the justice to say that you've spared me any reference to it during the last five years." She leaned towards him and put her hand on his knee. "Tell me, child, how much have you put by from your income in these five years?"

He cavorted like a clown, laughed, and rolled at Léa's feet, but she pushed him aside with her toe.

"No, tell me the truth . . . fifty thousand a year, or sixty? Tell me, sixty? Seventy?"

He sat down on the carpet facing away from Léa, and laid his head back on her lap. "Aren't I worth it, then?"

He stretched out to his full length, turned his head to look up at her, and opened his eyes wide. They looked black, but their true shade, Léa knew, was a dark almost reddish brown. As though to indicate her choice of what was rarest among so much beauty, she put her forefinger on his eyebrows, his eyelids and the corners of his mouth. At moments this lover, whom she slightly despised, inspired her with a kind of respect by his outward form. 'To be as handsome as that amounts to nobility,' she said to herself.

"Tell me, child, how does this young person feel about you?"

"She loves me. She admires me. She never says a word."

"And you—how do you behave with her?"

"I don't," he answered simply.

"Delightful love duets," Léa said, dreamily.

He sat up, crossing his legs tailor-fashion.

"You seem to me to be thinking a lot about her," he said severely. "Don't you think of yourself at all, in this upheaval?"

She gazed at Chéri with an astonishment that made her look years younger—eyebrows raised and lips half open.

"Yes, you, Léa. You, the victimized heroine. You, the one sympathetic character in all this, since you're being dropped."

He had become rather pale, and his tough handling of Léa seemed to be hurting him.

Léa smiled. "But, my darling, I've not the slightest intention of changing my life. Now and then, during the next week, I'll come across a pair of socks, a tie, a handkerchief on my shelves . . . and when I say a week . . . you know in what excellent order my shelves are kept! Oh, yes, and I'll have the bathroom re-done. I've got an idea of putting in encrusted glass. . . ."

She fell silent and assumed an almost greedy look as she traced a vague outline with her finger. Chéri continued to look vindictive.

"You aren't pleased! What do you want, then? Do you expect me to go to Normandy to hide my grief? To pine away? To stop dyeing my hair? To have Madame Peloux rushing to my bedside?" And she imitated Madame Peloux, flapping her arms and trumpeting: " 'The shadow of her former self, the shadow of her former self! The poor unfortunate creature has aged a hundred years, a hundred years!' Is that what you want?"

He had been listening with a smile that died on his lips, and a trembling of the nostrils that might be due to emotion. "Yes!" he cried.

Léa rested her smooth, bare, heavy arms on Chéri's shoulders.

"My poor boy! But at that rate, I ought to have died four or five times already! To lose a little lover. . . . To exchange one naughty little boy. . . ." She added in lower, lighter tones: "I've grown used to it!"

"We all know that," he said harshly. "I don't give a damn—d'you hear me?—I don't give a single damn that I wasn't your first lover. What I should have liked, or rather what would have been . . . fitting . . . decent . . . is to be your last." With a twist of his shoulders, he shrugged off her superb arms. "After all, what I am saying to you now is for your own good."

"I understand perfectly. You think only of me. I think only of your fiancée. That's all very nice, all very natural. It's clear that we both have hearts of gold."

She rose, waiting for some outrageous rejoinder. But he said nothing, and it hurt her to see for the first time a look of discouragement on his face.

She bent over and put her hands under his armpits.

"Now then, come along, get your clothes on. I've only to put on my dress, I'm ready underneath, and what in the world is there to do on a day like this except to go to Schwabe and choose a pearl for you? You see, I must give you a wedding-present."

He jumped up, his face aglow: "Top-hole! A pearl for my shirt-front! A pale pink pearl. I know the very one!"

"Not on your life! A white one, something masculine for pity's sake! Don't tell me, I know which one just as well as you. It'll ruin me, as usual. However, think of the money I'm going to save when you're out of the way!"

Chéri adopted a more reticent attitude. "Oh, that . . . that depends on my successor."

Léa turned back at the door of her boudoir and gave him

her gayest smile, showing her strong teeth and the fresh blue of her eyes skilfully darkened by bistre.

"Your successor? A couple of francs and a packet of cigarettes! And a glass of cassis on Sunday—that's all the job will be worth! And I'll settle money on your children."

They both became extremely gay for the next few weeks. Chéri's official duties as a fiancé separated them for a few hours each day, sometimes for a night or two. "We mustn't let them lose confidence," Chéri declared. Léa, kept by Madame Peloux at a safe distance from Neuilly, satisfied her curiosity by plying Chéri with a hundred questions. Whenever he came back to Léa's house, he was full of his own importance and heavy with secrets which he at once divulged. He was like a schoolboy playing truant.

"Oh my sainted aunt!" he shouted one day, cramming his hat down on Léa's portrait-bust. "The goings-on at the Peloux Palace Hôtel ever since yesterday!"

She began by scolding him, laughing already in anticipation.

"Take your hat off that, in the first place. And in the second, don't invoke your wretched aunt in my house. Well, what's been happening now?"

"A riot, Nounoune! A riot's broken out among the ladies. Marie-Laure and Ma'me Peloux are scratching each other's eyes out over the marriage settlement!"

"No!"

"Yes! It was a superb sight. (Look out for the olives. . . . I'm going to impersonate Ma'me Peloux as a windmill. . . .) 'Separate bank accounts! Separate bank accounts! Why not a trustee? It's a personal insult, a personal insult. You forget that my son has his own fortune! . . . May I inform you, Madame . . .' "

"She called her Madame?"

"She most certainly did. 'Let me tell you, Madame, that my son has never had a ha'porth of debts since he came of age and the list of his investments bought since 1910 is worth . . .' is worth this, that and the other, including the skin off my nose, plus the fat off my bottom. In short, Catherine de Medici in person! But even more artful, of course!"

Léa's blue eyes glistened with tears of merriment. "Oh Chéri! you've never been funnier in your life! What about the other? The fair Marie-Laure?"

"Her? Oh! terrible, Nounoune. That woman must have at least a dozen corpses in her wake. Dolled up in jade green, red hair, painted to look eighteen, and the inevitable smile. The trumpetings of my revered Mamma failed to make her bat an eyelid. She held her fire till the assault was over, then she came out with: 'It might perhaps be wiser, dear Madame, not to talk too loudly about all the money your son put by in 1910 and the years following. . . .' "

"Bang! Straight between the eyes! . . . Between yours. Where were you while all this was going on?"

"Me? In the large armchair."

"You were actually in the room?" She stopped laughing, and eating. "You were there? What did you do?"

"Cracked a joke, of course. Ma'me Peloux had just seized hold of a valuable piece of bric-à-brac, to avenge my honour, when I stopped her without even getting up. 'My adored mother, calm yourself. Follow my example, follow that of my charming mother-in-law, who's being as sweet as honey . . . as sweet as sugar.' And that's how I managed to arrange that the settlement should apply only to property acquired after marriage."

"I simply don't understand."

"The famous sugar plantations that the poor little Prince Ceste left to Marie-Laure by his will. . . ."

"Yes?"

"Forged will! Fury of the Ceste family! Lawsuit pending! Now d'you get it?"

He crowed.

"I get it. But how did you get hold of the story?"

"Ah! I'll tell you! Old Lili has just pounced with her full weight upon the younger of the Ceste boys, who's only seventeen and religious. . . ."

"Old Lili? What a nightmare!"

"And he babbles family secrets in her ear between every kiss. . . ."

"Chéri! I feel sick!"

"And old Lili tipped me off at Mamma's At Home last Sunday. She simply adores me! Besides, she respects me because I've never wanted to go to bed with her. . . ."

"I should hope not!" Léa sighed. "Yet all the same . . ." She broke off to reflect, and it seemed to Chéri her enthusiasm was flagging.

"Well, you must say it was pretty smart of me, eh?"

He leaned across the table; and the sunshine, playing over the silver and the white table-cloth, lit him up like a row of footlights.

"Yes . . ." 'All the same,' she was thinking, 'that poisonous Marie-Laure simply treated him like a ponce . . .'

"Is there any cream cheese, Nounoune?"

"Yes . . ." '. . . and he showed no more surprise than if she had thrown him a flower. . . .'

"Nounoune, will you let me have that address? the address of the place where you get your cream cheese—for the new cook I've engaged for October?"

"Are you mad? It's home-made. I *have* a cook, you know. Think of the *sauce aux moules* and *vol-au-vent!*" '. . . it's true I've practically kept the boy for the last five years. . . . But all the same he has an income of three hundred thousand francs a year. That's the point. Can you be a ponce with three hundred thousand a year? But why ever not? It doesn't depend on the amount, but on the man. . . . There are some men I could have given half a million to, and that wouldn't make them a ponce. But how about Chéri? After all, I have never actually given him any money. All the same . . .'

"All the same," she broke into speech. "She treated you like a gigolo!"

"Who did?"

"Marie-Laure!"

He brightened at once, like a child.

"Didn't she? Didn't she just, Nounoune? That's what she meant, wasn't it?"

"So it seems to me."

Chéri raised his glass of Château-Chalon, almost the colour of brandy. "So here's to Marie-Laure! What a compliment, eh? And if anyone can still say it of me when I'm your age, I shan't ask anything better!"

"If that's enough to make you happy . . ."

She listened to him absent-mindedly till the end of luncheon. Accustomed to her half-silences and her worldly wisdom, he asked for nothing better than the usual maternal homilies—"Take the brownest crusts. Don't eat so much new bread. . . . You've never learnt how to choose a fruit. . . ." All the time, secretly disgruntled, she was reproaching herself, 'I must make up my mind what I want! What would I really have liked him to do? Get up on his hind legs and hiss "Madame, you have insulted me! Madame, I am not what you take me for!" I'm responsible, when all's said and done. I've spoon-fed him, I've stuffed him with good things. . . . Who in the world would have thought that one day he'd want to play the paterfamilias? It never occurred to me! Even supposing it had—as Patron would say, "Nature will out." Even supposing Patron had accepted Liane's proposals, his nature would have come out all right if anyone had hinted at the fact in his hearing. But Chéri . . . has Chéri's nature. He's just Chéri. He's . . .'

"What were you saying, child?" she interrupted her thoughts to ask. "I wasn't listening."

"I was saying that never again—never, do you hear me—will anything make me laugh so much as my scene with Marie-Laure!"

—'There you are,' Léa concluded her thoughts, 'it . . . it merely made him laugh.'

Slowly she rose to her feet, as though tired. Chéri put an arm round her waist, but she pushed it away.

"What day is your wedding to be, now I come to think of it?"

"Monday week."

His candour and detachment terrified her. "That's fantastic!"

"Why fantastic, Nounoune?"

"You don't look as if you were giving it a thought!"

"I'm not," he said, calmly. "Everything's been arranged. Ceremony at two o'clock, saving us all the fuss and rush of a wedding breakfast. Instead, a tea party at Ma'me Peloux's. After that, sleepers, Italy, the Lakes. . . ."

"Are the Lakes back in fashion?"

"They are. There'll be villas, hotels, motor-drives, restaurants, like Monte-Carlo, eh?"

"But the girl! There's always the girl. . . ."

"Of course there's the girl. She's not much, but she's there!"

"And I'm no longer there."

Chéri had not expected her to say this and showed it. His face became disfigured, and he suddenly turned white about the mouth. He controlled his breath to avoid an audible gasp, and became himself again.

"Nounoune, you'll always be there."

"Monsieur overwhelms me."

"There'll always be you, Nounoune . . ." and he laughed awkwardly, "whenever I need you to do something for me."

She did not answer. She bent to pick up a tortoiseshell comb that had fallen to the floor and pushed it back in her hair, humming to herself. She went on humming a little snatch of a song in front of a looking-glass, pleased with herself, proud of having kept her self-control so easily, covered up so successfully the only emotional moment of their separation, proud of having held back words that must never be said: "Speak . . . beg for what you want, demand it, put your arms round my neck. . . . You have suddenly made me happy. . . ."

Madame Peloux must have been talking a great deal and for a long time before Léa appeared. The high colour on her cheeks emphasised the sparkle of her large eyes, which expressed only an indiscreet and inscrutable watchfulness. This Sunday she was wearing a black afternoon dress with a very narrow skirt, and nobody could fail to have observed that her feet were tiny and her stays too tight. She stopped talking, took a little sip from the petal-thin brandy glass warming in her hand, and nodded at Léa in lazy contentment.

"Isn't it a lovely day? Such weather, such weather! Would any one believe we're in the middle of October?"

"Oh, no, never. . . . Most certainly not!" two obsequious voices answered in chorus.

Beside the curving garden path a stream of red salvias wound between the banks of grey-mauve Michaelmas daisies. Golden butterflies flitted as if it were summer and the scent of chrysanthemums, strengthened by the hot sun, was wafted into the garden-room. A yellowing birch tree trembled in the wind above beds of tea roses, where the last of the bees still were busy.

"But what's this weather," yelled Madame Peloux, suddenly waxing lyrical, "but what's this weather, when compared to what *they* must be having in Italy?"

"Yes, indeed! . . . Just what I was thinking!" the attendant voices echoed.

Léa turned with a frown in their direction. 'If only they would hold their tongues,' she thought.

The Baroness de la Berche and Madame Aldonza were sitting at a card-table, playing piquet. Madame Aldonza, an aged ballerina, with legs eternally swathed in bandages, was distorted with rheumatism, and wore her shiny black wig a little askew. Opposite her, a head or more taller, the Baroness squared her rigid shoulders like a country priest's. Her face was large and had grown alarmingly masculine with age. She was a bristling bush of hair—hair in her ears, tufts in her nostrils and on her lip, and rough hairs between her fingers.

"Baroness, don't forget I made ninety," Madame Aldonza bleated like a goat.

"Score it, score it, my good friend! All I want is to see everyone happy."

An endless flow of honied words masked her savage cruelty. Léa looked at her closely as if for the first time, felt disgusted, and turned back to Madame Peloux. 'Charlotte, at least, *looks* human,' she thought.

"What's the matter with you, my Léa? You don't seem your usual self?" Madame Peloux enquired tenderly.

Léa drew up her handsome figure and answered: "Of course I am, Lolotte dear . . . it's so comfortable here in your house, I was merely relaxing," thinking all the while, 'Careful now . . . she's just as cruel as the other,' and she at once assumed an expression of flattering contentment, of dreamy repletion, and accentuated it by sighing, "I lunched too well. . . . I really must get thinner. I shall start a strict diet from to-morrow."

Madame Peloux flapped her hands and simpered.

"Isn't a broken heart enough to do that?"

"Oh, oh, oh! Ha-ha! Ho-ho!" guffawed Madame Aldonza and the Baroness de la Berche. "Ha-ha-ha!"

Léa rose to her full height in her autumn dress of sombre green, handsome under her satin hat trimmed with seal-skin, youthful among these old ruins over whom she cast a gentle eye. "Oh, la-la, my dears! Give me a dozen such heart-breaks, if that would help me to lose a couple of pounds!"

"Léa, you're astounding," the old baroness shot at her in a puff of smoke. "Madame Léa, think of me, please, when you throw away that hat," old Madame Aldonza begged. "Madame Charlotte, you remember your blue one? It lasted me two years. Baroness, when you've quite finished ogling Madame Léa, perhaps you'll be kind enough to deal the cards to me."

"Very well, my sweet, and may they bring you luck!"

Léa stopped for a moment by the door, then stepped out into the garden. She picked a tea rose, which shed its petals. She listened to the breeze in the birch, to the trams in the Avenue, to the whistle of the local train. The bench she sat on was warm, and she closed her eyes, letting her shoulders enjoy the warmth of the sun. When she opened her eyes again, she hurriedly turned her head in the direction of the house, feeling positive that she was going to see Chéri standing in the garden entrance with his shoulder against the doorway.

'What can be the matter with me?' she wondered. Piercing screams of laughter and a little chorus of greeting from indoors brought her, trembling slightly, to her feet. 'Can I be suffering from nerves?'

"Ah, here they are, here they are!" Madame Peloux trumpeted, and the deep bass of the Baroness chimed in "Here come the happy pair!"

Léa shivered, ran as far as the door and stopped short: there, in front of her, were old Lili and her adolescent lover, Prince Ceste, just arriving.

Perhaps seventy years of age, with the corpulence of a eunuch held in by stays, old Lili was usually referred to as 'passing all bounds', without these 'bounds' being defined. Her round pink painted face was enlivened by a ceaseless girlish gaiety, and her large eyes and small mouth, thin-lipped and shrunken, flirted shamelessly. Old Lili followed the fashion to an outrageous degree. A striking blue-and-white striped skirt held in the lower part of her body, and a little blue jersey gaped over her skinny bosom crinkled like the wattles of a turkey-cock; a silver fox failed to conceal the neck, which was the shape of a flower-pot and the size of a belly. It had engulfed the chin.

'It's terrifying,' Léa thought. She was unable to tear her eyes away from details that were particularly sinister—a white sailor hat, for instance, girlishly perched on the back of a short-cut, strawberry-roan wig; or, again, a pearl necklace visible one moment and the next interred in a deep ravine which once had been termed a *"collier de Vénus"*.

"Léa, Léa, my little chickabiddy!" old Lili exclaimed as she did her best to hasten towards Léa. She walked with difficulty on round swollen feet, tightly swaddled in high-heeled laced boots with paste buckles on the ankle-straps, and was the first to congratulate herself on this performance: "I waddle like a duckling! it is a special little way I have. Guido, my passion, you remember Madame de Lonval? Don't remember her too well or I'll tear your eyes out. . . ."

A slim youth with Italian features, enormous empty eyes and a weak receding chin, kissed Léa's hand hastily and retired into the shadows without a word. Lili caught him in flight, pulled his head down to her scaly chest, calling the onlookers to witness: "Do you know what this is, Madame, do you know what this is? This, ladies, is the love of my life!"

"Restrain yourself, Lili!" Madame de la Berche advised in her masculine voice.

"But why? But why?" from Charlotte Peloux.

"For the sake of decency," said the Baroness.

"Baroness, that's not nice of you! I think they're so sweet. Ah!" she sighed, "they remind me of my own children."

"I was thinking of them," Lili said, with a delighted smile. "It's our honeymoon too, Guido's and mine. Indeed, we've just come to ask about the other young couple! We want to hear all about them."

Madame Peloux became stern. "Lili, you don't expect me to go into details, do you?"

"Oh yes, yes, I do," Lili cried, clapping her hands. She tried to skip, but succeeded only in raising her shoulders and hips a little. "That's always been my besetting sin, and always will be! I adore spicy talk! I'll never be cured of it. That little wretch there knows how I adore it."

The silent youth, called to bear witness, did not open his mouth. The black pupils of his eyes moved up and down against the whites, like frantic insects. Léa watched him, rooted to the spot.

"Madame Charlotte told us all about the wedding ceremony," bleated Madame Aldonza. "The young Madame Peloux was a dream in her wreath of orange-blossom!"

"A madonna! A madonna!" Madame Peloux corrected at the top of her voice, with a burst of religious fervour. "Never, never, has anyone looked so divine. My son was in heaven! In heaven, I tell you! . . . What a pair they made, what a pair!"

"You hear that, my passion? Orange blossom!" Lili murmured. "And tell me, Charlotte, what about our mother-in-law, Marie-Laure?"

Madame Peloux's pitiless eyes sparkled: "Oh her! Out of place, absolutely out of place. In tight-fitting black, like an eel wriggling out of the water—you could see everything, breasts, stomach—everything!"

"By Jove!" muttered the Baroness de la Berche with military gusto.

"And that look of contempt she has for everybody, that look of having a dose of cyanide up her sleeve and half a pint of chloroform inside her handbag! As I said, out of place—that exactly describes her. She behaved as if she could only spare us five minutes of her precious time—she'd hardly brushed the kiss off her lips, before she said, 'Au revoir, Edmée, au revoir, Fred,' and off she flew."

Old Lili was breathing hard, sitting on the edge of her

chair, her little grandmotherly mouth, with its puckered corners, hanging half open. "And who gave the usual advice?" she threw out.

"What advice?"

"The little talk—oh, my passion, hold my hand while I say it!—instruction for the young bride. Who gave her that?"

Charlotte Peloux took offence and stared at her. "Things may well have been done in that way when you were young, but the practice has fallen into disuse."

The sprightly old girl plumped her fists on her thighs: "Disuse? Disuse or not, how would you know anything about it, my poor Charlotte? There's so little marrying in your family!"

"Ha-ha-ha!" the two toadies imprudently guffawed.

But a single glance from Madame Peloux made them tremble. "Peace, peace, my little angels! You're each enjoying your paradise on earth, so what more do you want?" The Baroness stretched out a strong arm, like a policeman keeping order, between the purple faces of Lili and Madame Peloux. But Charlotte scented battle like a war-horse. "If you're looking for trouble, Lili, you don't have to look further than me! Because of your age, I must treat you with respect, and if it weren't for that . . ."

Lili shook with laughter from chin to thigh. "If it weren't for that, you'd get married yourself just to give me the lie? I know—it's not so hard to get married! Why, I'd marry Guido like a shot, if only he were of age!"

"Not possible!" gasped Charlotte, so taken aback that she forgot her anger.

"But, of course . . . Princess Ceste, my dear! *la piccola principessa! Piccola principessa*, that's what my little Prince always calls me!"

She nipped hold of her skirt, and, in turning, displayed a gold curb-chain where her ankle ought to have been. "Only," she continued mysteriously, "his father . . ."

By now out of breath, she made a sign to the silent young man, who took up the tale in a low rapid voice as if he were reciting his piece: "My father, the Duke of Parese, threatens to put me in a convent if I marry Lili."

"In a convent!" Charlotte Peloux squealed. "A man in a convent!"

"A man in a convent!" neighed Madame de la Berche in her deep bass, "Egad! if that isn't exciting!"

"They're barbarians," Aldonza lamented, joining her misshapen hands together.

Léa rose so abruptly that she upset a glass.

"It's uncoloured glass," Madame Peloux observed with satisfaction. "You'll bring good luck to my young couple. Where are you running off to? Is your house on fire?"

Léa managed to squeeze out a sly little laugh: "On fire? In a sense, perhaps. Ssh! no questions! It's a secret."

"What? Already? It's not possible!" Charlotte Peloux cheeped enviously. "I was just saying to myself that you looked as if . . ."

"Yes, yes! You must tell us! Tell us everything," yapped the three old women.

Lili's quilted fists, old Aldonza's deformed stumps, Charlotte Peloux's hard fingers had seized upon her wrist, her sleeve, her gold-mesh bag. She snatched her arm away from all these claws and succeeded in laughing again, teasingly: "No, it's far too early in the day, it would spoil everything! It's my secret." And she rushed away to the hall.

But the door opened in front of her and a desiccated old fellow, a sort of playful mummy, took her into his arms: "Léa, lovely creature, a kiss for your little Berthellemy, or he won't let you pass!"

54

She gave a cry of fright and impatience, struck off the gloved bones retarding her progress, and fled.

Neither in the avenues of Neuilly, nor on the roads through the Bois, turning to blue in the fast-falling twilight, did she allow herself a moment's reflection. She shivered slightly and pulled

up the windows of the motor-car. She felt restored by the sight
of her clean house, the comfort of her pink bedroom and boudoir, overcrowded with furniture and flowers.

"Quick, Rose, light the fire in my room!"

"But, Madame, the pipes are already at their winter temperature. Madame should not have gone out with only a fur round
her neck. The evenings are treacherous."

"A hot-water bottle in my bed at once, and for dinner a cup
of thick chocolate beaten up with the yolk of an egg, some toast,
and a bunch of grapes. . . . Hurry, dear, I'm freezing. I caught
cold in that junk-shop at Neuilly. . . ."

Once under the sheets, she clenched her teeth to stop them
chattering. The warmth of the bed eased her stiffened muscles,
but still she did not altogether relax, and she went through the
chauffeur's expense book till the chocolate arrived. This she
drank at once, frothy and scalding. She chose her *chasselas*
grapes one by one, the long greenish-amber bunch dangling by
its stem against the light.

Then she turned out the bedside lamp, settled herself in her
favourite position, flat on her back, and gave way.

'What can be the matter with me?'

She succumbed again to anxiety and started to shiver. She
was obsessed by the vision of an empty doorway, with clumps of
red salvia on either side. 'I can't be well,' she thought, 'one
doesn't get into a state like this over a door!' Again she saw the
three old women, Lili's neck, and the beige rug that Madame
Aldonza had trailed about with her for the past twenty years.
'Which of them am I going to look like in ten years' time?'

Though she did not feel alarmed at this prospect, her anxiety increased still further. She let her mind wander from one
incident of her past life to another, from this scene to that,
trying to rid her thoughts of the empty doorway framed by red
salvia. She was growing restless in her bed and trembled
slightly. Suddenly she jumped as though shot, racked by a pain
so deep that at first she thought it must be physical, a pain that

twisted her lips and dragged from them, in a raucous sob, a single name: "Chéri!"

Tears followed, beyond all control at first. As soon as she had regained her self-control, she sat up, wiped her face, and turned on the lamp again. 'Ah! That's what it is! Now I understand!'

She took a thermometer from the drawer of her bedside table and put it under her arm. 'My temperature's normal, so it's nothing physical. I see. I'm just unhappy. Something must be done about it.'

She drank some water, got out of bed, bathed her inflamed eyes, put on a little powder, poked the fire, and went back to bed. She was on her guard, full of mistrust for an enemy she had never known: grief. She had just said goodbye to thirty years of easy living: years spent pleasantly, intent often on love, sometimes on money. This had left her, at almost fifty, still young and defenceless.

She made fun of herself, ceased to feel her grief, and smiled. 'I think I was out of my mind just now. There's nothing wrong with me any longer.'

But a movement of her left arm, which bent automatically to hold and shelter a sleeping head, brought back all her agony, and she sat up with a jump. "Well, this *is* going to be fun!" she said out loud and sternly.

She looked at the clock and saw that it was barely eleven. Overhead passed the slippered tread of the elderly Rose, on her way up the stairs to the attic floor. Then there was silence. Léa resisted the impulse to call out for help to this deferential old body. 'Don't give the servants anything to gossip about. We mustn't have that.'

She left her bed again, wrapped herself up warm in a quilted silk dressing-gown and toasted her feet. Then she half opened her window and listened for she knew not what. A moist and milder wind had brought clouds in its wake, and the lingering leaves in the neighbouring Bois sighed with every gust. Léa shut the window again, picked up a newspaper and looked at the date

—'October the twenty-sixth. Exactly a month since Chéri was married?' She never said 'Since Edmée was married.'

Following Chéri's example, she did not yet count his young wraith of a wife as really alive. Chestnut-brown eyes, ashy hair which was very lovely with the vestige of a crimp in it—all the rest melted away in her memory like the contours of a face seen in a dream.

'At this very moment, of course, they'll be in each other's arms in Italy. And . . . and I don't mind that in the least.'

She was not boasting. The picture of the young couple she had called up, the familiar attitudes it evoked—even Chéri's face, as he lay exhausted for a minute, with the white line of light between his tired eyelids—aroused in her neither curiosity nor jealousy. On the other hand, an animal convulsion again racked her body, bending her double, as her eye fell on a nick in the pearl-grey wainscot—the mark of some brutality of Chéri's. "The lovely hand which here has left its trace, has turned away from me for ever," she said. 'How grandly I'm talking! Soon grief will be turning me into a poet!'

She walked about, she sat down, she went to bed again and waited for daylight. At eight o'clock Rose found her writing at her desk, and this upset the old lady's-maid.

"Is Madame not well?"

"So-so, Rose. Age, you know. . . . Doctor Vidal thinks I ought to have a change of air. Will you come with me? It promises to be a cold winter here in Paris. We'll go south to the sun, and eat meals cooked in oil."

"Whereabouts will that be?"

"You want to know too much. Simply have my trunks brought down, and give my fur rugs a good beating."

"Madame will be taking the motor-car?"

"I think so. I'm sure of it, in fact. I'll need all my creature comforts now, Rose. Just think of it, this time I'm going all on my own. It's going to be a pleasure trip."

During the next five days Léa rushed all over Paris; wrote, telegraphed, and received telegrams and answers from the south. And she said goodbye to Paris, leaving behind a short letter addressed to Madame Peloux which she started no less than three times:

My dear Charlotte,
    You'll forgive me if I go away without saying goodbye to you, and keep my little secret to myself. I'm making a perfect fool of myself . . . and why not? It's a short life, let's make it a gay one.
    I send you an affectionate kiss. Remember me to the child when he comes back.

Your incorrigible
Léa.

    PS.—Don't trouble to come and interview my butler or concierge; no member of my household knows anything at all about it.

"**D**o you know, my adored treasure, I don't think you're looking very well."

"It's the night in the train," Chéri answered shortly.

Madame Peloux did not dare to say just what she thought. She found her son changed. 'He's . . . yes, he's sinister!' she decided; and she ended by exclaiming enthusiastically, "It's Italy!"

"If you like," Chéri conceded.

Mother and son had just finished breakfasting together, and Chéri had condescended to praise with an oath his cup of "housemaid's coffee", made with creamy milk, well sugared, slowly re-heated, with buttered toast crumbled into it and browned till it formed a succulent crust.

He felt cold in his white woollen pyjamas and was clasping his knees to his chest. Charlotte Peloux, anxious to look pretty for her son, had put on a brand new marigold négligée, and a boudoir-cap fitting tight across the forehead. This made her face stand out, bare and macabre.

Finding her son's eye fixed upon her, she simpered: "You see, I've adopted the grandmother style. Very soon, I'll powder my hair. Do you like this cap? Rather eighteenth-century, don't you think? Dubarry or Pompadour? How do I look in it?"

"Like an old convict," Chéri said witheringly. "Next time you must run up a warning signal."

She groaned, then shrieked with laughter: "Ha-ha-ha. You've a sharp tongue in your head and no mistake!"

But he did not laugh. He was staring out at the lawn powdered with snow after last night's fall. His nervous state was visible only in the spasmodic twitching of his jaw muscles. Madame Peloux was intimidated. She, too, was silent. The faint tinkle of a bell sounded.

"That's Edmée, ringing for her breakfast," said Madame Peloux.

Chéri did not answer. "What's wrong with the heating? It's freezing in here!" he said a moment later.

"It's Italy!" Madame Peloux repeated lyrically. "You come back here, your eyes and your heart full of the warm sun of the south, and find you've landed at the Pole—at the North Pole. There hasn't been a flower on the dahlias for the last week. But don't worry, my precious! Your love-nest will soon be finished. If the architect hadn't gone down with paratyphoid, it would be ready for you now. I warned him. If I told him once, I told him twenty times: 'Monsieur Savaron . . .' "

Chéri, who was standing by the window, turned round sharply. "What was the date on that letter?"

Madame Peloux opened her large child-like eyes: "What letter?"

"The letter from Léa you showed me."

"She put no date on it, my love; but I got it the night before my last Sunday At-home in October."

"I see. And you don't know who it is?"

"Who what is, my paragon?"

"Whoever it was she went away with, of course."

Malice clothed Madame Peloux's stark features. "No. Would you believe it, nobody has an idea! Old Lili is in Sicily, and none of my set has a clue! A mystery, an enthralling mystery! However, you know me, I've managed to pick up a few scraps here and there . . ."

Chéri's dark eyes expanded: "What's the tattle?"

"It seems it's a young man . . ." Madame Peloux whispered. "A young man not . . . not particularly desirable, if you know what I mean . . . very well made, of course!" She was lying, careful to insinuate the worst.

Chéri shrugged his shoulders.

"Well made, did you say. Don't make me laugh! My poor Léa! I can see him from here—a hefty little fellow from Patron's training-quarters—black hairs on his wrists and clammy hands. . . . Well, I'm going back to bed now; you make me tired."

Trailing his bedroom slippers, he went back to his room, dawdling in the long corridors and on the spacious landings of the house he seemed to be discovering for the first time. He ran into a pot-bellied wardrobe, and was amazed. 'Damned if I knew that thing was there. . . . Oh, yes, I vaguely remember. . . . And who the devil's this chap?' He was addressing an enlarged photograph, in a deep black frame, hanging funereally near a piece of coloured pottery, equally unfamiliar to Chéri.

Madame Peloux had been installed in this house for the last twenty-five years, and had kept every unfortunate result of her bad taste and acquisitiveness. "Your house looks just like the nest of a magpie gone batty," was old Lili's reproachful comment. She herself had a hearty appetite for modern pictures, and still more for modern painters. To this Madame Peloux had replied: "I believe in letting well alone."

If the muddy green paint—"The green of hospital corridors," Léa called it—flaked off in one of the passages, Madame Peloux would have it repainted a similar muddy green; or if the maroon velvet on a *chaise-longue* needed replacing, she was careful to choose the same maroon velvet.

Chéri paused by the open door of a dressing-room. Embedded in the dark red marble-topped wash-stand were jug and basin of plain white with a monogram, and over the two electric-light fittings were lily-shaped bead shades. Chéri shuddered as though caught in a violent draught—'Good God, how hideous, what an old junk-shop!'

He hurried away. At the end of the passage, he came upon a window edged with small pieces of red and yellow stained glass. 'That's the last straw!' he said grumpily.

He turned to the left and roughly opened a door—the door of his nursery—without knocking. A little cry came from the bed where Edmée was just finishing her breakfast. Chéri closed the door and stared at his wife without going any closer.

"Good morning," she said with a smile. "You do look surprised to see me here!"

She lay bathed in a steady blue light reflected from the snow outside. Her crimped ashy chestnut hair was down, but barely covered her prettily curved shoulders. With her pink-and-white cheeks matching her nightgown, and her rosy lips paler than usual from fatigue, she looked like a light toned picture, not quite finished and rather misty.

"Aren't you going to say good morning to me, Fred?" she insisted.

He sat down close beside his wife and took her in his arms. She fell back gently, dragging him with her. Chéri propped himself on his elbow to look down more closely at her. She was so young that even when tired she still looked fresh. He seemed astonished by the smoothness of her fully rounded lower eyelids, and by the silvery softness of her cheeks.

"How old are you?" he asked suddenly.

Edmée opened her eyes, which she had closed voluptuously. Chéri stared at the brown of their pupils and at her small square teeth.

"Oh, come! I shall be nineteen on the fifth of January, and do try and remember it."

He drew his arm away roughly and the young woman slipped into the hollow of the bed like a discarded scarf.

"Nineteen, it's prodigious! Do you know that I'm over twenty-five?"

"But of course I know that, Fred. . . ."

He picked up a pale tortoiseshell mirror from the bed-table and gazed at himself. "Twenty-five years old!"

Twenty-five years of age and a face of white marble that seemed indestructible. Twenty-five, but at the outer corners of the eye and beneath it—delicately plagiarising the classical design of the eyelid—were two lines, visible only in full light, two incisions traced by the lightest, the most relentless, of fingers.

He put back the mirror: "You're younger than I am. That shocks me."

"Not me!"

She had answered in a biting voice, full of hidden meaning. He took no notice.

"Do you know why my eyes are beautiful?" he asked in all seriousness.

"No," Edmée said. "Perhaps because I love them?"

"Stuff!" Chéri said, shrugging his shoulders. "It's because they're shaped like a sole."

"Like what?"

"Like a sole."

He sat down near her to give a demonstration.

"Look—here—the corner next the nose is the head of the sole. And then—the upper curve, that's the back of the sole; whereas the lower line runs perfectly straight and that's its belly. And the other corner that tapers up to my temples, that's the sole's tail."

"Oh?"

"Yes, but if I had an eye shaped like a flounder, that's to say, with the lower part as much curved as the top, then I should look silly. See? You've passed your matric., and you didn't know that?"

"No, I must admit . . ."

She broke off, feeling guilty, because he had spoken sententiously and with exaggerated passion, like someone with a mania. 'There are moments when he looks like a savage,' she thought, 'like a man from the jungle. Yet he knows nothing about plants or animals, and sometimes he doesn't seem even to know about human beings.'

Sitting close beside her, Chéri put one arm round her

shoulders and with his free hand began to finger the small, evenly matched, very round and very beautiful, pearls of her necklace. Intoxicated by the scent which Chéri used too much of, she began to droop like a rose in an overheated room.

"Fred! Come back to sleep! We're both tired. . . ."

He seemed not to have heard. He was staring at the pearls with obsessed anxiety.

"Fred!"

He shivered, leaped to his feet, furiously tore off his pyjamas and jumped naked into bed, seeking the place to rest his head on a shoulder where the delicate collar-bone was still youthfully sharp. The whole of Edmée's body obeyed his will as she opened her arms to him. Chéri closed his eyes and never moved. She took care to remain awake, a little smothered under his weight, and thinking him asleep. But almost at once he turned over away from her with a sudden pitch, imitating the groans of someone fast asleep, and rolled himself up in the sheet at the other side of the bed.

'He always does that,' Edmée noted.

All through the winter, she was to awaken in this square room with its four windows. Bad weather delayed the completion of the new house in the Avenue Henri-Martin—bad weather, and Chéri's whims. He wanted a black bathroom, a Chinese drawing-room, a basement fitted up with a swimming pool and gymnasium. To the architect's objections he would answer: "I don't care a damn. I pay, I want the work done. To hell with the cost." But every now and again he would cast a ruthless eye over an estimate and proclaim "You can't bamboozle young Peloux." Indeed, he held forth on standardisation, fibro-cement and coloured stucco with unexpected glibness and a memory for exact figures that compelled the contractor's respect.

Rarely did he consult his young wife, although he paraded his authority for her benefit and took pains, when occasion arose, to cover his deficiencies by giving curt commands. She was to find that he possessed an instinctive eye for colour, but had only contempt for beauty of shape and period differences.

"You simply clutter up your head with all that stuff and nonsense, what's your name, yes, you, Edmée. An idea for the smoking-room? All right, here's one: Blue for the walls—a ferocious blue. The carpet purple—a purple that plays second fiddle to the blue of the walls. Against that you needn't be afraid of using as much black as you like and a splash of gold in the furniture and ornaments."

"Yes, you're right, Fred. But it will be rather drastic with all those strong colours. It's going to look rather charmless without a lighter note somewhere . . . a white vase or a statue."

"Nonsense," he interrupted, rather sharply. "The white vase you want will be me—me, stark naked. And we mustn't forget a cushion or some thingumabob in pumpkin-red for when I'm running about stark naked in the smoking-room."

Secretly attracted and at the same time disgusted, she cherished these fanciful ideas for turning their future home into a sort of disreputable palace, a temple to the greater glory of her husband. She offered little resistance, just gently requested "some little corner" for a small and precious set of furniture upholstered with needle-work on a white ground—a present from Marie-Laure.

This gentleness masked a determination that was young yet far from inexperienced; it stood her in good stead during the four months of camping out in her mother-in-law's house. It enabled her to evade, throughout these four months, the enemy stalking her, the traps laid daily to destroy her equanimity, her still susceptible gaiety, and her tact. Charlotte Peloux, over-excited at the proximity of so tender a victim, was inclined to lose her head and squander her barbs, using her claws indiscriminately.

"Keep calm, Madame Peloux," Chéri would throw out from time to time. "What bones will there be left for you to pick next winter, if I don't stop you now?"

Edmée raised frightened, grateful eyes to her husband, and did her best not to think too much, not to look too much at Madame Peloux. Then one evening, Charlotte, almost heedlessly, three times tossed across the chrysanthemum table-piece Léa's name instead of Edmée's.

Chéri lowered his satanic eyebrows: "Madame Peloux, I believe your memory is giving way. Perhaps a rest-cure is indicated?"

Charlotte Peloux held her tongue for a whole week, but Edmée never dared to ask her husband: "Did you get angry on my behalf? Was it me you were defending? Or was it that other woman, the one before me?"

Life as a child and then as a girl had taught her patience, hope, silence; and given her a prisoner's proficiency in handling these virtues as weapons. The fair Marie-Laure had never scolded her daughter: she had merely punished her. Never a hard word, never a tender one. Utter loneliness, then a boarding-school, then again loneliness in the holidays and frequent relegations to a bedroom. Finally, the threat of marriage—any marriage—from the moment that the eye of a too beautiful mother had discerned in the daughter the dawn of a rival beauty, shy, timid, looking a victim of tyranny, and all the more touching for that. In comparison with this inhuman gold-and-ivory mother, Charlotte Peloux and her spontaneous malice seemed a bed of roses.

"Are you frightened of my respected parent?" Chéri asked her one evening.

Edmée smiled and pouted to show her indifference: "Frightened? No. You aren't frightened when a door slams, though it may make you jump. It's a snake creeping under it that's frightening."

"A terrific snake, Marie-Laure, isn't she?"

"Terrific."

He waited for confidences that did not come and put a brotherly arm round his wife's slender shoulders: "We're sort of orphans, you and I, aren't we?"

"Yes, we're orphans, and we're so sweet!"

She clung to him. They were alone in the big sitting-room, for Madame Peloux was upstairs concocting, as Chéri put it, her poisons for the following day. The night was cold and the window panes reflected the lamp-light and furnishings like a pond. Edmée felt warm and protected, safe in the arms of this unknown man. She lifted her head and gave a cry of alarm. He was staring up at the chandelier above them with a look of desperation on his magnificent features, and two tears hung glistening between the lids of his half-closed eyes.

"Chéri, Chéri, what's the matter with you?" On the spur of the moment she had called him by the too endearing nickname she had never meant to pronounce. He answered its appeal in bewilderment and turned his eyes down to look at her.

"Chéri, oh God! I'm frightened. What's wrong with you?"

He pushed her away a little, and held her facing him.

"Oh! Oh! You poor child, you poor little thing! What are you frightened of?"

He gazed at her with his eyes of velvet, wide-open, peaceful, inscrutable, all the more handsome for his tears. Edmée was about to beg him not to speak, when he said, "How silly we are! It's the idea that we're orphans. It's idiotic. It's so true."

He resumed his air of comic self-importance, and she drew a breath of relief, knowing that he would say no more. He began switching off all the lights with his usual care, and then turned to Edmée with a vanity that was either very simple or very deceitful: "Well, why shouldn't I have a heart like everybody else?"

"What are you doing there?"

He had called out to her almost in a whisper, yet the sound of Chéri's voice struck Edmée so forcibly that she swayed forward as if he had pushed her. She was standing beside a big open writing-desk and she spread her hands over the papers scattered in front of her.

"I'm tidying up . . ." she said in a dazed voice. She lifted a hand and it remained poised in mid-air as though be-numbed. Then she appeared to wake up, and stopped lying.

"It's like this, Fred. You told me that when we came to move house you'd hate to be bothered over what you'd want to take with you, all the things in this room . . . the furniture. I honestly wanted to tidy, to sort things. Then the poison, temptation came . . . evil thoughts . . . one evil thought. . . . I implore your forgiveness. I've touched things that don't belong to me. . . ."

She trembled bravely and waited.

He stood with his forehead jutting forward, his hands clenched in a threatening attitude; but he did not seem to see his wife. His eyes were strangely veiled, and ever after she was to retain the impression of having spoken with a man whose eyes were deathly pale.

"Ah, yes," he said at length. "You were looking . . . you were looking for love-letters." She did not deny it. "You were hunting for my love-letters."

He laughed his awkward, constrained laugh.

Edmée felt hurt, and blushed. "Of course you must think me a fool. As if you were the kind of man not to lock them away in a safe place or burn them! And then, anyhow, they're none of my business. I've only got what I deserved. You won't hold it too much against me, Fred?"

Her pleading had cost her a certain effort, and she tried deliberately to make herself look appealing, pouting her lips a little and keeping the upper half of her face shadowed by her fluffy hair. But Chéri did not relax his attitude, and she noticed for the first time that the unblemished skin of his cheeks had taken on the transparence of a white rose in winter, and that their oval contour had shrunk.

"Love-letters," he repeated. "That's howlingly funny."

He took a step forward, seized a fistful of papers and scattered them: post-cards, restaurant bills, tradespeople's announcements, telegrams from chorus girls met one night and never seen again, *pneumatiques* of four or five lines from sponging friends; and several close-written pages slashed with the sabre-like script of Madame Peloux.

Chéri turned round again to his wife: "I have no love-letters."

"Oh!" she protested. "Why do you want . . ."

"I have none," he interrupted; "you can never understand. I've never noticed it myself until now. I can't have any love-letters because——" He checked himself. "But wait, wait. . . . Yes, there was one occasion, I remember, when I didn't want to go to La Bourboule, and it . . . Wait, wait."

He began pulling out drawers and feverishly tossing papers to the floor.

"That's too bad! What can I have done with it? I could have sworn it was in the upper left-hand . . . No. . . ."

He slammed back the empty drawers and glowered at Edmée.

"You found nothing? You didn't take a letter which began 'But what do you expect, I'm not in the least bored. There's nothing better than to be separated one week in every month,' and then went on to something else. I don't remember what, something about honey-suckle climbing high enough to look in at the window."

He broke off, simply because his memory refused to come to his aid, and he was left gesticulating in his impatience.

Slim and recalcitrant, Edmée did not quail before him. She took refuge in caustic irritability. "No, no, I *took* nothing. Since when have I been capable of *taking* things? But if this letter is so very precious to you, how is it you've left it lying about? I've no need to enquire whether it was one of Léa's?"

He winced, but not quite in the manner Edmée had expected. The ghost of a smile hovered over his handsome, unresponsive features; and, with his head on one side, an expectant look in his eyes, and the delicious bow of his mouth taut-stretched, he might well have been listening to the echo of a name.

The full force of Edmée's young and ill-disciplined emotions burst forth in a series of sobs and tears, and her fingers writhed and twisted as if ready to scratch. "Go away! I hate you! You've never loved me. I might not so much as exist, for all the notice you take of me! You hurt me, you despise me, you're insulting, you're, you're . . . You think only of that old woman! It's not natural, it's degenerate, it's . . . You don't love me! Why, oh why, did you ever marry me? . . . You're . . . you're . . . "

She was tossing her head like an animal caught by the neck, and as she leaned back to take a deep breath, because she was suffocating, the light fell on her string of small, milky, evenly matched pearls. Chéri stared in stupefaction at the uncontrolled movements of the lovely throat, at the hands clasped together in appeal, and above all at the tears, her tears. . . . He had never seen such a torrent of tears. For who had ever wept in front of him, or wept because of him? No one. Madame Peloux? 'But,' he thought, 'Madame Peloux's tears don't count.' Léa? No. Searching his memory, he appealed to a pair of honest blue eyes; but they had sparkled with pleasure only, or malice, or a rather mocking tenderness. Such floods of tears poured down the cheeks of this writhing young woman. What could be done about all these tears? He did not know. All the same, he stretched out an arm, and as Edmée drew back, fearing some brutality perhaps, he placed his beautiful, gentle, scented hand on her head and patted her ruffled hair. He did his best to copy the tone and speech of a voice whose power he knew so well: "There, there. . . . What's it all about? What's the matter, then? There . . . there. . . ."

Edmée collapsed suddenly, fell back huddled in a heap on a settee, and broke out into frenzied and passionate sobbing that sounded like yells of laughter or howls of joy. As she lay doubled up, her graceful body heaved and rocked with grief, jealousy, fury and an unsuspected servility. And yet, like a wrestler in the heat of a struggle, or a swimmer in the hollow of a wave, she felt bathed in some strange new atmosphere, both natural and harsh.

She had a good long cry, and recovered by slow degrees, with periods of calm shaken by great shudders and gasps for breath. Chéri sat down by her side and continued to stroke her hair. The crisis of his own emotion was over, and he felt bored. He ran his eyes over Edmée as she lay sideways upon the unyielding settee. This straggling body, with its rucked-up frock and trailing scarf, added to the disorder of the room; and this displeased him.

Soft as was his sigh of boredom, she heard it and sat up. "Yes," she said, "I'm more than you can stand. . . . Oh! it would be better to . . ."

He interrupted her, fearing a torrent of words: "It's not that. It's simply that I don't know what you want."

"What I want? How d'you mean, what I . . ."

She lifted her face, still wet with tears.

"Now listen to me." He took her hands.

She tried to free herself. "No, no, I know that tone of voice. You're going to treat me to another of those nonsensical outbursts. When you put on that tone of voice and face, I know you're going to prove that your eye is shaped like a striped super-mullet, or that your mouth looks like the figure three on its side. No, no, I can't stand that!"

Her recriminations were childish, and Chéri relaxed, feeling that after all they were both very young. He pressed her warm hands between his own.

"But you must listen to me! . . . Good God! I'd like to know what you've got to reproach me with! Do I ever go out in the evenings without you? No! Do I often leave you on your own during the day? Do I carry on a secret correspondence?"

"I don't know—I don't think so——"

He turned her this way and that like a doll.

"Do I have a separate room? Don't I make love to you well?"

She hesitated, smiling with exquisite suspicion. "Do you call that love, Fred?"

"There are other words for it, but you wouldn't appreciate them."

"What you call love . . . isn't it possible that it may be, really, a . . . kind . . . of alibi?" She hastened to add, "I'm merely generalising, Fred, of course . . . I said 'may be', in certain cases. . . ."

He dropped Edmée's hands. "That," he said coldly, "is putting your foot right in it."

"Why?" she asked in a feeble voice.

He whistled, chin in air, as he moved back a step or two. Then he advanced upon his wife, looking her up and down as if she were a stranger. To instil fear a fierce animal has no need to leap. Edmée noticed that his nostrils were dilating and that the tip of his nose was white.

"Ugh!" he breathed, looking at his wife. He shrugged his shoulders, turned, and walked away. At the end of the room he turned round and came back again. "Ugh!" he repeated, "Look what's talking!"

"What are you saying?"

"Look what's talking, and what it says. Upon my word, it actually has the cheek to . . ."

She jumped up in a rage. "Fred," she said, "don't dare to speak to me again in that tone? What do you take me for?"

"For a woman who knows exactly how to put her foot in it, as I've just had the honour of informing you."

He touched her on the shoulder with a rigid forefinger, and this hurt her as much as if he had inflicted a serious bruise. "You've matriculated; isn't there somewhere some kind of a proverb which says, 'Never play with knives or daggers' or whatever it may be?"

"Cold steel," she answered automatically.

"That's right. Well, my child, you must never play with cold steel. That's to say, you must never be wounding about a man's . . . a man's favours, if I may so express it. You were wounding about the gifts, about the favours, I bestow on you."

"You . . . you talk like a cocotte," she gasped.

She blushed, and her strength and self-control deserted her. She hated him for remaining cool and collected, for keeping his superiority: its whole secret lay in the carriage of his head, the sureness of his stance, the poise of his arms and shoulders.

The hard forefinger once more pressed into Edmée's shoulder.

"Excuse me, excuse me . . . It'll probably come as a great surprise when I state that, on the contrary, it's you who have the mentality of a tart. When it comes to judging such matters, there's no greater authority than young Peloux. I'm a connoisseur of 'cocottes', as you call them. I know them inside out. A 'cocotte' is a lady who generally manages to receive more than she gives. Do you hear what I say?"

What she heard above all was that he was now addressing her like a stray acquaintance.

"Nineteen years old, white skin, hair that smells of vanilla; and then, in bed, closed eyes and limp arms. That's all very pretty, but is there anything unusual about it? Do you really think it so very unusual?"

She had started at each word, and each sting had goaded her towards the duel of female *versus* male.

"It may be very unusual," she said in a steady voice, "how could *you* know?"

He did not answer, and she hastened to take advantage of a hit. "Personally, I saw much handsomer men than you when we were in Italy. The streets were full of them. My nineteen years are worth those of any other girl of my age, just as one good-looking man is as good as the next. Don't worry, everything can be arranged. Nowadays, marriage is not an important undertaking. Instead of allowing silly scenes to make us bitter . . ."

He put a stop to what she had to say by an almost pitying shake of the head.

"My poor kid, it's not so simple as that."

"Why not? There's such a thing as quick divorce, if one's ready to pay."

She spoke in the peremptory manner of a runaway school-girl, and it was pathetic. She had pushed back the hair off her forehead, and her anxious, intelligent eyes were made to look all the darker by the soft contours of her cheeks now fringed with hair: the eyes of an unhappy woman, eyes mature and definitive in a still undeveloped face.

"That wouldn't help at all," Chéri said.

"Because?"

"Because . . ." He leaned forward with his eyelashes tapered into pointed wings, shut his eyes and opened them again as if he had just swallowed a bitter pill. "Because you love me."

She noticed that he had resumed the more familiar form of addressing her, and above all the fuller, rather choked tones of their happiest hours. In her heart of hearts she acquiesced: 'It's true, I love him. At the moment, there's no remedy.'

The dinner bell sounded in the garden—a bell which was too small, dating from before Madame Peloux's time, a sad clear bell reminiscent of a country orphanage. Edmée shivered. "Oh, I don't like that bell. . . ."

"No?" said Chéri, absent-mindedly.

"In our house, dinner will be announced. There'll be no bell. There'll be no boarding-house habits in our home—you'll see."

She spoke these words without turning round, while walking down the hospital-green corridor, and so did not see, behind her, either the fierce attention Chéri paid to her last words, or his silent laughter.

He was walking along with a light step, stimulated by the rathe spring, perceptible in the moist gusty wind and the exciting earthy smells of squares and private gardens. Every now and again a fleeting glimpse in a glass would remind him that he was wearing a becoming felt hat, pulled down over the right eye, a loose-fitting spring coat, large light-coloured gloves and a terracotta tie. The eyes of women followed his progress with silent homage, the more candid among them bestowing that passing stupefaction which can be neither feigned nor hidden. But Chéri never looked at women in the street. He had just come from his house in the Avenue Henri-Martin, having left various orders with the upholsterers: orders contradicting one another, but thrown out in a tone of authority.

On reaching the end of the Avenue, he took a deep breath of the good spring scents carried up from the Bois on the heavy moist wing of the west wind, and then hurried on his way to the Porte Dauphine. Within a few minutes he had reached the lower end of the Avenue Bugeaud, and there he stopped. For the first time in six months his feet were treading the familiar road. He unbuttoned his coat.

'I've been walking too fast,' he said to himself. He started off again, then paused and, this time, trained his eyes on one particular spot: fifty yards or so down the road: bareheaded, shammy-leather in hand, Ernest the concierge—Léa's concierge—was "doing" the brass-work of the railings in front of

Léa's house. Chéri began to hum, realised from the sound of his voice that he never did hum, and stopped.

"How are things, Ernest? Hard at work as usual?"

The concierge brightened respectfully.

"Monsieur Peloux! It's a pleasure to see Monsieur again. Monsieur has not changed at all."

"Neither have you, Ernest. Madame is well, I hope?"

He turned his head away to gaze up at the closed shutters on the first floor.

"I expect so, Monsieur, all we've had has been a few post-cards."

"Where from? Was it Biarritz?"

"I don't think so, Monsieur."

"Where is Madame?"

"It wouldn't be easy for me to tell you, Monsieur. We forward all letters addressed to Madame—and there's none to speak of—to Madame's solicitor."

Chéri pulled out his note-case, and cocked an eye at Ernest.

"Oh, Monsieur Peloux, money between you and me? Don't think of it. A thousand francs won't make a man tell what he doesn't know. But if Monsieur would like the address of Madame's solicitor?"

"No thanks, there's no point. And when does she return?"

Ernest threw up his hands: "That's another question that's beyond me. Maybe to-morrow, maybe in a month's time. . . . I keep everything in readiness, just the same. You have to watch out where Madame is concerned. If you said to me now, 'There she comes round the corner of the Avenue,' I shouldn't be surprised."

Chéri turned round and looked towards the corner of the Avenue.

"That's all Monsieur Peloux wants? Monsieur just happened to be walking by? It's a lovely day. . . ."

"Nothing else, thank you, Ernest. Good-bye, Ernest."

"Always at Monsieur's service."

Chéri walked up as far as the Place Victor-Hugo, swinging his cane as he went. Twice he stumbled and almost fell, like people who imagine their progress is being followed by hostile eyes. On reaching the balustraded entrance to the Métro, he leaned over the ramp to peer down into the pink-and-black recesses of the Underground, and felt utterly exhausted. When he straightened his back, he saw that the lamps had been lighted in the square and that the blue of dusk coloured everything around him.

'No, it can't be true. I'm ill.'

He had plumbed the depths of cavernous memories and his return to the living world was painful. The right words came to him at last. 'Pull yourself together, Peloux, for God's sake! Are you losing your head, my boy? Don't you know it's time to go back home?'

This last word recalled a sight that one hour had sufficed to banish from his mind: a large square room—his own nursery; an anxious young woman standing by the window; and Charlotte Peloux, subdued by a Martini.

"Oh, no," he said aloud. "Not that! That's all over."

He signalled to a taxi with his raised stick.

"To the . . . er . . . to the Restaurant du Dragon Bleu."

Chéri crossed the grill-room to the sound of violins in the glare of the atrocious electric light, and this had a tonic effect. He shook the hand of a maître d'hôtel who recognised him. Before him rose the stooping figure of a tall young man. Chéri gave an affectionate gasp. "Desmond, the very man I wanted to see! Howdydo?"

They were shown to a table decorated with pink carnations. A small hand and a towering aigrette beckoned towards Chéri from a neighbouring table.

"It's La Loupiote," Vicomte Desmond warned him.

Chéri had no recollection of La Loupiote, but he smiled towards the towering aigrette and, without getting up, touched the small hand with a paper fan lying on his table. Then he put on his most solemn "conquering hero" look, and swept his eyes over an unknown couple. The woman had forgotten to eat since he had sat down in her vicinity.

"The man with her looks a regular cuckold, doesn't he?"

He had leaned over to whisper into his friend's ear, and his eyes shone with pleasure as if with rising tears.

"What d'you drink, now you're married?" Desmond asked, "Camomile tea?"

"Pommery," Chéri said.

"And before the Pommery?"

"Pommery, before and after." And, dilating his nostrils, he sniffed as he remembered some sparkling, rose-scented old champagne of 1889 that Léa kept for him alone.

He ordered a meal that a shop-girl out on the spree might choose—cold fish *au porto*, a roast bird, and a piping hot soufflé which concealed in its innards a red ice, sharp on the tongue.

"Hello!" La Loupiote shouted, waving a pink carnation at Chéri.

"Hello," Chéri answered, raising his glass.

The chimes of an English wall-clock struck eight. "Blast!" Chéri grumbled, "Desmond, go and make a telephone call for me."

Desmond's pale eyes were hungry for revelations to come.

"Go and ask for Wagram 17-08, tell them to put you through to my mother, and say we're dining together."

"And supposing young Madame Peloux comes to the telephone?"

"Say the same thing. I'm not tied to her apron-strings. I've got her well trained."

He ate and drank a lot, taking the greatest care to appear serious and blasé; but his pleasure was enhanced by the least sound of laughter, the clink of glasses, or the strains of a syrupy valse. The steely blue of the highly glazed woodwork reminded him of the Riviera, at the hour when the too blue sea grows dark around the blurred reflection of the noonday sun. He forgot that very handsome young men ought to pretend indifference; he began to scrutinise the dark girl opposite, so that she trembled all over under his expert gaze.

"What about Léa?" Desmond asked suddenly.

Chéri did not jump: he was thinking of Léa. "Léa? She's in the South."

"Is all over between you?"

Chéri put his thumb in the armhole of his waistcoat.

"Well, of course, what d'you expect? We parted in proper style, the best of friends. It couldn't last a lifetime. What a charming, intelligent woman, old man! But then, you know her yourself! Broadminded . . . most remarkable. My dear fellow, I confess that if it hadn't been for the question of age . . . But there *was* the question of age, and you agree . . ."

"Of course," Desmond interrupted.

This young man with lack-lustre eyes, though he knew just how to perform the wearing and difficult duties of a parasite, had just yielded to curiosity and blamed himself for such rashness. Chéri, circumspect and at the same time highly elated, never stopped talking about Léa. He made all the right remarks, showed all the sound sense of a married man. He spoke in praise of marriage, while giving Léa's virtues their due. He extolled the submissive sweetness of his young wife, and thus found occasion to criticise Léa's independence of character. "Oh, the old devil, she had her own ideas about everything, I can tell you!"

He went a step further in his confidences, speaking of Léa with severity, and even impertinence. He was sheltering behind idiotic words, prompted by the suspicions of a deceived lover, and at the same time enjoying the subtle pleasure of being able to speak of her without danger. A little more, and he would have sullied her name, while his heart was rejoicing in his own memories of her: sullied the soft sweet name which he had been unable to mention freely during the last six months, and the whole gracious vision he had of Léa, leaning over him with her two or three irreparable wrinkles, and her beauty, now lost to him, but—alas—ever present.

About eleven o'clock they rose to go, chilled by the emptiness of the almost deserted restaurant. However, at the next table, La Loupiote was busy writing letters and had called for telegraph-forms. She raised her white, inoffensive, sheep-like head as the two friends passed by. "Well, aren't you even going to say good evening?"

"Good evening," Chéri condescended to say.

La Loupiote drew her friend's attention to Chéri's good looks. "Would you believe it! And to think that he's got such pots of money. Some people have everything!"

But when Chéri merely offered her an open cigarette-case, she became vituperative. "They have everything, except the knowledge of how to make proper use of it. Go back home to your mother, dearie!"

"Look here," Chéri said to Desmond when they were outside in the narrow street, "Look here, I was about to ask you, Desmond . . . Wait till we get away from this beastly crowd. . . ."

The soft damp evening air had kept people lingering in the streets, but the theatre-goers from the Rue Caumartin onwards had not yet packed the Boulevard. Chéri took his friend by the arm: "Look here, Desmond . . . I wanted you to make another telephone call."

Desmond stopped, "Again?"

"You'll ask for Wagram . . ."

"17-08."

"You're marvellous . . . Say that I've been taken ill in your flat. Where are you living?"

"Hôtel Morris."

"Splendid—and that I won't be back till morning, and that you're making me some mint tea. Go on, old man. Here, you can give this to the telephone-girl, or else keep it yourself. But come back quickly. I'll be sitting waiting for you outside Weber's."

The tall young man, arrogant and serviceable, went off crumpling the franc-notes in his pocket, without permitting

81
.....

himself a comment. When Desmond rejoined him, Chéri was slouched over an untouched orangeade in which he appeared to be reading his fortune.

"Desmond . . . Who answered you?"

"A lady," the laconic messenger replied.

"Which?"

"Dunno."

"What did she say?"

"That it was all right."

"In what tone of voice?"

"Same as I'm speaking to you in."

"Oh, good. Thanks."

'It was Edmée,' thought Chéri.

They were walking towards the Place de la Concorde and Chéri linked arms with Desmond. He did not dare to admit that he was feeling dog-tired.

"Where do you want to go?" Desmond asked.

"Well, old man," Chéri sighed in gratitude, "to the Morris; and as soon as we can. I'm fagged out."

Desmond forgot to be impassive. "What? It can't be true. To the Morris? What d'you want to do? No nonsense! D'you want to . . ."

"To go to bed," Chéri answered. And he closed his eyes as though on the point of dropping off, then opened them again. "Sleep, I want to sleep, got it?"

He gripped his friend's arm too hard.

"Let's go there, then," Desmond said.

Within ten minutes they were at the Morris. The sky-blue and white bedroom and the imitation Empire furniture of the sitting-room smiled at Chéri like old friends. He took a bath, borrowed one of Desmond's silk night-shirts which was too tight for him, got into bed, and, wedged between two huge soft pillows, sank into dreamless bliss, into the dark depths of a sleep that protected him from all attacks.

He began to count the shameful days as they went by. "Sixteen . . . seventeen . . . When three weeks are up, I'll go back to Neuilly." He did not go back. Though he saw the situation quite clearly, he no longer had the strength to cure it. At night, and in the morning sometimes, he flattered himself that he would get over his cowardice within an hour or two. "No strength left? . . . Please, please, I beg of you . . . Not yet strength enough. But it's coming back. What's the betting I'll be in the Boulevard d'Inkermann dining-room at the stroke of twelve? One, two . . ." The stroke of twelve found him in the bath, or else driving his motor, with Desmond at his side.

At every mealtime, he felt optimistic for a moment about his marriage. This feeling was as regular as a recurrent fever. As he sat down facing Desmond at their bachelor table, the ghost of Edmée would appear, and plunge him into silent thoughts of his young wife's inconceivable deference. "Really, that young thing's too sweet! Did you ever see such a dream of a wife? Never a word, never a complaint! I'll treat her to one of those bracelets when I get back. . . . Upbringing, that's what does it! Give me Marie-Laure every time for bringing up a daughter!" But one day in the grill-room at the Morris, abject terror was written on his face when he caught sight of a green dress with a chinchilla collar just like one of Edmée's dresses.

Desmond found life wonderful and was getting a little fat. He reserved his arrogance for moments when Chéri—encouraged by him to pay a visit to some "prodigious English girl, riddled with vice", or to some "Indian potentate in his opium palace"—refused point blank or else consented with unconcealed scorn. Desmond had long since despaired of understanding Chéri's ways; but Chéri was paying—and better than during the best of their bachelor days together. They ran across the blonde La Loupiote a second time, when they visited a friend of hers, a woman who boasted such an ordinary name that nobody ever remembered it; "What's-her-name . . . you know perfectly well . . . that pal of La Loupiote's."

The Pal smoked opium, and gave it to others. The instant you came into her modest, ground-floor flat, you smelt escaping gas and stale drugs. She won the hearts of her guests by a tearful cordiality and by a constant incitement to self-pity—both objectionable traits. She treated Desmond, when he paid her a visit, as "a great big desperately lonesome boy," . . . and Chéri as "a beauty who has got everything and it only makes him more miserable." Chéri never touched the pipe; he looked at the small box of cocaine with the repugnance of a cat about to be dosed, and spent most of the night with his back against the cushioned dado, sitting up on a straw mat between Desmond, who went to sleep, and the Pal, who never stopped smoking. For most of the night he breathed in the fumes that satisfy all hunger and thirst, but his self-control and distrust persisted. He appeared to be perfectly happy, except that he stared now and then, with pained and questioning intensity, at the Pal's withered throat—a skinny, far too red throat, round which shimmered a string of false pearls.

Once, he stretched out a hand and with the tip of his fingers touched the henna-tinted hair on the nape of her neck. He judged the weight of the big light hollow pearls with his hand, then snatched it back with the nervous shiver of someone who catches his finger-nail on a piece of frayed silk. Not long after, he got up and went.

"Aren't you sick to death of all this," Desmond asked Chéri, "sick of these poky holes where we eat and drink and never have any girls? Sick of this hotel with the doors always slamming? Sick of the night-clubs where we go in the evenings, and of dashing in that fast car of yours from Paris to Rouen, Paris to Compiègne, Paris to Ville d'Avray? . . . Why not the Riviera for a change? The season down there isn't December and January, it's March, April, or . . ."

"No," said Chéri.

"Then what?"

"Then nothing."

Chéri affected to become amiable and put on what Léa used to call "his air of worldly superiority".

"Dear old boy . . . you don't seem to appreciate the beauty of Paris at this time of the year. . . . This . . . er . . . indecisive season, this spring that doesn't seem willing to smile, the softness of the light . . . as opposed to the commonplace Riviera. . . . No, don't you see, I like it here."

Desmond all but lost his lackey patience. "Yes, and besides, it may be that the young Peloux's divorce will . . ."

Chéri's sensitive nostrils blenched. "If you've arranged to touch a commission from some lawyer friend, you can drop the idea at once. There'll be no such thing as 'young Peloux's divorce'."

"My dear fellow! . . ." Desmond protested, doing his best to look hurt, "You have a very curious way of behaving to a man who has been a friend since your childhood, and who has always . . ."

Chéri was not listening. Instead, he pushed towards Desmond's face a pointed chin and a mouth pursed like a miser's. For the first time in his life he had heard a stranger disposing of his possessions.

He began to reflect. Young Peloux's divorce? Many nights and days had he spent in thinking over these words till they had come to spell liberty, a sort of second boyhood, perhaps something even better. But Desmond's voice, with its affected nasal twang, had just called up the image he had been looking for: Edmée, resolute in her little hat with its long motoring veil, moving out of the house at Neuilly on her way to an unknown house to join an unknown man. "Of course, that would settle everything," and his Bohemian side was delighted. At the same time a surprisingly timorous Chéri jibbed, "That's not the sort of way one behaves!" The image became focused in sharper colour and movement. Chéri could hear the heavy musical note of the iron gate swinging to, and could see beyond it fingers wearing a grey pearl and a white diamond. "Farewell," the small hand said.

Chéri jumped up, pushing back his seat. "Those are mine, all of them! The woman, the house, the rings . . . they all belong to me!"

He had not spoken out loud, but his features expressed such savage violence that Desmond thought his last hour of prosperity had struck. Chéri spoke to him pityingly but without kindness.

"Poor pussy-cat, did I scare you? What it is to be descended from the Crusaders! Come along, and I'll buy you pants as fine as my shirts, and shirts as fine as your pants. Desmond, is to-day the seventeenth?"

"Yes, why?"

"The seventeenth of March. In other words, spring. Desmond, people who think themselves smart, I mean those in the height of fashion, women or men—can they afford to wait any longer before buying their spring wardrobes?"

"Hardly——"

"The seventeenth, Desmond! Come along at once; everything's all right. We're going to buy a huge bracelet for my wife, an enormous cigarette-holder for Madame Peloux, and a tiny tie-pin for you."

On more than one such occasion he had felt an overwhelming presentiment that Léa was on the point of returning; that she was already back in her house; that the first-floor shutters had been opened, allowing a glimpse of the flowered pink net curtains across the windows, the lace of the full-length curtains at each side and the glint of the looking-glasses. . . . The fifteenth of April went by and still there was no sign of Léa.

The mournful monotony of Chéri's existence was tempered by several provoking incidents. There was a visit from Madame Peloux, who thought she was breathing her last when she found Chéri looking as thin as a greyhound, eyes wandering and mouth tight shut. There was the letter from Edmée: a letter all in the same surprising tone, explaining that she would stay on at Neuilly "until further orders," and had undertaken to pass on to Chéri "Madame de la Berche's best regards." . . . He thought she was laughing at him, did not know what to answer, and ended by throwing away the enigmatic screed; but he did not go to Neuilly.

April advanced, leafy, cold, bright, and scenting all Paris with tulips, bunches of hyacinths, paulownias and laburnums like dropping-wells of gold. Chéri buried himself all the deeper in austere seclusion. The harassed, ill-treated, angry but well-paid Vicomte Desmond was given his orders: now to protect Chéri from familiar young women and indiscreet young men; now to recruit both sections and form a troop, who ate, drank, and rushed screaming at the top of their voices between Montmartre, the restaurants in the Bois, and the cabarets on the left bank.

One night the Pal was alone in her room, smoking opium and bewailing some shocking disloyalty of La Loupiote's, when her door opened to reveal the young man, with satanic eyebrows tapering towards his temples. He begged for "a glass of really cold water" to allay some secret ardour that had parched his beautiful lips. He showed not the slightest interest in the Pal and the woes she poured out. She pushed towards him the lacquer tray with its pipe: he would accept nothing, and took up his usual position on the mat, to share with her the semi-obscurity in silence. There he stayed till dawn, moving as little as possible, like a man who fears that the least gesture may bring back his pain. At dawn, he questioned the Pal: "Why weren't you wearing your pearls to-day; you know, the big ones?" and politely took his leave.

Walking alone at night was becoming an unconscious habit with him. With rapid lengthy strides he would make off towards some positive but inaccessible goal. Soon after midnight he would escape from Desmond, who discovered him again only towards daybreak, asleep on his hotel bed, flat on his stomach, his head pillowed on his folded arms, in the posture of a fretful child.

"Oh, good, he's here all right," Desmond would say with relief. "One can never be sure with such a crack-pot."

One night, when out on a tramp, his eyes wide open in the darkness, Chéri had felt compelled to walk up the Avenue Bugeaud; for during the day he had disregarded the superstition that made him return there once every twenty-four hours. There are maniacs who cannot go to sleep without having first touched the door-knob three times; a similar obsession made him run his hand along the railings, then put his first finger to the bell-push, and call out Hullo! under his breath, as if in fun, before making off in haste.

But one night, that very night, as he stood before the railings, his heart jumped almost into his mouth: there, in the court, the electric globe shone like a mauve moon above the front door steps, the back-door stood wide open shedding a glow on the paved courtyard, while, on the first floor, the bedroom lights filtered through the shutters to make a golden comb. Chéri supported himself against the nearest tree and lowered his head.

"It can't be true. As soon as I look up, it will all be dark again."

He straightened up at the sound of a voice. Ernest, the concierge, was shouting in the passage: "At nine to-morrow, Marcel will help me carry up the big black trunk, Madame."

Chéri turned round in a flash and ran as far as the Avenue du Bois. There he sat down. In front of his eyes danced the image of the electric globe he had been staring at—a dark purple ball fringed with gold, against a black group of trees in bud. He pressed his hand to his heart, and took a deep breath. Early lilac blossom scented the night air. He threw his hat away, undid the buttons of his overcoat and, leaning back on a seat, let himself go, his legs outstretched and his hands hanging feebly by his sides. A crushing yet delicious weight had just fallen upon him. "Ah!" he whispered, "so this is what they call happiness. I never knew."

For a moment he gave way to self-pity and self-contempt. How many good things had he missed by leading such a pointless life—a young man with lots of money and little heart! Then he stopped thinking for a moment, or possibly for an hour. Next, he persuaded himself there was nothing in the world he wanted, not even to go and see Léa.

When he found himself shivering in the cold, and heard the blackbirds carolling the dawn, he got up and, stumbling a little but light-hearted, set off towards the Hôtel Morris without passing through the Avenue Bugeaud. He stretched himself, filled his lungs with the morning air, and overflowed with good-will to all.

"Now," he sighed, the devil driven out of him, "now . . . Oh now you'll see just how nice to the girl I shall be."

Shaved, shod and impatient—he had been up since eight—Chéri shook Desmond. Sleep gave him a swollen look, livid and quite frightful, like a drowned man. "Desmond! Hey, Desmond! Up you get. . . . You look too hideous when you're asleep!"

The sleeper woke, sat up, and turned towards Chéri eyes the colour of clouded water. He pretended to be fuddled with sleep so that he could make a long and close examination of Chéri—Chéri dressed in blue, pathetic, superb, and pale under the lightest coat of powder.

There were still moments when Desmond felt painfully aware of the contrast between his ugly mask and Chéri's good looks. He pretended to give a long yawn. 'What's he up to

89
.....

now?' he wondered; 'The idiot is in far better looks than yester-day—especially his eyelashes, and what eyelashes he has . . .' He was staring at the lustrous sweep of Chéri's thick lashes and the shadow they shed on the dark pupils and bluish whites of his eyes. Desmond noticed also that, this morning, the contemptu-ously arched lips were moist and fresh, and that he was breath-ing through them as if he had just that moment finished making love.

Quickly he relegated his jealousy to the back of his mind—where he kept his personal feelings—and asked Chéri in tones of weary condescension: "May one enquire whether you are going out at this hour of the morning, or just coming in?"

"I'm going out," Chéri said. "Don't worry about me. I'm off shopping. I'm going to the florist's, the jeweller's, to my mother's, to my wife's, to . . ."

"Don't forget the Papal Nuncio!"

"I know what's what," Chéri answered. "He shall have some imitation gold studs and a sheaf of orchids."

It was rare for Chéri to respond to jokes: he usually ac-cepted them in stony silence. His facetious reply proved that he was pleased with himself, and revealed this unaccustomed mood to Desmond. He studied Chéri's reflection in the looking-glass, noted the pallor of his dilated nostrils, observed that his eyes were continually on the rove, and ventured to put the most discreet of questions.

"Will you be coming back for luncheon? . . . Hey, Chéri, I'm speaking to you. Are we lunching together?"

Chéri answered by shaking his head. He whistled softly, arranging himself in front of the pier-glass so that it framed his figure exactly like the one between the two windows in Léa's room—the one which would soon frame in its heavy gold, against a sunny pink background, the reflection of his body—naked or loosely draped in silk—the magnificent picture of a young man, handsome, loved, happy, and pampered, playing with the rings and necklaces of his mistress. 'Perhaps her young man's reflection is already there, in Léa's looking-glass!' This sudden thought cut so fiercely into his exhilaration that it dazed him, and he fancied he had heard it actually spoken.

"What did you say?" he asked Desmond.

"I never said a word," his well-trained friend said stiffly. "It must have been someone talking outside in the courtyard."

Chéri went out, slamming the door behind him, and returned to his own rooms. They were filled with the dim continual hubbub of the fully awakened Rue de Rivoli, and Chéri, through the open window, could see the spring foliage, the leaves stiff and transparent like thin jade knives against the sun. He closed the window and sat down on a useless little chair which stood against the wall in a dingy corner between his bed and the bathroom door.

"How can it be? . . ." he began in a low voice, and then said no more. He did not understand why it was that during the last six and a half months he had hardly given a thought to Léa's lover. *"I'm making a perfect fool of myself,"* were the actual words of the letter so piously preserved by Charlotte Peloux.

'A perfect fool?' Chéri shook his head. 'It's funny, but that's not how I see her at all. What sort of a man can she be in love with? Somebody like Patron—rather than like Desmond, of course. An oily little Argentine? Maybe. Yet all the same . . .' He smiled a simple smile. 'Apart from me, who is there she could possibly care for?"

A cloud passed over the sun and the room darkened. Chéri leaned his head against the wall. "My Nounoune . . . My Nounoune . . . Have you betrayed me? Are you beastly enough to deceive me? . . . Have you really done that?"

He tried to give a sharper edge to his suffering by a misuse of his imagination: the words and sights it presented left him more astonished than enraged. He did his best to evoke the elation of early morning delights when he was living with Léa, the solace of the prolonged and perfect silences of certain afternoons, with Léa—the delicious sleepy hours in winter spent in a warm bed in a freshly aired room, with Léa . . . ; but, all the time, in the suffused cherry-coloured afternoon light aflame behind the curtains of Léa's room, he saw in Léa's arms one lover and one lover only—Chéri. He jumped up, revived by a spontaneous act of faith. 'It's as simple as that! If I'm unable to see anyone but myself beside her, then it's because there is no one else to see.'

He seized the telephone, and was on the point of ringing her up, when he gently replaced the receiver. "No nonsense. . . ."

He walked out into the street, erect, with shoulders squared. He went in his open motor to the jeweller's, where he became sentimental over a slender little bandeau of burning blue sapphires invisibly mounted on blue steel, "so exactly right for Edmée's hair," and took it away with him. He bought some stupid, rather pompous flowers. As it had only just struck eleven, he frittered away a further half-hour, drawing money from the Bank, turning over English illustrated papers at a kiosk, visiting his scent-shop and a tobacconist's that specialised in Oriental cigarettes. Finally, he got back into his motor, and sat down between his sheaf of flowers and a heap of little beribboned parcels.

"Home."

The chauffeur swivelled round on his basket-seat.

"Monsieur? . . . What did Monsieur say? . . ."

"I said Home—Boulevard d'Inkermann. D'you require a map of Paris?"

The motor went full speed towards the Champs-Elysées. The chauffeur drove much faster than usual and his thoughts could almost be read in his back. He seemed to be brooding uneasily over the gulf which divided the flabby young man of the past months—with his "As you like," and his "Have a glass of something, Antonin?"—from young Monsieur Peloux, strict with the staff and mindful of the petrol.

"Young Monsieur Peloux" leaned back against the morocco leather, hat on knees, drinking in the breeze and exerting all his energy in an effort not to think. Like a coward, he closed his eyes between the Avenue Malakoff and the Porte Dauphine to avoid a passing glimpse of the Avenue Bugeaud, and he congratulated himself on his resolution.

The chauffeur sounded his horn in the Boulevard d'Inkermann for the gate to be opened, and it sang on its hinges with a heavy musical note. The capped concierge hurried about his business, the watch-dogs barked in recognition of their returning master. Very much at his ease, sniffing the green smell of the newly mown lawns, Chéri entered the house and with a master's step climbed the stairs to the young woman whom he had left behind three months before, much as a sailor from Europe leaves behind, on the other side of the world, a little savage bride.

éa sat at her bureau, throwing away photographs from the last trunk to be unpacked. "Heavens, how hideous people are! The women who had the nerve to give me these! And they think I'm going to put them up in a row on the mantel-piece—in plated frames or little folding-cases. Tear them all up quick, and straight into the waste-paper basket!"

She picked up the photographs again and, before throwing them away, subjected each to the closest scrutiny of which her blue eyes were capable. A post-card with a dark background of a powerful lady encased in full-length stays, doing her best to veil her hair and the lower part of her face with a wisp of tulle, in the teeth of a strong sea-breeze. "*To dearest Léa, in memory of exquisite hours spent at Guéthary. Anita.*" Another photograph, stuck on the middle of a piece of cardboard with a surface like dried mud, portrayed a large and lugubrious family. They might have been a penal colony, with a dumpy, heavily-painted grand-mother in charge. Holding above her head a tambourine tricked out with favours, she was resting one foot on the bent knee of what looked like a robust and crafty young butcher-boy. "That should never have seen the light of day," Léa said decisively, crumpling the rough-cast cardboard.

She smoothed out an unmounted print, to disclose two old provincial spinsters. An eccentric, loud-voiced and aggressive couple, they were to be found every morning on a bench some-where along a promenade, and every evening between a glass of

Cassis and their needle-work-frames, on which they were embroidering black pussy-cats, fat toads, or a spider. *"To our beautiful fairy! From her little friends at Le Trayas, Miquette and Riquette."*

Léa destroyed these souvenirs of her travels—and brushed a hand across her forehead. "It's horrible. And there'll be dozens and dozens more after these, just as there were dozens before them, all much the same. There's nothing to be done about it. It's life. Maybe wherever a Léa is to be found, there at once spring from the earth a myriad creatures like Charlotte Peloux, de la Berche, and Aldonza, or old horrors who were once handsome young men, people who are . . . well, who are impossible, impossible, impossible. . . ."

She heard, so fresh was her memory, voices that had called out to her from the top of hotel steps or hailed her with a "Hoo-hoo" from afar, across golden sands, and she lowered her head in anger like a bull.

She had returned, after an absence of six months, thinner, more flabby, less serene. Now and again a nervous twitch of the jaw jerked her chin down against her neck, and careless henna-shampooing had left too orange a glint in her hair; but her skin had been tanned to amber by sea and wind. This gave her the glowing complexion of a handsome farmer's wife, and she might have done without rouge. All the same, she would have to arrange something carefully round her neck, not to say cover it up completely; for it had shrunk and was encircled with wrinkles that had been inaccessible to sunburn.

Still seated, she dawdled over tidying away her various odds and ends, and her eyes began to glance round the room, as if some chair were missing. But what she was looking for was her old energy, the old anxiety to see at once that everything was as it should be in her comfortable home.

'Oh! That trip!' she sighed. 'How could I? How exhausting it all is!'

She frowned, once again with that irritable jerk of her chin, when she noticed the broken glass of a little picture by Chaplin which she thought perfectly lovely—the head of a young girl, all silver and rose.

"And I could put both hands through that tear in the lace curtains. . . . And that's only the beginning. . . . What a fool I was to stay away so long! And all in *his* honour! As if I couldn't just as well have nursed my grief here, in peace and comfort!"

She rose, disgruntled, and, gathering up the flounces of her tea-gown, went over to ring the bell, saying to herself, "Get along with you, you old baggage!"

Her maid entered, under a heap of underclothes and silk stockings.

"Eleven o'clock, Rose. And my face hasn't been done yet. I'm late."

"There's nothing to be late for. There aren't any old maids now to drag Madame off on excursions, or turn up at crack of dawn to pick every rose in the place. There's no Monsieur Roland to drive Madame mad by throwing pebbles through her window. . . ."

"Rose, there's only too much to keep us busy in the house. The proverb may well be true that three moves are as bad as a fire, but I'm quite convinced that being away from home for six months is as bad as a flood. I suppose you've noticed the hole in the curtain?"

"That's nothing. . . . Madame has not yet seen the linen-room: mouse-droppings everywhere and holes nibbled in the floor. And it's a funny thing that I left Émérancie with twenty-eight glass-cloths and I come back to find twenty-two."

"No!"

"It's the truth—every word I say, Madame."

They looked at each other, sharing the same indignation, both of them deeply attached to this comfortable house, muffled in carpets and silks, with its well-stocked cupboards and its shiny white basement. Léa gave her knee a determined slap.

"We'll soon change all that, my friend. If Ernest and Émérancie don't want their week's notice, they'll manage to find those six glass-cloths. And did you write to Marcel, and tell that great donkey which day to come back?"

"He's here, Madame."

Léa dressed quickly, then opened the window and leaned out, gazing complacently at her avenue of trees in bud. No more of those fawning old maids, and no more of Monsieur Roland—the athletic young heavy-weight at Cambo. . . . 'The idiot,' she sighed.

She forgave this passing acquaintance his silliness, and blamed him only for having failed to please her. In her memory —that of a healthy woman with a forgetful body—Monsieur Roland was now only a powerful animal, slightly ridiculous and, when it came to the point, so very clumsy. Léa would now have denied that, one rainy evening when the showers were falling in fragrance on the rose-geraniums, a flood of blinding tears had served to blot out Monsieur Roland behind the image of Chéri.

This brief encounter had left Léa unembarrassed and un-regretful. In the villa she had taken at Cambo, the "idiot" and his frolicking old mother would have been made just as wel-come as before. They could have gone on enjoying the well-arranged meals, the rocking-chairs on the wooden balcony, all the creature comforts that Léa dispensed with such justifiable pride. But the idiot had felt sore and gone away, leaving Léa to the attentions of a stiff, handsome officer, greying at the tem-ples, who aspired to marriage with "Madame de Lonval".

"Our years, our fortunes, the taste we both have for inde-pendence and society, doesn't everything show that we were destined for each other?" murmured the colonel, who still kept his slim waist.

She laughed, and enjoyed the company of this dry, dapper man, who ate well and knew how to hold his liquor. He mistook her feelings and he read into the lovely blue eyes, and the trustful, lingering smiles of his hostess, the acceptance he was expecting. The end of their dawning friendship was marked by a decisive gesture on her part: one she regretted in her heart of hearts and for which she was honest enough to accept the blame. 'It's my own fault. One should never treat a Colonel Ypoustègue, descendant of an ancient Basque family, as one would treat a Monsieur Roland. I've never given anyone such a snub. All the same, it would have been gentlemanly, and intelligent too, if he had come back as usual the next day in his dogcart, to smoke his cigar, meet the two old girls and pull their legs.'

She failed to understand that a middle-aged man could accept his dismissal, but not certain glances—glances appraising his physique, comparing him in that respect so unmistakably with another, unknown and invisible. Léa, caught in his sudden kiss, had subjected him to the searching, formidable gaze of a woman who knows exactly where to find the tell-tale marks of age. From the dry, well cared-for hands, ribbed with veins and tendons, her glance rose to the pouched chin and furrowed brows, returning cruelly to the mouth entrapped between double lines of inverted commas. Whereupon all the aristocratic refinement of the "Baroness de Lonval" collapsed in an "Oh, la la," so insulting, so explicit, so common, that the handsome figure of Colonel Ypoustègue passed through her door for the last time.

'The last of my idylls,' Léa was thinking, as she leaned out over her window-ledge. But the weather over Paris was fine, her echoing courtyard was dapper, with its trim bay trees rising ball-shaped in green tubs, and from the room behind her a breath of scented warmth came playing over the nape of her neck: all this gradually helped her to recover her good humour, and her sense of mischief. She watched the silhouettes of women passing on their way down to the Bois. 'So skirts are changing again,' Léa observed, 'and hats are higher.' She planned sessions with her dressmaker, others with her milliner; the sudden desire to look beautiful made her straighten her back. 'Beautiful? For whom? Why, for myself, of course. And then to aggravate old Ma Peloux!'

Léa had heard about Chéri's flight, but knew no more than

that. While disapproving of Madame Peloux's private-detective methods, she did not scruple to listen to a young *vendeuse*, who would show her gratitude for all Léa's kindnesses by pouring gossip in her ear at a fitting, or else by sending it to her, with "a thousand thanks for the delicious chocolates" on a huge sheet of paper embossed with the letter-head of her establishment. A postcard from Lili, forwarded to Léa at Cambo—a postcard scribbled by the dotty old harridan in a trembling hand without commas or full stops—had recounted an incomprehensible story of love and flight and a young wife kept under lock and key at Neuilly.

'It was weather like this,' Léa recalled, 'the morning I read Lili's postcard in my bath at Cambo.'

She could see the yellow bathroom, the sunlight dancing on the water and ceiling. She could hear the thin-walled villa re-echoing with a great peal of laughter—her own laughter, rather ferocious and none too spontaneous—then the cries that followed it: "Rose! Rose!"

Breasts and shoulders out of water, dripping, robust, one magnificent arm outstretched, looking more than ever like a naiad on a fountain, she had waved the card with the tips of her wet fingers. "Rose, Rose! Chéri . . . Monsieur Peloux has done a bunk! He's left his wife!"

"That doesn't surprise me, Madame," Rose had said. "The divorce will be gayer than the wedding, when the dead seemed to be burying the dead."

All through that day Léa had given way to unseemly mirth. "Oh! that fiendish boy. Oh! the naughty child! Just think of it!"

And she shook her head, laughing softly to herself, like a mother whose son has stayed out all night for the first time.

A bright varnished park-phaeton flashed past her gates, sparkled behind its prancing high-steppers and vanished almost without a sound on its rubber wheels.

'There goes Spéleïeff,' Léa observed; 'he's a good sort. And there goes Merguillier on his piebald: eleven o'clock. It won't be long before that dried-up old Berthellemy passes on his way to thaw out his bones on the Sentier de la Vertu. Curious how people can go on doing the same thing day after day! I could almost believe I'd never left Paris, except that Chéri isn't here. My poor Chéri! He's finished with, for the present. Night-life, women, eating at any hour, drinking too much. It's a pity. He might have turned into a decent sort, perhaps, if he'd only had pink chaps like a pork-butcher and flat feet. . . .'

She left the window, rubbing her numbed elbows, and shrugged her shoulders. 'Chéri could be saved once, but not a second time.' She polished her nails, breathed on a tarnished ring, peered closely at the disastrous red of her hair and its greying roots, and jotted down a few notes on a pad. She did everything at high speed and with less composure than usual, trying to ward off an attack of her old insidious anxiety. Familiar as this was, she denied its connection with her grief and called it "her moral indigestion". She began wanting first one thing, then suddenly another—a well-sprung victoria with a quiet horse appropriate to a dowager; then a very fast motor-car; then a suite of Directoire furniture. She even thought of doing her hair differently; for twenty years she had worn it high, brushed straight off the neck. 'Rolled curls low on the neck, like Lavallière? Then I should be able to cope with this year's loose-waisted dresses. With a strict diet, in fact, and my hair properly hennaed, I can hope for ten—no, let's say five years more of . . .'

With an effort she recovered her good sense, her pride, her lucidity. 'A woman like me would never have the courage to call a halt? Nonsense, my beauty, we've had a good run for our money.' She surveyed the tall figure, erect, hands on hips, smiling at her from the looking-glass. She was still Léa.

'Surely a woman like that doesn't end up in the arms of an old man? A woman like that, who's had the luck never to soil her hands or her mouth on a withered stick! Yes, there she stands, the "vampire", who needs must feed off youthful flesh.'

She conjured up the chance acquaintances and lovers of her

early days: always she had escaped elderly lechers; so she felt pure, and proud of thirty years devoted to radiant youths and fragile adolescents.

'And this youthful flesh of theirs certainly owes me a great debt. How many of them have me to thank for their good health, their good looks, the harmlessness of their sorrows! And then their egg-nogs when they suffered from colds, and the habit of making love unselfishly and always refreshingly! Shall I now, merely to fill my bed, provide myself with an old gentleman of . . . of . . .' She hunted about and finished up with majestic forgetfulness of her own age, 'An old gentleman of forty?'

She rubbed her long shapely hands together and turned away in disgust. 'Pooh! Farewell to all that! It's much prettier. Let's go out and buy playing-cards, good wine, bridge-scorers, knitting-needles—all the paraphernalia to fill a gaping void, all that's required to disguise that monster, an old woman.'

In place of knitting-needles, she bought a number of dresses, and négligées like the gossamer clouds of dawn. A Chinese pedicure came once a week, the manicurist twice, the masseuse every day. Léa was to be seen at plays, and before the theatre at restaurants where she never thought of going in Chéri's time.

She allowed young women and their friends—as well as Kühn, her former tailor, now retired—to ask her to their box or to their table. But the young women treated her with a deference she did not appreciate; and when Kühn, at their first supper together, called her "my dear friend," she retorted: "Kühn, I assure you it doesn't suit you at all to be a customer."

She sought refuge with Patron, now a referee and boxing promoter. But Patron was married to a young person who ran a bar, a little creature as fierce and jealous as a terrier. To join the susceptible athlete, Léa went as far out as the Place d'Italie, at considerable risk to her dark sapphire-blue dress, heavy with gold embroidery, to her birds of paradise, her impressive jewels, and her new rich red-tinted coiffure. She had had enough after one sniff of the sweat, vinegar and turpentine exuded by Patron's "white hopes", and she left, deciding never to venture again inside that long low gas-hissing hall.

An unaccountable weariness followed her every attempt to get back into the bustling life of people with nothing to do.

'What can be the matter with me?'

She rubbed her ankles, a little swollen by evening, looked at her strong teeth, and gums that had hardly begun to recede; and thumped her strong ribs and healthy stomach as if sounding a cask. Yet some undefinable weight, now that the chock had been knocked from under her, was shifting within her, and dragging her down. It was the Baroness de la Berche—met by chance in a "public bar" where she was washing down two dozen snails with cabbies' white wine—who in the end informed her of the prodigal's return to the fold, and of the dawn of a crescent honeymoon in the Boulevard d'Inkermann. Léa listened calmly to this Moral Tale; but she turned pale with emotion the following day when she recognised the blue limousine outside her gates and saw Charlotte Peloux on her way to the house.

"At last, at last! Here you are again, Léa, my beauty! . . . Lovelier than ever! Thinner than last year! Take care, Léa, we mustn't get too thin at our age! So far, and no further! And yet . . . But what a treat it is to see you!"

Never had that bitter tongue sounded so sweet to Léa. She let Madame Peloux prattle on, thankful for the breathing-space afforded by this acid stream. She had settled Charlotte Peloux into a deep armchair, in the soft light of the little pink-panelled salon, as in the old days. Automatically she had herself taken the straight-backed chair, which forced her to lift her shoulders and keep up her chin, as in the old days. Between them stood the table covered by a cloth of heavy embroidery, and on it, as in the old days, the large cut-glass decanter half full of old brandy, the shimmering petal-thin goblets, iced water, and shortbread biscuits.

"My beauty, now we'll be able to see each other again in peace, in peace. You know my motto: 'When in trouble, shun your friends: let them only share your luck!' All the time Chéri was playing truant, I purposely didn't show you any sign of life, you understand. Now that all's well and my children are happy again, I shout it aloud, I throw myself into your arms, and we start our pleasant existence all over again. . . ." She broke off and lit a cigarette, as clever with her pauses as an actress, ". . . without Chéri, of course."

"Of course," Léa acquiesced with a smile.

She was watching and listening to her old enemy in satisfied astonishment. The huge inhuman eyes, the chattering lips, the restless, tight little body—all that was facing her across the table had come simply to test her powers of resistance, to humiliate her, as in the old days, always as in the old days. But, as in the old days, Léa knew when to answer, when to be scornful, when to smile, and when to retaliate. Already that sorry burden, which had weighed so heavily the day before and the days before that, was beginning slowly to lift. The light seemed normal once more, and familiar, as it played over the curtains and suffused the little drawing-room.

'Here we are again,' Léa thought, in lighter vein. 'Two women, both a little older than a year ago, the same habits of backbiting and the same stock phrases; good-natured wariness at meals shared together; the financial papers in the morning, scandalmongering in the afternoon: all this will have to be taken up again, since it's Life, my life. The Aldonzas and the de la Berches, the Lilis and a few homeless old gentlemen: the whole lot squeezed round a card table, with the packs jostling the brandy-glasses, and perhaps, thrown in, a pair of little woollen shoes, begun for a baby who's soon to be born. . . . We'll start all over again, since it is ordained. Let's enter on it cheerfully. After all, it's only too easy to sink back into the grooves of the old life.'

And she settled back, eyes bright and mouth relaxed, to listen to Charlotte Peloux, who was greedily expatiating upon her daughter-in-law.

"My Léa, you should know, if anyone, that what I've always

longed for is peace and quiet. Well now, I've got them. Chéri's escapade, you see, was nothing more than sowing a few wild oats. Far be it from me to reproach you, Léa dear, but as you'll be the first to admit, from eighteen to twenty-five he really never had the time to lead the life of a bachelor! And now he's done it with a vengeance!"

"It's a very good thing that he did," Léa said, without the flicker of a smile; "it acts as a sort of guarantee to his wife for the future."

"The very word, the very word I was hunting for!" barked Madame Peloux, beaming. "A guarantee! And ever since that day—one long dream! And, you know, when a Peloux does come home again after being properly out on the spree, he never goes off again!"

"Is that a family tradition?" Léa asked.

But Charlotte took no notice.

"And what's more, he was very well received when he did return home. His little wife—ah, there's a little wife for you, Léa!—and I've seen a fair number of little wives in my time, you know, and I don't mind telling you I've never seen one to hold a candle to Edmée!"

"Her mother is so remarkable," Léa said.

"Think, just think, my beauty—Chéri left her on my hands for very nearly three months! and between you and me she was very lucky to have me there."

"That's exactly what I was thinking," Léa said.

"And then, my dear, never a word of complaint, never a scene, never a tactless word! Nothing, nothing! She was patience itself, and sweetness . . . and the face of a saint, a saint!"

104

"It's terrifying," Léa said.

"And then, what d'you suppose happened when our young rascal walked in one morning, all smiles, as though he'd just come in from a stroll in the Bois? D'you suppose she allowed herself a single comment? Not one. Far from it. Nothing. As for him, though at heart he must have felt just a little ashamed . . ."

"Oh, why?" Léa asked.

"Well, really! After all . . . He was welcomed with open arms, and the whole thing was put right in their bedroom—in two ticks—just like that—no time lost! Oh, I can assure you, for the next hour or so there wasn't a happier woman in the world than me."

"Except, perhaps, Edmée," Léa suggested.

But Madame Peloux was all exaltation, and executed a superb soaring movement with her little arms: "I don't know what you can be thinking of. Personally, I was only thinking of the happy hearth and home."

She changed her tune, screwed up her eyes and pouted: "Besides, I can't see that little girl frantic with passion, or sobbing with ecstasy. Twenty, and skinny at that. . . . Pah! at that age they stammer and stutter. And then, between ourselves, I think her mother's cold."

"Aren't you being carried away by your sense of family?" Léa said.

Charlotte Peloux expanded her eyes to show their very depths, but absolutely nothing was to be read there.

"Certainly not, certainly not! Heredity, heredity! I'm a firm believer in it. Look at my son, who is fantasy incarnate . . . What? You don't know that he's fantasy incarnate?"

"It must have escaped my memory," Léa apologised.

"Well, I have high hopes for my son's future. He'll love his home as I love mine, he'll look after his fortune, he'll love his children, as I loved him. . . ."

"For goodness' sake, don't paint such a depressing picture," Léa begged. "What's it like, the young people's home?"

"Sinister!" shrieked Madame Peloux. "Positively sinister. Purple carpets. Purple! A black-and-gold bathroom. A salon with no furniture in it, full of Chinese vases larger than me! So, what happens is that they're always at Neuilly. Besides, without being conceited, I must say that girl adores me."

"Her nerves have not been upset at all?" Léa asked, anxiously.

Charlotte Peloux's eyes brightened. "No danger of that! She plays her hand well, and we must face the fact."

"Who d'you mean by 'we'?"

"Forgive me, my beauty, pure habit. We're dealing here with what I call a brain, a real brain. You should see the way she gives orders without raising her voice, and takes Chéri's teasing, and swallows the bitterest pills as if they were lollipops. . . . I begin to wonder, I really begin to wonder, whether there is not positive danger lying ahead for my son. I'm afraid, Léa dear, I'm afraid she may prove a damper on his originality, on his . . ."

"What? Is he being an obedient little boy?" Léa interrupted. "Do have some more of my brandy, Charlotte, it comes from Spéleïeff and it's seventy-four years old—you could give it to a new-born babe."

" 'Obedient' is hardly the right word, but he's . . . interimpertur . . ."

"Imperturbable?"

"That's the word! For instance, when he knew I was coming to see you . . ."

"Did he know, then?"

An impetuous blush leapt to Léa's cheeks, and she cursed her hot blood and the bright daylight of the little drawing-room. Madame Peloux, a benign expression in her eyes, fed on Léa's confusion.

"But of course he knew. That oughtn't to bring a blush to your cheeks, my beauty. What a child you are!"

"In the first place, how did you know I was back?"

"Oh, come, Léa, don't ask such foolish questions. You've been seen about everywhere."

"Yes, but Chéri—did you tell him I was back?"

"No, my beauty, it was he who told me."

"Oh, it was he who . . . That's funny."

She heard her heart beating in her voice and dared not risk more than the shortest answers.

"He even added: 'Madame Peloux, you'll oblige me by

going to find out news of Nounoune.' He's still so fond of you, the dear boy."

"How nice!"

Madame Peloux, crimson in the face, seemed to abandon herself to the influence of the old brandy and talked as in a dream, wagging her head from side to side. But her russet eyes remained fixed and steely, and she kept a close watch on Léa, who was sitting bolt upright, armed against herself, waiting for the next thrust.

"It's nice, but it's quite natural. A man doesn't forget a woman like you, Léa dear. And . . . if you want to know what I really think, you've only to lift a finger and . . ."

Léa put a hand on Charlotte Peloux's arm. "I don't want to know what you really think," she said gently.

The corners of Madame Peloux's mouth fell: "Oh, I can understand, I approve," she sighed in a passionless voice. "When one has made other arrangements for one's life, as you have . . . I haven't even had a word with you about yourself!"

"But it seems to me that you have."

"Happy?"

"Happy."

"Divinely happy? A lovely trip? Is *he* nice? Where's his photo?"

Léa, relieved, sharpened her smile and shook her head. "No, no, you'll find out nothing, search where you will. Have your detectives let you down, Charlotte?"

"I rely on no detectives," Charlotte answered. "It's certainly not because anyone has told me . . . that you'd been through another heart-breaking desertion . . . that you'd been terribly worried, even over money. . . . No, no, you know what small attention I pay to gossip!"

107

"No one knows it better than me. My dear Lolotte, you can go back home without any fears on my behalf. And please reassure our friends, and tell them that I only wish they had made half what I did out of Oil shares between December and February."

The alcoholic cloud-screen, which softened the features of Madame Peloux, lifted in a trice; a clear, sharp, thoroughly alert face emerged. "You were in on Oil? I might have known it! And you never breathed a word to me."

"You never asked me about it. . . . You were thinking only of your family, as was natural. . . ."

"Fortunately, I was thinking of Compressed Fuel at the same time." The muted trumpet resembled a flute.

"Ah! and you never let on to me either!"

"Intrude upon love's young dream? Never! Léa, my dear, I'm off now, but I'll be back."

"You'll come back on Thursday, because at present, my dear Lolotte, your Sundays at Neuilly . . . they're finished for me. Would you like it if I started having a few people here on Thursdays? Nobody except old friends, old Ma Aldonza, our Reverend-Father-the-Baroness—poker for you, knitting for me. . . ."

"Do you knit?"

"Not yet, but it will soon come. Well?"

"I jump for joy at the idea! See if I'm not jumping! And you may be sure I won't say a word about it at home. That bad boy would be quite capable of coming and asking for a glass of port on one of your Thursdays. Just one more little kiss, my beauty. . . . Heavens, how good you smell. Have you noticed that as the skin gets less firm, the scent sinks in better and lasts much longer? It's really very nice."

'Be off, be off . . .' Quivering, Léa stood watching Madame Peloux as she crossed the courtyard. 'Go on your mischievous way! Nothing can stop you. You twist your ankle, yes—but it never brings you down. Your chauffeur is careful not to skid, so you'll never crash into a tree. You'll get back safely to Neuilly, and you'll choose your moment—to-day, or to-morrow, or one day next week—to come out with words that should never pass your lips. You'll try and upset those who, perhaps, are happy and at peace. The least harm you'll do is to make them tremble a little, as you made me, for a moment. . . .'

She was trembling at the knees, like a horse after a steep pull, but she was not in pain. She felt overjoyed at having kept so strict a control over herself and her words. Her looks and her colour were enhanced by her recent encounter, and she went on pulping her handkerchief to release her bottled-up energy.

She could not detach her thoughts from Madame Peloux. 'We've come together again,' she said to herself, 'like two dogs over an old slipper which both have got used to chewing. How queer it is! That woman is my enemy, and yet it's from her I now draw my comfort. How close are the ties that bind us!'

Thus, for a long time, she mused over her future, veering between alarm and resignation. Her nerves were relaxed, and she slept for a little. As she sat with one cheek pressed against a cushion, her dreams projected her into her fast-approaching old age. She saw day follow day with clockwork monotony, and herself beside Charlotte Peloux—their spirited rivalry helping the time to pass. In this way she would be spared, for many years, the degrading listlessness of women past their prime, who abandon first their stays, then their hair-dye, and who finally no longer bother about the quality of their underclothes. She had a foretaste of the sinful pleasures of the old—little else than a concealed aggressiveness, day-dreams of murder, and the keen recurrent hope for catastrophes that will spare only one living creature and one corner of the globe. Then she woke up, amazed to find herself in the glow of a pink twilight as roseate as the dawn.

"Ah, Chéri!" she sighed.

But it was no longer the raucous hungry cry of a year ago. She was not now in tears, nor was her body suffering and rebellious, because threatened by some sickness of the soul. Léa rose from her chair, and rubbed her cheek, embossed by the imprint of the embroidered cushion.

'My poor Chéri! It's a strange thought that the two of us—

you by losing your worn old mistress, and I by losing my scandalous young lover—have each been deprived of the most honourable possession we had upon this earth!'

Two days went by after the visit of Charlotte Peloux: two grey days that passed slowly for Léa. She faced this new life with the patience of an apprentice. 'Since this is going to be my new life,' she said to herself, 'I'd better make a start.' But she set about it clumsily, altogether too conscientiously, so that it was a strain on her perseverance. On the second day, about eleven in the morning, she was seized with a desire to go for a walk through the Bois as far as the Lakes.

'I'll buy a dog,' she thought. 'He'll be a companion, and force me to walk.' And Rose had to hunt through the bottom of the summer cupboards for a pair of strong-soled brown boots and a tweed coat and skirt, smelling of alpine meadows and pine forests. Léa set off with the resolute stride proper to the wearer of heavy footwear and rough country clothes.

'Ten years ago, I should not have feared to carry a stick,' she said to herself. When still quite near the house, she heard behind her a brisk light tread, which she thought she recognised. She became unnerved, almost paralysed by a compelling fear; and before she could recover she let herself unwittingly be overtaken, and then passed, by an unknown young man. He was in a hurry, and never even glanced at her.

'I really am a fool,' she breathed in her relief.

She bought a dark carnation to pin on her jacket and started off again. But thirty yards ahead of her, looming out of the diaphanous mist above the grass verges of the Avenue, the silhouette of a man was waiting.

'This time I do recognise the cut of that coat and that way of twirling a cane. . . . Oh, no thank you, the last thing I want is for him to see me shod like a postman and wearing a thick jacket that makes me look stocky. If I must run into him, I'd far rather he saw me in something else . . . and he never could

stand me in brown, anyhow. . . . No, no . . . I'm off home.
. . . I . . .'

At that moment the waiting man hailed an empty taxi,
stepped in, and drove past Léa: he was a young man with fair
hair and a small close-clipped moustache. But this time Léa did
not smile or feel relief. She turned on her heel and walked back
home.

"One of my off-days, Rose. . . . Bring me the peach-blos-
som tea-gown, the new one, and the big embroidered cloak. I'm
stifling in these woollen things."

'It's no good being obstinate,' Léa thought. 'Twice in suc-
cession it's turned out not to be Chéri: the third time it would
have been. I know the little jokes Fate plays on one. There's
nothing to be done about it. I've no fight left in me to-day, I'm
feeling limp.'

She spent the rest of the day once more trying patiently to
learn to be alone. After luncheon she enjoyed a cigarette and a
look at the papers, and welcomed with a short-lived joy a telephone call from Baroness de la Berche, then another from
Spéleïeff, her former lover, the handsome horse-coper, who had
seen her in the street the previous evening and offered to sell
her a spanking pair.

There followed an hour of complete and frightening silence. 'Come, come . . .' She began to walk up and down, with
her hands on her hips, her arms free of the heavy gold rose-
embroidered cloak, its magnificent train sweeping the floor behind her.

'Come, come. . . . Let's try to take stock. This isn't the
moment to become demoralised—now that I'm no longer in
love with the boy. I've been living on my own now for six
months. I managed perfectly well when I was in the south. To
start with, I moved about from place to place. And the people I
got to know on the Riviera or in the Pyrenees did me good; I
felt positively refreshed each time any of them went away.
Starch poultices may not cure a burn, but they do bring relief

when constantly renewed. My six months of keeping on the move reminds me of the story of that hideous Sarah Cohen, who married a monster of ugliness. "Each time I look at him, I think that I am pretty."

'But I knew what it was like to live alone before these last six months. What sort of life did I lead after I'd left Spéleïeff, for instance? Oh yes, I went chasing round bistros and bars with Patron, and then all of a sudden Chéri came into my life. But before Spéleïeff, there was little Lequellec: when his family dragged him away from me to lead him to the altar, his beautiful eyes were brimming with tears, poor boy. . . . After him, I was all alone for four months, I remember. The first month, I cried a great deal. Oh, no, it was for Bacciocchi I cried so much. But when I was through with my tears, there was no holding me. It was so delightful to find myself alone. Yes, but at the Bacciocchi time I was twenty-eight, and thirty after Lequellec, and in between these two, I had known . . . Well, no matter. After Spéleïeff, I became disgusted—so much money so ill spent. Whereas now, after Chéri, I'm . . . I'm fifty, and I was unwise enough to keep him for six whole years!"

She wrinkled her forehead, and looked ugly with her mouth in a sulky droop.

'It serves me right. At my age, one can't afford to keep a lover six years. Six years! He has ruined all that was left of me. Those six years might have given me two or three quite pleasant little happinesses, instead of one profound regret. A liaison of six years is like following your husband out to the colonies: when you get back again nobody recognises you and you've forgotten how to dress.'

To relieve the strain, she rang for Rose, and together they went through the contents of the little cupboard where she kept her lace. Night fell, set the lamps blossoming into light, and called Rose back to the cares of the house.

'To-morrow,' Léa said to herself, 'I'll order the motor and drive out to Spéleïeff's stud-farm in Normandy. I'll take old La Berche, if she wants to come: it will remind her of the past glories of her own carriages. And, upon my word, should the younger Spéleïeff cast an eye in my direction, I'm not saying I . . .'

She carefully smiled a mysterious and provocative smile, to delude what ghosts there might be hovering round the dressing-table or round the formidable bed, glimmering in the shadows. But she felt entirely frigid, and full of contempt for the pleasures other people found in love.

She dined off grilled sole and pastries, and found the meal a recreation. She chose a dry champagne in place of the Bordeaux, and hummed as she left the table. Eleven o'clock caught her by surprise, still taking the measurements of the space between the windows in her bedroom, where she planned to replace the large looking-glasses with old painted panels of flowers and balustrades. She yawned, scratched her head, and rang for her maid to undress her. While Rose knelt to take off her silk stockings, Léa reviewed her achievements of the day already slipping into the pages of the past, and was as pleased with her performance as if she had polished off an imposition. Protected for the night against the dangers of idleness, she could look forward to so many hours of sleep, so many when she would lie awake. Under cover of night, the restless regain the privilege of yawning aloud or sighing, of cursing the milkman's cart, the street-cleaners, and the early morning sparrows.

During her preparations for the night, she thought over a number of mild projects that would never come into being.

'Aline Mesmacker has a restaurant bar and is simply coining money. . . . Obviously, it gives her something to do, as well as being a good investment. . . . But I can't see myself sitting at a cash-desk; and if one employs a manageress, it's no longer worth while. Dora and that fat Fifi run a night-club together, Mother La Berche told me. Everybody's doing it now. And they wear stiff collars and dinner jackets, to attract a special clientèle. Fat Fifi has three children to bring up—they're her excuse. . . . Then there's Kühn, who's simply kicking his heels, and would gladly take some of my capital to start a new dressmaker's.'

113

Naked, and brick-pink from the reflection of her Pompeian bathroom, she sprayed herself with her favourite sandalwood, and, without thinking about it, enjoyed unfolding a long silk night-gown.

'All that's so much poppycock! I know perfectly well that I dislike working. To bed with you, Madame! You'll never have any other place of business, and all your customers are gone!'

The coloured lining of the white gandoura she put on was suffused with a vague pink. She went back to her dressing-table, and combed and tugged at the hairs stiffened by dye, lifting both her arms, and thus framing her tired face. Her arms were still so beautiful, from the full deep hollow of the armpit up to the rounded wrists, that she sat gazing at them in the looking-glass.

"What lovely handles for so old a vase!"

With a careless gesture she thrust a pale tortoiseshell comb into the back of her hair, and, without much hope, picked a detective story from the shelf of a dark closet. She had no taste for fine bindings and had never lost the habit of relegating books to the bottom of a cupboard, along with cardboard boxes and empty medicine bottles.

As she stood smoothing the cool linen sheets on her huge uncovered bed, the big bell in the courtyard rang out. The full, solemn, unwonted peal jarred on the midnight hour.

"What in the world . . . ?" she said out loud.

She held her breath while listening, her lips parted. A second peal sounded even louder than the first, and Léa, with an instinctive movement of self-preservation and modesty, ran to powder her face. She was about to ring for Rose when she heard the front door slam, followed by footsteps in the hall and on the stairs, and the sound of two voices mingling—her maid's and someone else's. She had no time to make up her mind: the door of her room was flung open by a ruthless hand. Chéri stood before her—his top-coat unbuttoned over evening clothes, his hat on his head—pale and angry-looking.

He leaned back against the door now shut behind him, and

did not move. He looked not so much at Léa as all round the room, with the quick shifting glance of a man about to be attacked.

Léa, who that morning had trembled at the half-surmised outline of a figure in the mist, felt at first only the resentment of a woman caught at her toilet. She drew her wrap more closely about her, settled her comb, and with one foot hunted for a missing slipper. She blushed, yet by the time the high colour died down she had already recovered the semblance of calm. She raised her head and appeared taller than the young man who was leaning, all in black, against the white of the door.

"That's a nice way to come into a room," she said in a rather loud voice. "You might at least take your hat off and say good evening."

"Good evening," Chéri said in surly tones.

The sound of his voice seemed to astonish him. He looked all round less like an angry animal, and a sort of smile drifted from his eyes down to his mouth, as he repeated a gentler "Good evening."

He took off his hat and came forward a few steps.

"May I sit down?"

"If you like," Léa said.

He sat down on a pouffe and saw that she remained standing.

"Are you in the middle of dressing? Aren't you going out?"

She shook her head, sat down far away from him, picked up her nail-buffer and never said a word. He lit a cigarette, and asked her permission only after it was alight.

"If you like," Léa repeated indifferently.

He said nothing more and dropped his gaze. Noticing that his hand with the cigarette in it was shaking, he rested it on the edge of a table. Léa continued polishing her nails deliberately and from time to time cast a brief glance at Chéri's face, especially at his lowered eyelids and the dark fringe of his lashes.

"It was Ernest who opened the front door to me as usual," Chéri said at last.

"And why shouldn't it have been Ernest? Ought I to have changed my staff because you got married?"

"No . . . I mean, I simply said that . . ."

Again silence fell, broken by Léa.

"May I know whether you intend to remain for some time, sitting on that pouffe? I don't even ask why you take the liberty of entering my house at midnight. . . ."

"You may ask me why," he said quickly.

She shook her head. "It doesn't interest me."

He jumped up precipitately, sending the pouffe rolling away behind him, and bore down upon Léa. She felt him bending over her as if he were going to strike her, but she did not flinch. The thought came to her: 'What in this world is there for me to be frightened of?'

"So you don't know what brings me here! You don't want to know what brings me here!"

He tore off his coat and sent it flying on to the chaise-longue, then he crossed his arms, and shouted quite close to Léa's face, in a strained but triumphant voice, "I've come back!"

She was using a delicate pair of tweezers, and these she carefully put away before wiping her fingers. Chéri dropped into a chair, as though his strength was completely exhausted.

"Good," Léa said. "You've come back. That's very nice! Whose advice did you take about that?"

"My own," Chéri said.

She got up in her turn, the better to dominate him. Her surging heartbeats had subsided, allowing her to breathe in comfort. She wanted to play her role without a mistake.

"Why didn't you ask me for my advice? I'm an old friend who knows all your clownish ways. Why did it never occur to you that your coming here might well embarrass . . . some-one?"

Lowering his head, he searched every corner of the room from under his eyebrows—the closed doors, the bed, metal-girt and heaped with luxurious pillows. He found nothing exceptional, nothing new, and shrugged his shoulders.

Léa expected more than that and drove home her point. "You understand what I mean?"

"Perfectly," he answered. " 'Monsieur' has not come in yet? 'Monsieur' is sleeping out?"

"That's none of your business, child," she said calmly.

He bit his lip and nervously knocked off his cigarette ash into a jewel tray.

"Not in that, I keep on telling you!" Léa cried. "How many times must I . . . ?"

She broke off to reproach herself for having unconsciously adopted the tone of their old familiar quarrels. But he did not appear to have heard and went on examining one of Léa's rings —an emerald she had purchased on her recent trip.

"What's . . . what's this?" he stammered.

"That? It's an emerald."

"I'm not blind. What I mean is, who gave it you?"

"No one you know."

"Charming!" Chéri said bitterly.

The note in his voice was enough to restore Léa's authority, and she pressed her advantage, taking pleasure in leading him still further astray.

"Isn't it charming? I get compliments on it wherever I go. And the setting, you've seen it . . . the filigree of diamonds . . ."

"Enough!" bawled Chéri furiously, smashing his fist down on the fragile table.

A few roses shed their petals at the impact, and a china cup slithered without breaking on to the thick carpet. Léa reached for the telephone, but Chéri caught her hand in a rough grasp. "What are you going to do with that telephone?"

117

"Call the police," Léa said.

He took hold of both her arms, pretending to be up to some playful nonsense as he pushed her away from the instrument.

"Oh go on with you, that's all right. Don't be silly! Can't I even open my mouth without your getting all melodramatic?"

She sat down and turned her back on him. He remained

standing, with nothing in his hands: his parted lips were swollen, giving him the look of a sulky child; one black lock hung down over his eyebrow. Surreptitiously, Léa watched him in a looking-glass, till his reflection vanished when he sat down. In her turn, Léa was embarrassed when she felt him staring at her back, broadened by the loose folds of her gandoura. She returned to her dressing-table, smoothed her hair, rearranged her comb, and, as if for want of something better to do, began unscrewing the top of a scent-bottle. Chéri turned his head as the first whiff reached his nostrils.

"Nounoune!" he called.

She did not answer.

"Nounoune!"

"Beg my pardon," she ordered, without turning round.

"Not likely!" he sneered.

"I can't force you. But you'll leave the house. And at once. . . ."

"I beg your pardon," he said at once, peevishly.

"Better than that."

"I beg your pardon," he repeated, quite low.

"That's better."

She went over to him and ran her hand lightly over his bowed head. "Come, tell me all about it."

He shivered, trembling under her touch. "What do you want me to tell you? It's not very complicated. I've come back, that's all."

"Tell me! Come along, tell me!"

He rocked backwards and forwards on his seat, pressing his hands between his knees, and raised his head towards Léa without meeting her eyes. She watched the quivering of his nostrils, and she heard him trying to control his rapid breathing. She had only to say once more, "Come, tell me all about it," and give him a prod with her finger, as if to push him over. At once he cried out, "Nounoune darling! Nounoune darling!" and threw all his weight upon her, clasping her long legs, so that they gave way under her.

118

Once seated, she let him slither to the floor and sprawl over her with tears, and inarticulate words, and groping fingers that caught at her lace and her pearls and hunted feverishly under her dress for the shape of her shoulder and under her hair to touch her ears.

"Nounoune darling! We're together again, my Nounoune! Oh, my Nounoune! your shoulder, and your scent, and your pearls, my Nounoune, oh, it's so stunning . . . and that little burnt taste your hair has, oh, it's . . . it's stunning. . . ."

He leaned back to breathe out this silly word with what might have been the last breath of his body: then, still on his knees, he clasped Léa in his arms, offering her a forehead shadowed under tousled hair, a trembling mouth moist with tears, and eyes bright with weeping and happiness. She was so lost in contemplating him, so perfectly oblivious of everything that was not Chéri, that she never thought of kissing him. She twined her arms round his neck and gently hugged him to her, rocking him to the rhythm of murmured words.

"My pet . . . my naughty boy . . . You're here . . . You've come back again. . . . What have you been up to now? You're so naughty . . . my pretty. . . ."

He was moaning softly, keeping his lips together and hardly speaking, as he listened to Léa. He rested his cheek on her breast and begged her to go on, if for a moment she ceased her tender lullaby. And Léa, fearful that her own tears would flow, went on with her scolding.

"Wicked monster . . . heartless little devil . . . Get along with you, you great slut!"

He looked at her in gratitude: "That's right . . . Go on slanging me! Oh, Nounoune!"

She held him at arm's length to see him properly. "So you love me, then?"

He lowered his eyes in childish confusion: "Yes, Nounoune."

A little burst of uncontrollable laughter warned Léa that she was on the verge of giving way to the most terrible joy of her life. An embrace, followed by collapse, the uncovered bed, two bodies joined together like the two living halves of an animal that has been cut through. 'No, no,' she said to herself, 'not yet, oh, not yet. . . .'

"I'm thirsty," Chéri sighed. "Nounoune, I'm thirsty."

She rose quickly and put a hand on the now tepid jug of water; hardly had she hurried from the room before she was back again. Chéri, curled up in a ball, was lying with his head on the pouffe. "Rose will bring you some lemonade," Léa said. "Don't stay there. Come and sit on the chaise-longue. Does the lamp hurt your eyes?"

She was trembling with delight in her imperious solicitude. She sat down at the other end of the chaise-longue and Chéri half stretched out to nestle against her.

"Perhaps now you'll tell me a little . . ."

They were interrupted by the entry of Rose. Chéri, without getting up, languidly turned his head in her direction: "Evening, Rose."

"Good evening, Monsieur," Rose said, discreetly.

"Rose, to-morrow at nine, I'd like . . ."

"Brioches and chocolate," Rose finished for him.

Chéri shut his eyes again with a sigh of contentment. "And that's that. . . . Rose, where am I going to dress to-morrow morning?"

"In the boudoir," Rose answered accommodatingly. "Only I had better take the settee out, I suppose, and put back the shaving-mirror, as it used to be?"

She sought confirmation in the eye of Léa, who was proudly displaying her spoilt child, supported by her arm as he drank.

"If you like," Léa said. "We'll see. You can go, Rose."

Rose retired, and during the ensuing moment's silence nothing could be heard except the vague murmuring of the wind and the cry of a bird bewildered by the brightness of the moon.

"Chéri, are you asleep?"

He gave one of his long-drawn sighs like an exhausted re-
triever. "Oh, no, Nounoune, I'm too happy to sleep."

"Tell me, child . . . You haven't been unkind over there?"

"At home? No Nounoune, far from it. I swear to you."

He looked up at her, without raising his trusting head.

"Of course not, Nounoune. I left because I left. The girl's
very nice. There was no fuss at all."

"Ah!"

"I wouldn't swear that she didn't have an inkling all the
same. This evening she was wearing what I call her 'orphanage
look', you know, pathetic dark eyes under her pretty head of
hair. . . . You know how pretty her hair is?"

"Yes."

She threw out these monosyllables in a whisper as if intent
on the words of someone talking in his sleep.

"I even think," Chéri continued, "that she must have seen
me going through the garden."

"Oh?"

"Yes. She was on the balcony, in her white sequin dress,
congealed whiteness. Oh! I don't like that dress. . . . Ever
since dinner it had been making me long to cut and run."

"No."

"Yes it had, Nounoune. I can't say whether she saw me.
The moon wasn't up. It came up while I was waiting."

"Where were you waiting?"

Chéri waved a vague hand in the direction of the avenue.
"There. I was waiting, don't you understand. I wanted to see.
I'd waited a long time."

"But what for?"

He hastily jumped away and sat further off. He resumed his
expression of primitive distrust. "I wanted to be sure there was
nobody here."

"Oh, yes. . . . You thought that . . ."

She could not resist a scornful laugh. A lover in her house!
A lover while Chéri was still living! It was grotesque. 'How
stupid he is!' she thought in her enthusiasm.

"You're laughing?"

He stood up in front of her and put his hand on her forehead, forcing back her head. "You're laughing! You're making fun of me. You're . . . Then you have a lover! There is someone!"

He leaned over her as he spoke, pushing her head back against the end of the chaise-longue. She felt the breath of an insulting mouth on her eyelids, and made no effort to be free of the hand that was crushing her hair against her forehead.

"I dare you to say you have a lover!"

She fluttered her eyelids, dazzled by the radiance of the face bearing down on her, and finally, in a toneless voice, she said: "No, I have no lover. I . . . love you. . . ."

He relaxed his hold and began pulling off his dinner jacket and waistcoat; his tie whistled through the air and ended up round the neck of Léa's bust—up on the mantelpiece. Meanwhile, he never moved away from her, and kept her, wedged between his knees, where she sat on the chaise-longue.

When she saw him half-naked, she asked, with a note of sadness: "Do you really want to? . . . Do you? . . ."

He did not answer, carried away by the thought of his approaching pleasure and the consuming desire to take her again. She gave way and served her young lover like a good mistress, with devout solicitude. Nevertheless, she anticipated with a sort of terror the moment of her own undoing; she endured Chéri as she might a torture, warding him off with strengthless hands, and holding him fast between strong knees. Finally, she seized him by the arm, uttered a feeble cry and foundered in the deep abyss, whence love emerges pale and in silence, regretful of death.

122

They remained enfolded in their close embrace and no words troubled the prolonged silence of their return to life. The upper part of his body had slipped down and he lay across Léa's thigh, his pendent head, with eyes closed, resting upon the sheets as if he had been stabbed to death over the body of his mistress. She, meanwhile, partly turned away from him, bore almost the full weight of this unsparing body. She breathed softly but unevenly. Her left arm ached, crushed beneath her. Chéri could feel the back of his neck growing numb. Both were waiting, concentrated and motionless, for the abating tempest of their pleasure to recede.

'He's asleep,' Léa thought. With her free hand, she was still clinging to Chéri's wrist and she squeezed it gently. One of her knees was being crushed by a knee—how well she knew its lovely shape! About the level of her own heart she could feel the steady muffled beating of another. Chéri's favourite scent—insistent, clinging, reminding her of fat waxy flowers and exotic glades—was all pervasive. 'He is here!' she whispered, immersed in a feeling of blind security. 'He is here for ever!' her senses re-echoed. The well-ordered prudence, the happy common sense that had been her guide through life, the humiliating vagaries of her riper years and the subsequent renunciations, all beat a retreat and vanished into thin air before the presumptuous brutality of love. 'He is here!' she thought. 'He has left his own home and his pretty silly little wife to come back, to come back to me! Who can take him from me now? Now at last I'll be able to organise our existence. He doesn't always know what he wants; but I do. No doubt we shall have to go away. We shan't go into hiding, but we'll look for somewhere peaceful. For I must find time to look at him. When I was unaware I loved him, I can't ever have looked at him properly. I must find a place where there'll be room enough for his whims and my wishes. I'll do the thinking for both of us—let him do the sleeping.'

While she was painstakingly withdrawing her left arm, cramped and pricking with pins and needles, and her numbed shoulder, she glanced at Chéri's averted face and found that he was not asleep. She could see the whites of his eyes and the flutter of the little black wings of his long eyelashes.

"Why, you're not asleep!"

She felt him tremble against her, before he turned over in a single movement.

"But you're not asleep, either, Nounoune!"

He stretched a hand out to the bedside table and switched on the lamp: a flood of rosy light covered the big bed, throwing the patterns of the lace into high relief, hollowing out shadowed valleys between swelling hills in the quilted folds of the eiderdown. Chéri, stretched out at full length, surveyed the field of his victory and of his peace. Léa, leaning on one elbow beside him, stroked his beloved, long eyebrows, and swept back the rebellious locks. Lying with his hair dishevelled over his forehead, he looked as if he had been blown over by a raging wind.

The enamel clock struck. Chéri straightened himself at a bound and sat up. "What time is it?"

"I don't know. What difference can it make to us?"

"Oh, I just asked. . . ."

He gave a short laugh, and did not immediately lie down again. Outside, the first milkcart clinked out its tinkling carillon, and he made a vague movement in the direction of the avenue. The strawberry-coloured curtains were slit through by the cold blade of dawning day. Chéri turned back to look at Léa, and stared at her with the formidable intensity of a suspicious dog or a puzzled child. An undecipherable thought appeared in the depths of his eyes; their shape, their dark wallflower hue, their harsh or languorous glint, were used only to win love, never to reveal his mind. From sheets crumpled as though by a storm, rose his naked body, broad-shouldered, slim-waisted; and his whole being breathed forth the melancholy of perfect works of art.

"Ah, you . . . ." sighed the infatuated Léa.

He did not smile, accustomed as he was to accepting personal praise.

"Tell me, Nounoune. . . ."

"What, my pretty?"

He hesitated, fluttered his eyelids, and shivered. "I'm tired . . . and then to-morrow, how will you manage about——"

Léa gave him a gentle push and pulled the naked body and drowsy head down to the pillows again.

"Don't worry. Lie down and go to sleep. Isn't Nounoune

here to look after you? Don't think of anything. Sleep. You're cold, I'm sure. . . . Here, take this, it's warm. . . ."

She rolled him up in the silk and wool of a little feminine garment, retrieved from somewhere in the bed, and put out the light. In the dark, she lent him her shoulder, settled him happily against her side, and listened till his breathing was in rhythm with her own. No desires clouded her mind, but she did not wish for sleep. 'Let him do the sleeping; it's for me to do the thinking,' she repeated to herself. 'I'll contrive our flight with perfect tact and discretion; I believe in causing as little suffering and scandal as possible. . . . For the spring we shall like the south best. If there were only myself to be considered, I'd rather stay here, in peace and quiet; but there's Ma Peloux and the young Madame Peloux. . . .' The vision of a young wife in her nightgown, anxiously standing beside a window, checked Léa only long enough for her to shrug her shoulders with cold impartiality. 'I can't help that. What makes one person's happiness . . .'

The black silky head stirred on her breast, and her sleeping lover moaned in his dream. With a zealous arm, Léa shielded him against nightmares, and rocked him gently so that—without sight, without memory, without plans for the future—he might still resemble that "naughty little boy" never born to her.

He had lain awake for some little while, taking great care not to stir. Cheek on folded arms, he tried to guess the time. Under a clear sky, the avenue must be vibrating with heat too insistent for early morning, since no shadow of a cloud passed across the lambent rose-red curtains. 'Ten o'clock, perhaps?' He was tormented by hunger; he had eaten little the previous evening. A year ago he would have bounded out of bed, roughly aroused Léa from sleep by ferocious shouts for cream-frothed chocolate and butter off the ice.

He did not stir. He was afraid, did he move, of crumbling away what remained to him of his rapture, the visual pleasure he derived from the shining curtains and from the steel and brass spirals of the bed, twinkling in the coloured aura of the room. Last night's great happiness had dwindled, it seemed, had melted, and sought refuge in the dancing iridescence of a cut glass jug.

On the landing, Rose trod the carpet with circumspect step; a discreet besom was sweeping the courtyard; and Chéri heard the tinkle of china coming from the pantry. 'How the morning drags on,' he said to himself. 'I'll get up'. But he remained without moving a muscle, for, behind him, Léa yawned and stretched her legs. He felt the touch of a gentle hand on his back. He shut his eyes again, and, for no good reason, his whole body began to act a lie, feigning the limpness of sleep. He was aware of Léa leaving the bed and of her dark silhouette between him and the curtains, which she drew half apart. She turned round to look at him, and with a toss of the head smiled in his direction—in no sense a smile of triumph, but a resolute smile, ready to accept all dangers. She was in no hurry to leave the room, and Chéri kept watch on her through hardly parted eyelashes. He saw her open a railway time-table and run her finger down the columns; then she seemed absorbed in some calculation, brow puckered and face upturned. Not yet powdered, a meagre twist of hair at the back of her head, double chin and raddled neck, she was exposing herself rashly to the unseen observer.

She moved away from the window, and, taking her cheque-book from a drawer, wrote and tore out several cheques. Then she put a pair of white pyjamas at the foot of the bed, and silently left the room.

Alone, Chéri took several deep breaths, realising that he had hardly dared to breathe since Léa had left the bed. He got up, put on the pyjamas, and opened a window. 'It's stifling in here,' he gasped. He had the vague uncomfortable feeling of having done something reprehensible. 'Because I pretended to be asleep? But I've watched Léa a hundred times just after she's got out of bed. Only, this time, I made the pretence of being asleep.'

The dazzling light restored the rose-pink glow of the room, and the delicate nacreous tints of the picture by Chaplin smiled down at him from the wall. Chéri bowed his head and shut his eyes, in an effort to remember the room as it had looked the night before—the mysterious colour, like the inside of a watermelon, the enchanted dome of lamp-light, and, above all, his exaltation when reeling under the intensity of his pleasures.

"You're up! The chocolate's already on its way."

He was pleased to note that it had taken Léa only these few moments to do her hair, touch up her face, and spray herself with the familiar scent. The room seemed suddenly to be filled with the cheerful sound of her lovely voice, and with the smell of chocolate and hot toast. Chéri sat down beside the two steaming cups and was handed the thickly buttered toast by Léa.

She did not suspect that he was trying to find something to say, for she knew that he was seldom talkative, especially when he was eating. She enjoyed a good breakfast, eating with the haste and preoccupied gaiety of a woman who, her trunks packed, is ready to catch her train.

"Your second piece of toast, Chéri?"

"No, thank you, Nounoune."

"Not hungry any more?"

"Not hungry."

With a smile, she shook her finger at him. "You know what you're in for! You're going to swallow down two rhubarb pills!"

He wrinkled his nose, shocked. "Listen, Nounoune. You've got a mania for fussing . . ."

"Ta ti ta ta! That's my look out. Put out your tongue. You won't show it me! Then wipe off your chocolate moustache, and let's have a quick sensible talk. Tiresome subjects can't be dealt with too quickly."

She stretched across the table to take Chéri's hand and hold it between her own.

"You've come back. That was our fate. Do you trust yourself to me? I'll be responsible for you."

She could not help breaking off, and closed her eyes as if hugging her victory. Chéri noticed the flush on his mistress's face.

"Oh!" she continued in a lower voice, "When I think of all that I never gave you, all that I never said to you! When I think that I believed you merely a passing fancy, like all the others— only a little more precious than all the others! What a fool I was not to understand that you were my love, *the* love, the great love that comes only once!"

When she opened her blue eyes, they seemed to have become bluer, gaining depth in the shade of her eyelids, and her breathing was uneven.

'Oh,' Chéri prayed inwardly, 'Don't let her ask me a question, don't let her expect an answer from me now! I couldn't speak a single word.'

128

She gave his hand a little shake. "Come along, let's be serious. As I was saying—we're leaving, we've already left. What will you do about *over there*? Let Charlotte arrange all the settlement details—it's much the wisest—and make her be generous, I beg of you. How will you let them know *over there*? A letter, I imagine. None too easy, but the less ink spilled, the better. We'll see about that between us. Then there's the question of your luggage. I've none of your things here any more. Such little details are far more upsetting than a major decision, but don't worry too much. . . . Will you kindly stop tearing the skin off the side of your toe all the time! That's the way to get an ingrowing toe-nail!"

Automatically, he let his foot drop to the floor. Under the weight of his sullen taciturnity, he found it a strain to focus his jaded attention on what Léa was saying. He stared at his mistress's happy, animated, imperious features, and asked himself vaguely: 'Why does she look so happy?'

His bewilderment became so obvious that Léa stopped in the middle of her monologue on their chances of buying old Berthellemy's yacht from him. "Could anyone believe that you've not got one word of advice to give? Oh, you might still be twelve!"

Chéri, snatched from his stupor, put a hand to his forehead and looked at Léa, his eyes filled with melancholy.

"Being with you, Nounoune, is likely to keep me twelve for half a century."

She blinked her eyes several times as if he had breathed on their lids, and let silence settle again.

"What are you trying to say?" she asked at last.

"Nothing, except what I did say, Nounoune. Nothing but the truth. And can you deny it, you, the most honest person alive?"

She decided to laugh, but her gaiety masked a terrible fear.

"But half your charm lies in your childishness, stupid! Later on it will be the secret of your eternal youth. Why complain of it? And you have the cheek to complain of it to *me*!"

129
....

"Yes, Nounoune. Do you expect me to complain to anyone but you?" and he caught hold of the hand she had taken away. "My own Nounoune, dearest, darling Nounoune, I'm not only complaining of myself: I'm accusing you!"

She felt the grip of his firm hand. Instead of looking away, his large dark eyes with lashes gleaming clung pitifully to hers. She was determined not to tremble, yet. 'It's nothing, it's nothing,' she thought. 'It calls only for two or three sharp words and he'll become insulting, then sulky, and then I'll forgive him. . . . It's no more than that.' But she failed to find the quick rebuke which would change the expression on his face. "Come, come, child . . . You know quite well there are certain jokes I will not tolerate." But at the same moment she knew her voice to be sounding false and feeble. 'How badly I said that . . . bad theatre. . . .'

It was half-past ten, and the sun was now shining on the table between them. Léa's polished nails twinkled in its beams; but the light fell also on the soft flabby skin on the back of her well-shaped hands and on her wrists. This emphasised—like criss-crossings on a clay soil when heavy rain is followed by a dry spell—the complicated network of tiny concentric grooves and miniature parallelograms. Léa rubbed her hands absent-mindedly, turning her head to make Chéri look out of the window; but he persisted in his miserable, hang-dog moodiness. The two hands were pretending, as if in disgrace, to toy with a loop of her belt. Brusquely he pounced upon them, kissed and kissed them again, then pressed his cheek against them, murmuring "My Nounoune. . . . Oh, my poor Nounoune . . ."

"Let me alone," she cried with inexplicable anger, snatching her hands away from him.

She took a moment to regain her control, frightened of her weakness, for she had been on the verge of tears. As soon as she was able, she smiled and spoke.

"So now it's me you're sorry for! Why did you accuse me a moment ago?"

"I was wrong," he said, humbly. "For me you have been

always . . ." He made a gesture to express his inability to find words worthy of her.

"*You have been?*" she underlined in a biting voice. "That sounds like an obituary notice, my good child!"

"You see . . ." he began reproachfully.

He shook his head, and she saw only too well that she could not rouse any anger in him. She tightened all her muscles, and reined in her thoughts with the help of those few words, ever the same, and inwardly repeated again and again: 'Here he is, in front of my eyes. I've only to look to see he's still there. He's not out of reach. But is he still here, with me, really and truly?'

Her thoughts escaped from the domination of these repeated phrases, only to sink into a great unvoiced lament. 'Oh! if only, if only I could somehow be returned to the moment when I was saying, "Your second piece of toast, Chéri!" for that moment's only just round the corner—it's not yet lost and gone for ever! Let's start again from there. The little that's taken place since won't count—I'll wipe it out, I'll wipe it out. I'm going to talk to him as though we're back where we were a moment ago. I'm going to talk to him about our departure, our luggage.'

She did, in fact, speak, and said, "I see . . . I see I cannot treat as a man a creature who, from sheer feebleness of character, can drive two women to distraction. Do you think that I don't understand? You like your journeys short, don't you? Yesterday at Neuilly, here to-day, but to-morrow! To-morrow, where? Here? No, no, my child, no need to lie, that guilty look would never take in even a woman stupider than I am, if there is one like that over there. . . ."

She threw out an arm to indicate Neuilly with so violent a gesture that she upset a cake-stand, which Chéri picked up again. Her words had sharpened her grief into anguish, an angry jealous anguish pouring forth like a young wife's outburst. The rouge on her cheek turned to the deep purple of wine-lees; a strand of her hair, crimped by the curling-tongs, wriggled down her neck like a small dry snake.

131

"And even the woman over there, even your wife won't be found waiting there every time you choose to come back home! A wife, my child, may not always be easy to find, but she's much easier to lose! You'll have yours kept under lock and key by Charlotte, eh? That's a marvellous idea! Oh, how I'll laugh, the day when . . ."

Chéri got up, pale and serious. "Nounoune! . . ."

"Why Nounoune? What d'you mean, Nounoune? Do you think you're going to frighten me? You want to lead your own life, do you? Go ahead! You're bound to see some pretty scenes, with a daughter of Marie-Laure's. She may have thin arms and a flat behind, but that won't prevent her from . . ."

"I forbid you, Nounoune!"

He seized her by the arm; but she rose, vigorously shook herself free, and broke into hoarse laughter: "Why, of course, 'I forbid you to say a word against my wife!' Isn't that it?"

He walked round the table, trembling with indignation, and went straight up to her. "No, I forbid you—d'you hear me?—I forbid you to spoil my Nounoune!" She retreated to the end of the room, babbling, "What's that? what's that?" He followed her as though bent on chastising her. "You heard what I said. Is that the way for Nounoune to speak? What do you mean by such behaviour? Cheap little jibes like Madame Peloux's, is that what you go in for? To think they could come from you, Nounoune, from you. . . ."

Arrogantly he threw back his head. "I know how Nounoune should speak. I know how she ought to think. I've had time to learn. I've not forgotten the day when you said to me, just before I married, 'At least don't be cruel. Try not to make her suffer. I have the feeling that a doe is being thrown to a greyhound.' Those were your words. That's really you. And the night before I married, when I ran away to come and see you, I remember you said to me . . ."

He could not go on, but all his features were bright with the memory.

"Darling, pull yourself together." He put his hands on

Léa's shoulders. "And even last night," he went on, "it wasn't the first time you asked me whether I might not have hurt somebody *over there!* My Nounoune, I knew you as a fine woman, and I loved you as a fine woman, when we first started. If we have to make an end of it, must you start behaving like all the other women?"

She dimly felt the cunning behind the compliment and sat down, hiding her face in her hands.

"How hard you are, how hard," she stammered. "Why did you come back? . . . I was so calm on my own, getting so used to . . ."

She heard herself lying and stopped.

"Well, *I* wasn't!" Chéri said quickly. "I came back because . . . because . . ."

He raised his arms, let them drop and lifted them again. "Because I couldn't go on without you, there's no point in looking for any other explanation."

For a moment no word was spoken.

Quite overcome, she looked at this impatient young man, who with light feet and open arms, as white as a seagull, seemed poised for flight.

Chéri let his dark eyes rove all over her body.

"Oh, you can be proud of yourself," he said suddenly. "You can be proud of yourself for having made me—and what's more for three months—lead such a life, such a life!"

"I did?"

"Who else, if it wasn't you? If a door opened, it was Nounoune; the telephone rang, Nounoune; a letter in the garden postbox, perhaps Nounoune. . . . In the very wine I drank, I looked for you, and I never found a Pommery to equal yours. And then at nights . . . Oh, heavens above!"

He was walking up and down the carpet with rapid, noiseless steps. "I know now what it is to suffer for a woman, and no mistake! After you, I know what all the other women will be . . . dust and ashes! Oh, how well you've poisoned me!"

She drew herself up slowly in her chair, and, letting her

body turn now this way, now that, followed Chéri's movements. Her cheeks were dry, rather shiny, and their fevered flush made the blue of her eyes almost intolerable. He was walking up and down, head lowered, and he never stopped talking.

"Imagine Neuilly with you not there, the first days after my return! For that matter, everything—with you not there! I almost went mad. One night, the child was ill—I no longer remember what it was, headache, pains, something. I felt sorry for her, but I had to leave the room; otherwise nothing in the world could have stopped me saying, 'Wait, don't cry, I'll go and fetch Nounoune and she'll make you well'—and you would have come, wouldn't you, Nounoune? Great heavens, what a life it was. . . . I took on Desmond at the Hôtel Morris, paid him well into the bargain, and sometimes at night I would tell him stories. . . . I used to speak as if you were unknown to him. 'Old boy, there's never been a skin like hers. . . . Take one look at that cabochon sapphire of yours, and then hide it away for ever, because no light can turn the blue of *her* eyes to grey!' I used to tell him how you could be tough when you wanted to be; and that no one had ever got the better of you, least of all me! I used to say, 'That woman, old boy, when she's wearing just the right hat—the dark blue one with the white wing, Nounoune, last summer's—and with the way she has of putting on her clothes—you can match her against any other woman you may choose—and she'll put every one of them in the shade!' And then that wonderful manner you have of walking—of talking—your smile—the erect way you hold yourself, I used to say to him—to Desmond: 'Ah! A woman like Léa *is* something!'"

He snapped his fingers with proprietary pride and stopped, quite out of breath from his talking and walking. 'I never said all that to Desmond,' he thought, 'and yet I'm not telling lies. Desmond understood all right.'

He wanted to go on and glanced at Léa. She was still ready to listen. Sitting bolt upright now, she exposed to him in the full light her noble face in its disarray, the skin shining like wax where the hot tears had dried. Her cheeks and chin were pulled down by an invisible weight, and this added a look of sadness to the trembling corners of her mouth. Chéri found intact amidst this wreckage of beauty the lovely commanding nose and the eyes as blue as a blue flower.

"And so you see, Nounoune, after months of that sort of life, I come back here, and . . ." He pulled himself up, frightened by what he had nearly said.

"You come back here, and find an old woman," Léa said calmly, in a whisper.

"Nounoune! Listen, Nounoune!"

He threw himself on his knees beside her, looking like a guilty, tongue-tied child no longer able to hide his misdemeanour.

"And you find an old woman," Léa repeated. "So what are you afraid of, child?"

She put her arms round his shoulders, and felt his body rigid and resistant, in sympathy with the hurt she was suffering. "Come, cheer up, my Chéri. Don't cry, my pretty. . . . What is it you're afraid of? Of having hurt me? Far from it: I feel so grateful to you."

He gave a sob of protestation, finding no strength to gainsay her.

She put her cheek against his tousled black hair. "Did you say all that, did you really think all that of me? Was I really so lovely in your eyes, tell me? And so kind? At the age when a woman's life is so often over, was I really the loveliest for you, the most kind, and were you really in love with me? How grateful I am to you, my darling! The finest, did you say? . . . My poor child."

He let himself go, while she supported him in her arms.

135

"Had I really been the finest, I should have made a man of you, and not thought only of the pleasures of your body, and my own happiness. The finest! Oh no, my darling, I certainly wasn't that, since I kept you to myself. And now it's almost too late. . . ."

He seemed to be asleep in Léa's arms; but his obstinately

tight-shut eyelids quivered incessantly, and with one lifeless hand he was clutching hold of her négligée and slowly tearing it.

"It's almost too late, it's almost too late. But all the same . . ." She leaned over him. "Listen to me, my darling. Wake up, my pretty, and listen to me with your eyes open. Don't be afraid of looking at me. I am, after all, the woman you were in love with, you know, the finest woman . . ."

He opened his eyes, and his first tearful glance was already filled with a selfish, mendicant hope.

Léa turned away her head. 'His eyes . . . Oh, we must get this over quickly. . . .' She put her cheek against his forehead.

"It was I, child, it was my real self who said to you, 'Don't cause unnecessary pain; spare the doe. . . .' I had quite forgotten, but luckily you remembered. You are breaking away from me very late in the day, my naughty little boy; I've been carrying you next to my heart for too long, and now you have a load of your own to carry: a young wife, perhaps a child. . . . I am to blame for everything you lack. . . . Yes, yes, my pretty, here you are, thanks to me, at twenty-five, so light-hearted, so spoilt, and at the same time so sad. . . . I'm very worried about you. You're going to suffer and make others suffer. You who have loved me. . . ."

His fingers tightened their grip on her négligée, and Léa felt the sharp nails of her "naughty child" bite into her breast.

"You who have loved me," she went on after a pause, "will you be able to? . . . I don't know how to explain what I mean. . . ."

He drew back in order to listen: and she could barely restrain herself from saying, "Put your hand back on my breast and your nails where they have left their mark; my strength abandons me as soon as your flesh is parted from mine." Instead, she leaned over him as he knelt in front of her, and continued: "You have loved me, and you will regret . . ."

She smiled at him, looking down into his eyes.

"What vanity, eh! . . . But you will regret me! I beg of you, when you're tempted to terrify the girl entrusted to your care and keeping, do restrain yourself! At such moments, you must find for yourself the wisdom and kindness you never learned from me. I never spoke to you of the future. Forgive me, Chéri—I've loved you as if we were both destined to die within the same hour. Because I was born twenty-four years before you, I was doomed, and I dragged you down with me. . . ."

He was listening very attentively, which made his face look hard. She put her hand on his forehead to smooth the furrows of anxiety.

"Can you see us, Chéri, going out to lunch together at Armenonville! . . . Can you see us inviting Monsieur and Madame Lili! . . ."

She gave a sad little laugh, and shivered.

"Oh, I'm just about as done for as that old creature. . . . Quick, quick, child, run off after your youth! Only a small piece of it has been snipped off by ageing women: all the rest is there for you and the girl who is waiting for you. You've now had a taste of youth! It never satisfies, but one always goes back for more. Oh, you had started to make comparisons before last night. . . . And what am I up to now, doling out all this advice and displaying the greatness of my soul! What do I know of you two? She loves you: it's her turn to tremble; but her misery will come from passion and not from perverted mother love. And you will talk to her like a master, not capriciously, like a gigolo. Quick, quick, run off. . . ."

She spoke in tones of hasty supplication. He listened, standing planted before her, his chest bare, his hair tempestuous: and so alluring, that she had to clasp her hands to prevent their seizing hold of him. He guessed this, perhaps, and did not move away. For an instant they shared a lunatic hope—do people feel like this in mid-air when falling from a tower?—then the hope vanished.

"Go," she said in a low voice. "I love you. It's too late. Go away. But go away at once. Get dressed!"

She rose and fetched him his shoes, spread out his crumpled

137

shirt and his socks. He stood helpless, moving his fingers awkwardly as if they were numb. She had to find his braces and his tie; but she was careful not to go too close to him and offered him no further help. While he was dressing, she glanced into the courtyard several times, as if she were expecting a carriage at the door.

He looked even paler when he was dressed, and a halo of fatigue round his eyes made them seem larger.

"You don't feel ill?" she asked him. And she added timidly, lowering her eyes, "You could always lie down for a little." But at once she pulled herself together and came over to him, as though he were in great danger. "No, no, you'll be better at home. Hurry, it's not yet midday; a good hot bath will soon put you to rights, and then the fresh air . . . Here are your gloves. . . . Your hat? On the floor, of course. Put your coat on, there's a nip in the air. Au revoir, my Chéri, au revoir. That's right. And tell Charlotte that . . ." She closed the door behind him, and silence put an end to her vain and desperate words. She heard Chéri stumble on the staircase and she ran to the window. He was going down the front steps and then he stopped in the middle of the courtyard.

"He's coming back! He's coming back!" she cried, raising her arms.

An old woman, out of breath, repeated her movements in the long pier-glass, and Léa wondered what she could have in common with that crazy creature.

Chéri continued on his way towards the street. On the pavement he buttoned up his overcoat to hide his crumpled shirt. Léa let the curtain fall back into place; but already she had seen Chéri throw back his head, look up at the spring sky and the chestnut trees in flower, and fill his lungs with the fresh air, like a man escaping from prison.

The Last of Chéri

Chéri closed the iron gate of the little garden behind him and sniffed the night air: "Ah! it's nice out here!" In the same breath, he changed his mind: "No, it isn't."

The thickly planted chestnut trees weighed heavily upon the heat pent up beneath. A dome of rusted leaves vibrated above the nearest gas-lamp. The Avenue Henri-Martin, close-set with greenery, was stifling; only with the dawn would a breath of fresh air come up from the Bois de Boulogne.

Bare-headed, Chéri turned back to look at the house, empty now but still lit up. He heard the clink of roughly handled glass, followed by the clear ring of Edmée's voice, sharp with reproof. He saw his wife come to the window of the gallery on the first floor and lean out. The frosted beads on her evening dress lost their snowy whiteness, caught for a moment a greenish glint from the lamp, then flamed into yellow as she touched the gold lamé curtains.

"Is that you on the pavement, Fred?"

"Who else could it be?"

"You didn't take Filipesco home, then?"

"No, I didn't; he'd hopped it already."

"All the same, I'd rather have liked . . . Oh well, it doesn't matter. Are you coming in now?"

"Not just yet. Far too hot. I'll just stretch my legs."

"But . . . Oh well, just as you like."

She broke off a moment, and must have been laughing, for he could see the quiver of her frost-spangled dress.

"All I can see of you from here is a white shirt-front and a white face cut out on black. Exactly like a poster for a night club. It looks devastating."

"How you adore my mother's expressions!" he said reflectively. "You can tell everyone to go to bed. I've got my key."

She waved a hand in his direction. He watched the lights go out one by one in all the windows. One particular light—a dull blue gleam—told Chéri that Edmée was going through her boudoir into their bedroom, which looked out on the garden at the back of the house.

'The boudoir will soon come to be known as the study, and no mistake,' he thought.

The clock of Janson-de-Sailly began to strike and Chéri cocked his ear to catch the chiming notes in flight, like drops of rain. 'Midnight! She's in a hurry to get to bed. . . . Yes, of course, she has to be at her Hospital by nine to-morrow morning.' He took a few nervous steps, shrugged his shoulders, and grew calmer.

'It's as if I'd married a ballet-dancer. Nine o'clock sharp, the class: it's sacrosanct. It has to come before everything else.'

He walked on as far as the entrance to the Bois. The day's dust, hanging in the pallid sky, dimmed the brightness of the stars. Step for step, a second tread echoed Chéri's: he stopped and waited for it to catch up with him. He disliked anyone walking behind him.

"Good evening, Monsieur Peloux," said the night-watchman, touching his cap.

Chéri answered by raising a finger to his forehead with the condescension of an officer—a trick he had picked up during the war from his fellow quartermaster-sergeants—and walked on past the night-watchman, who was trying the locks on the iron gates to the little private gardens.

From a couple of lovers on a bench just inside the Bois, came the rustle of crushed clothes and the whisper of smothered endearments. Chéri listened for an instant to the clasped bodies and invisible lips, a sound like the ripple of a ship's prow cleaving calm waters.

'The man's a soldier,' he noticed. 'I've just heard him unbuckle his belt.'

He was not thinking, which left his every sense on the alert. On many a calm night during the war Chéri had derived complex pleasure and subtle terror from his primitive keenness of hearing; his fingers, even when caked with mud and pocket fug, had been quick to distinguish the image on medal or coin, and to tell, by leaf or stalk, plants whose name he did not know. "Hi, there, Peloux lad, just tell us what I've got ahold of here?" Chéri recalled the ginger-headed lad who, under cover of darkness, would push into his hand a dead mole, a small snake, a tree-frog, an over-ripe fruit, or some piece of filth, and then exclaim, "Blimey, he gets it every time!" The memory made him smile, but with no pity for the ginger-headed lad, now dead. Yet he was haunted sometimes by the picture of his pal Pierquin, lying there on his back asleep for ever, with a look of distrust still on his face. He often spoke of him.

This very evening, at home, when dinner was over, Edmée had deftly steered the conversation round to the pathetic little tale, put together with such studied clumsiness. Chéri had it off by heart and it ended with the words: "And then Pierquin said to me, 'I had a dream about cats, old lad; and then I'd another dream about our river at home and it looked fair mucky. . . . The meaning of that's pretty clear. . . .' It was at this very moment he was picked off, by the smallest scrap of shrapnel. I wanted to carry him back. They found the two of us, him on the top of me, not a hundred yards from the spot. I tell you about him because he was a rare good sort . . . and he had quite a lot to do with my being given this."

And, as he ended on this modest note, Chéri had lowered his eyes to his green-and-red riband and knocked the ash off his cigarette, as though to keep himself in countenance. He considered it nobody's business that a chance explosion had thrown one of them across the other's shoulders, leaving Chéri alive and Pierquin dead. The truth—more ambiguous than falsehood —was that the terrific weight of a Pierquin, suddenly struck dead, had kept Chéri alive and half-suffocated, indignant and resentful. Chéri still bore a grudge against Pierquin. And, further, he had come to scorn the truth ever since the day when, years ago, it had suddenly fallen from his mouth like a belch, to spatter and wound one whom he had loved.

But at home this evening, the Americans—Majors Marsh-Meyer and Atkins, and Lieutenant Wood—had not appeared to listen to him. With the vacant faces of athletic first-communicants, with fixed and expressionless eyes, they had simply been waiting to go to a night club, waiting with almost painful anxiety. As for Filipesco! 'Needs watching,' Chéri decided laconically.

The lake in the Bois was encircled with a fragrant mist that rose rather from the scythed slopes of its banks than from the stagnant water. Chéri was about to lean against a tree, when, from the shadows, a woman boldly brushed against him. "Good evening, kid . . ." The last word made him start; it was uttered in a low parched voice, the very voice of thirst, of dusty roads, of this dry hot night. . . . He made no answer, and the dim figure came a step nearer on soft-soled shoes. But he caught a whiff of black woollens, soiled linen, dank hair, and turned back with long springy strides towards his own home.

The dull blue light was still on: Edmée had not yet left her boudoir-study. In all probability she would still be seated at her desk, signing chits for drugs and dressings, reading through the day's notes and the short reports made by her secretary. Her pretty school-marm head, crimped hair with a reddish tint, would be bent over her papers.

Chéri pulled out the small flat key on the end of its thin gold chain. 'Here we go. In for another carefully measured dose of love. . . .'

144

* * *

As was his habit, he entered his wife's boudoir without knocking. Edmée showed no sign of surprise, but went on with her telephone conversation. Chéri listened.

"No, not to-morrow. . . . You won't want me there for that. The General knows you perfectly well. And at the Ministry of Commerce, there's . . . What do you mean? 'Have I got Lémery?' No, certainly not! He's charming, but . . . Hullo? . . . Hullo? . . ." She laughed, showing her small teeth. "Oh come! that's going too far. . . . Lémery makes up to every woman, provided she's not blind or lame. . . . What? Yes, he's come in, he's here at my elbow. No, no, I'll be very discreet. . . . Goodbye. . . . See you to-morrow. . . ."

A plain white wrap, the white of her pearl necklace, was slipping off one shoulder. She had taken the pins from her chestnut hair, which, slightly frizzed by the dry atmosphere, followed every movement of her head.

"Who was that?" Chéri asked, as she put back the receiver and turned to ask him:

"Fred, you'll let me have the Rolls to-morrow morning, won't you? It will look better for bringing the General back here to lunch."

"What General?"

"General Haar."

"Is he a Boche?"

Edmée frowned. "Really, Fred, you're too old for such jokes! General Haar is coming to inspect my Hospital to-morrow. Then he can go back to America and tell them all that my Hospital can compare with any effort of the sort over there. Colonel Beybert will be showing him round, and they'll both come back here for luncheon afterwards."

Chéri took off his dinner-jacket and sent it flying in the direction of a chair.

"I don't give a damn! I'm lunching out."

"What d'you mean. What's all this?"

A spasm of rage crossed Edmée's face; but she smiled,

145

picked up the dinner-jacket with care, and changed her tone of voice. "Didn't you ask me a moment ago who that was on the telephone? Your mother."

Chéri collapsed into an armchair and said nothing. His features were set in their most beautiful and impassive mould. Over his forehead hovered an air of serene disapproval. This was apparent, too, on his lowered eyelids, faintly shadowed now at the approach of his thirtieth year, and on his mouth, which he was careful never to compress too tightly, keeping his lips gently apart as in sleep.

"You know," Edmée continued, "she wants Lémery, of the Ministry of Commerce, to do something about her three cargo-loads of leather. There are three ships filled with leather, at present held up in harbour at Valparaiso. There is something in the idea, you know! The only thing is that Lémery won't grant the necessary import licence . . . at least, that's what he says. Do you know how much money the Soumabis offered your mother as a minimum commission?"

With a wave of the hand, Chéri brushed aside ships, leather, and commission.

"Not interested," he said simply.

Edmée dropped the subject, and affectionately approached her husband.

"You will have luncheon here to-morrow, won't you? There'll probably be Gibbs—the reporter from *Excelsior*, who's going to photograph the Hospital—and your mother."

Chéri shook his head with no sign of impatience.

"No," he said. "General Hagenbeck . . ."

"Haar."

". . . and a Colonel, and my mother in her uniform. Her tunic—what d'you call it? her jacket?—with its little leather buttons; her elastic uplift-belt; epaulettes; high colonel's collar and her chin cascading over . . . and her cane. No, really, I don't pretend to be braver than I am. I'd rather go out."

He was laughing quietly to himself, and his laugh seemed

mirthless. Edmée put a hand, already trembling with irritation, upon his arm; but her touch was light.

"You can't mean that seriously?"

"Certainly I can. I shall go for lunch to *Brekekekex*, or somewhere else."

"With whom?"

"With whom I choose."

He sat down and kicked off his pumps. Edmée leant against a black lacquer cabinet and racked her brain for words to make him behave sensibly. The white satin front of her dress rose and fell in rhythm to the quickened pace of her breathing, and she crossed her hands behind her back like a martyr. Chéri looked at her with an air of pretended indifference. 'She really does look a lady,' he thought. 'Hair all anyhow, in her chemise, on her way to the bath—she always looks a lady.'

She lowered her eyes, caught Chéri's, and smiled.

"You're teasing me," she said plaintively.

"No," Chéri replied. "I shan't lunch here to-morrow, that's all."

"But why?"

He rose, walked as far as the open door into their room—which was in darkness and filled with night scents from the garden—and then came back to her.

"Because I shan't. If you compel me to explain myself, I shall speak out and perhaps be rude. You'll burst into tears, and 'in your distress', as the saying goes, you'll let your wrap slip to the floor and . . . and unfortunately it won't have the slightest effect on me."

Another spasm of rage passed over his wife's features, but her much-tried patience was not yet exhausted. She smiled and shrugged the one bare shoulder peeping from under her hair.

"It's quite easy to *say* that it won't have any effect on you."

He was walking to and fro, clad in nothing but his short white silk pants. All the time he was testing the elasticity of his instep and calf muscles, and kept rubbing his hand over the twin brown scars under his right breast, as if to preserve their fading hue. Lean, with less flesh on his body than he had had at twenty, at the same time in better shape and training, he liked to parade up and down in front of his wife as a rival rather than a lover. He knew himself to be the more perfect specimen and, as a connoisseur, could condescend to admire in her the slim hips, the small breasts, and the graceful, almost imperceptible lines which Edmée knew so well how to clothe in tubular frocks and slinky tunics. "Are you fading away, then?" he would sometimes ask her, just for the fun of annoying her. He would watch her whole body writhe in anger, and note its sudden and unsuspected vigour.

This reply of his wife's was distasteful to him. He wanted her to look well-bred, and to be silent, if not unresponsive, in his arms. He came to a halt, puckered his brow, and looked her up and down. "Pretty manners, I must say. Do you learn them from your Physician-in-charge? The war, Madame!"

She shrugged her bare shoulder.

"What a child you are, my poor Fred! It's lucky we're by ourselves. To go on at me like that just because of a little joke . . . which was really a compliment. And for you to try and teach me manners, you . . . you! And after seven years of marriage!"

"Where do you get the seven years from?"

He sat down, naked as he was, as though for a prolonged discussion, his legs wide apart with all the ostentation of an athlete.

"Well . . . really . . . nineteen-thirteen . . . nineteen-nineteen . . ."

"Excuse me! it's clear that we don't reckon by the same calendar. Now, I count from . . ."

Edmée arched a knee, taking the weight of her body on the other leg, a confession of her weariness; but Chéri interrupted her with: "Where's all this talk leading us? Come on, let's go to bed. You've got your ballet-class at nine to-morrow, haven't you?"

"Oh! Fred!"

Edmée crushed a rose from a black vase and threw away its petals. Chéri fanned the flames of anger still smouldering in her eyes, now moist with tears, by saying: "That's the name I give that job-lot of wounded, when I'm not thinking."

Without looking at him, she murmured through trembling lips: "You brute . . . you brute . . . you loathsome monster!"

He laughed, quite untouched.

"What d'you want me to say? As far as you're concerned, we all know you're carrying out a sacred mission. But what about me? You might just as well *have* to go to the Opera every day and practise in the Rotunda, for all the difference it would make. That would leave me just as much . . . just as much out of it. And those men I called your 'job-lot,' well, they're wounded, aren't they? Wounded who are a little luckier than others, perhaps. I've got absolutely nothing to do with them either. With them, too, I'm . . . out of it."

She turned round to face him so impulsively that it made her hair fly out from her temples: "My darling, don't be so unhappy! You're not out of it at all, you're above all that!"

He got up, drawn towards a jug of iced water, on the sides of which the moisture was slowly condensing into bluish tears. Edmée hurried forward: "With or without lemon, Fred?"

"Without, thanks."

He drank, she took the empty glass from his hands, and he went towards the bathroom.

"By the way," he said. "About that leak in the cement of the bathing-pool. It ought . . ."

"I'm having it seen to. The man who makes those glass mosaics happens to be a cousin of Chuche, one of my wounded, and he won't need to be asked twice, believe me."

"Good." Then, as he was moving away, he turned round. "Tell me, this business of the Ranch shares we were talking about yesterday morning, ought we to sell or not? Supposing I went to see old Deutsch about them to-morrow morning, and had a chin-wag with him?"

Edmée gave a shriek of schoolgirl laughter.

149

"Do you think I waited for you about that? Your mother had a stroke of genius this morning, while we were giving the Baroness a lift home."

"You mean that old La Berche woman?"

"Yes, the Baroness. Your mother, as you so elegantly put it, had a chin-wag with her. The Baroness is one of the original shareholders, and never leaves the Chairman of the Board alone for a moment. . . ."

"Except to cover her face in flour."

"Must you interrupt me the whole time? . . . and by two o'clock, my dear, the whole lot had been sold—every bit of it! The little flare up on the Bourse this afternoon—it lasted only a very short time—raked us in something like two hundred and sixteen thousand francs, Fred! That'll pay for piles of medicine and bandages. I wanted to keep the news till to-morrow, and then give you one of these topping note-cases. Kiss?"

He stood, naked and white-skinned, holding back the folds of the door-curtain, and looking closely at the expression on his wife's face.

"That's all very well . . ." he said at last, "but where do I come in?"

Edmée gave a mischievous shake of the head: "Your power of attorney still stands, my love. 'The right to sell, purchase, draw up or sign an agreement made out in my name . . . et cetera'—which reminds me, I must send the Baroness something as a souvenir."

"A briar pipe," said Chéri, after pretending to have given the matter his attention.

"No, don't laugh. The good soul is so valuable to us."

"And who are 'us'?"

"Your mother and me. The Baroness knows how to talk to the men in a way they understand. She speaks their language. She tells them rather risky stories, but in such a way . . . They dote on her."

The strangest of laughs trembled on Chéri's lips. He let go his hold on the dark curtain, and it fell back into place behind him, thus obliterating him completely, as sleep obliterates the figment of a dream. He walked along a passage dimly lit by a blue globe, without making a sound, like a figure floating on air; for he had insisted upon having thick carpets laid on every floor, from top to bottom of the house. He loved silence, and furtiveness, and never knocked at the door of the boudoir, which his wife, since the war, called her study. She showed no annoyance, and sensing Chéri's presence, never jumped when he came into the room.

He took a shower bath without lingering under the cool water, sprayed himself with scent absent-mindedly, and returned to the boudoir.

He could hear the sound of someone rumpling the sheets in the bedroom next door, and the tap of a paper-knife against a cup on the bedside table. He sat down and rested his chin in his hand. On the little table beside him, he caught sight of the morrow's menu, duly made out for the butler, according to daily routine. On it he read: *"Homard Thermidor, Côtelettes Fulbert-Dumonteil, Chaud-froid de canard, salade Charlotte, Soufflé au curaçao, Allumettes au Chester."* . . . 'No alteration required,' he murmured to himself. *"Six places?"*—'Ah, yes, that I must alter.' He corrected the number, and once more cupped his chin in his hand.

"Fred, do you know what time it is?"

He did not answer the soft voice, but went into their room and sat down facing the bed. With one shoulder bare and the other half-hidden by a wisp of white nightgown, Edmée was smiling, despite her tired state, aware that she looked prettier in bed than out. But Chéri remained seated, and once again cupped his chin in his hand.

151

"Rodin's *Penseur*," said Edmée, to encourage him to smile or to move.

"There's many a true word spoken in jest," he answered sententiously.

He pulled the folds of his Chinese dressing-gown closer over his knees and savagely crossed his arms.

"What the hell am I doing here?"

She did not understand, or had no wish to do so.

"That's what I'd like to know, Fred. It's two o'clock, and I get up at eight. To-morrow's going to be another of those pleasant little days. . . . It's unkind of you to dawdle like this. Do come along; there's a nice breeze rising. We'll go to bed with it on our faces, and imagine we're sleeping out of doors."

He weakened, and hesitated only an instant before hurling his silk wrap to a far corner of the room, while Edmée switched out the remaining light. She nestled up against him in the dark, but he neatly turned her over with her back to him and held her round the waist with strong arms, murmuring, "Like that. That's like being on a bob-sleigh," and fell asleep.

The following day, from the little window of the linen-room where he was hidden, he watched them leave. The duck's-egg green motor and another long American automobile were purring very quietly in the avenue under the thick overhanging chestnut trees. The green shade and the recently watered pavement exuded a pretence of freshness, but Chéri knew very well that in the garden at the back of the house the heat of this June morning—the month that scorches Paris—was already shrivelling the lovely deep blue of a pool of forget-me-nots within their edging of pinks.

His heart began to beat with a sort of nervousness when he saw, approaching the iron gates to his house, two figures in khaki, with gold stars on their breast and crimson velvet bands round their caps.

"In uniform, of course, the crackpot!"

This was the nickname Chéri had bestowed on the Physician-in-Charge at Edmée's Hospital, and without really knowing it, he loathed the man and his red-gold hair and the caressing tones he put into technical terms when talking to Edmée. He muttered vague hearty curses, against the Medical Corps in particular, and against all who insisted on wearing uniform in peacetime. The American officer was growing fat, so

Chéri sneered: "I thought the Americans went in for sport. What's he doing with a belly like that?" but he said not a word when Edmée, in a white dress and white shoes, vivaciously held out her white-gloved hand to the Doctor. She greeted him in loud, quick, cheerful tones. Chéri had not missed a single word that fell from her red mouth, which parted in a smile over such tiny teeth. She had walked out as far as the motors, come back to tell a footman to fetch a notebook she had forgotten and stood chatting while she waited for it. She had spoken in English to the American Colonel, and lowered her voice, in automatic deference, when replying to Doctor Arnaud.

Chéri was keeping a sharp look-out from behind the muslin curtains. His characteristic mistrust and slyness froze his features into immobility directly he concealed a strong emotion, and he kept a strict watch on himself, even when alone. His eyes travelled from Edmée to the Doctor, and then from the American Colonel back to Edmée, who had more than once looked up to the first floor, as though she knew of his hiding-place.

'What are they waiting for?' he grumbled under his breath. 'Ah, so this is it. . . . God in heaven!'

Charlotte Peloux had arrived, in a sports-car driven by an impersonal and impeccable young chauffeur. Bursting out of her gabardine uniform, she held her head stiffly upright under its little tight-fitting hat with a military peak, and the ends of her bobbed red hair could be seen popping out at the back. She did not set foot to ground, but suffered them to come and pay their respects to her. She received Edmée's kiss and apparently asked after her son, for she too raised her head in the direction of the first floor, thus unveiling her magnificent eyes, over which drifted, as over the huge eyes of an octopus, some dark inhuman dream.

153

"She's wearing her little military cap," Chéri murmured.

He gave a curious shudder, which made him angry with himself, and smiled when the three motors drove away. He waited patiently until his "bachelor's runabout" drew up against the kerb punctually at eleven o'clock, and he kept it waiting for some considerable time. Twice he stretched out his hand to lift the receiver of the telephone, and twice he let it fall again to his side. His sudden impulse to invite Filipesco soon vanished and he thought he would like to collect young Maudru and his girl. 'Or, better still, Jean de Touzac. . . . But at this hour he'll still be furiously snoring. Gosh! all that lot . . . not one of them, I must be fair, a patch on Desmond. . . . Poor old boy.'

He regarded Desmond as a war casualty; but with greater compassion than he ever vouchsafed the dead. Desmond, who was alive yet lost to him, had the power of inspiring him with an almost tender melancholy, as well as with the jealous respect due to a man with a "job". Desmond ran a night club, and sold antiques to Americans. A gutless wash-out during the whole of the war, when he had carried anything and everything but a rifle —official papers, billy-cans, any dirty hospital receptacle—Desmond had bitten deep into peacetime with a warlike fervour, and rich had been his immediate reward, very much to Chéri's astonishment. *Desmond's* had been started in quite a small way in a private house in the Avenue d'Alma, and now it sheltered frenzied and silent couples behind its heavy ashlar masonry, beneath ceilings decorated with swallows and hawthorn, and hemmed in by the bulrushes and flamingoes of its stained-glass windows. They danced at *Desmond's*, night and day, as people dance after war: the men, young and old, free from the burden of thinking and being frightened—empty-minded, innocent; the women, given over to a pleasure far greater than any more definite sensual delight, to the company of men: that is to say, to physical contact with them, their smell, their tonic sweat, the certain proof of which tingled in every inch of their bodies—the certainty of being the prey of a man wholly alive and vital, and of succumbing in his arms to rhythms as personal, as intimate, as those of sleep.

'Desmond will have got to bed at three, or three-thirty,' Chéri reckoned. 'He'll have had enough sleep.'

But once again he let drop the hand he had stretched out to the telephone. He went down the stairs in double quick time, aided by the springy thick pile that covered every floor board in his house. As he passed by the dining-room he looked without anger at the five white plates set in a diadem round a black crystal bowl, in which floated pink water-lilies, matching the pink of the tablecloth; and he did not pause till face to face with the looking-glass, fixed to the back of the heavy door of the reception-room on the ground floor. He feared, yet was attracted by, this looking-glass, which drew what little light it had from the french windows immediately facing it across the corridor, their opaque blue panes further obscured by the dark foliage of the garden. Every time he bumped into his own image, Chéri was brought up sharp by a slight shock when he recognised it as his own. He never could understand why this glass did not reflect the faithful image of a young man of twenty-four. He could not detect the precise points where time, with invisible finger, marks first the hour of perfection on a handsome face, and then the hour of that more blatant beauty, the herald of a majestic decline.

To Chéri's mind, there could be no question of a decline, and he could never have noticed it on his own features. He had just happened to bump into a thirty-year-old Chéri and failed to recognise him; and he sometimes asked himself "What's wrong with me?" as though he were feeling a little off-colour or had thrown his clothes on anyhow. Now he hurried past the reception-room door, and thought no more about it.

Desmond's, being a properly organised establishment, was up and doing by midday, despite the late hours it kept. The concierge was hosing the paved courtyard, a waiter was sweeping the steps clean, brushing away a heap of high-class rubbish—fine light dust, silver paper, corks with metal caps, stub-ends of gold-tipped cigarettes, and crumpled drinking-straws—rubbish which bore daily witness to the prosperity of *Desmond's*.

Chéri cleared at a bound the residue of last night's brisk business; but the smell inside the house barred further progress like a rope stretched across his path. Forty couples, packed like sardines, had left behind the smell—the memory of their sweat-soaked clothes—stale, and tainted with tobacco fumes. Chéri plucked up courage and leapt up the staircase, narrowed by heavy oak banisters supported on caryatids. Desmond had wasted no money on changing the stuffy sumptuosities of 1880. After removing two dividing walls, installing a refrigerator in the basement, engaging a jazz-band regardless of cost, no further outlay would be necessary for at least another year. "I'll bring it up to date to attract customers," so Desmond said, "when dancing isn't such a rage."

He slept on the second floor, in a room where convolvulus ran riot on the walls and storks on the stained-glass windows; his bath was of enamelled zinc, bordered by a tiled frieze of river-plants, and the ancient heating-apparatus wheezed like a bulldog past its prime. But the telephone shone as brightly as a weapon kept polished by daily use, and Chéri, after bounding up four steps at a time, discovered his friend, lips to the chalice, apparently imbibing the murky breath of its mouthpiece. His wandering glance came down to earth, and hardly settled on Chéri before it was off and up again to the convolvulus-wreathed cornice. His yellow-gold pyjamas cast a blight over a morning-after-the-night-before face, but Desmond was inflated by prosperity and no longer worried about being ugly.

"Good morning," said Chéri. "I came through all right. What a stench there is on your stairs. Worse than a dug-out."

". . . You'll never get *Desmond's* custom at twelve," Desmond was saying to an invisible listener. "I have no difficulty in buying Pommery at that price. And for my private cellar, Pommery ought to be eleven when minus labels . . . hullo . . . yes, the labels that came off in the general rumpus. That's what I want . . . hullo?"

"You're coming out to lunch. I've got the runabout at the door," Chéri said.

"No, and twice times no," said Desmond.

"What?"

"No, and a thousand times no. Hullo? . . . Sherry! What

156

d'you take me for? This isn't a bar. Champagne, or nothing. Don't go on wasting your time and mine. Hullo. . . . That's quite possible. Only I'm all the rage at the moment. Hullo. . . . At two o'clock precisely. A very good day to you, Monsieur."

He stretched himself, before offering a limp hand. He still looked like Alfonso XIII, but thirty summers and the war had rooted this uncertain creature in the soil he needed. To have come through the war without firing a shot, to have eaten regularly, taken every advantage of it, and malingered in general, were so many personal victories from which he had emerged strengthened and self-confident. Assurance and a full pocket had made him less ugly, and you could be sure that, at sixty, he would give the illusion of having once passed for a handsome man with a large nose and long legs. He looked at Chéri condescendingly, but with a friendlier eye. Chéri turned away his head and said: "What! Are you reduced to this? Come on, old boy. It's midday and you're not up yet."

"In the first place, I *am* ready," Desmond replied, unbuttoning his pyjamas to show a white silk shirt and a bronze-coloured bow tie. "And in the second, I'm not going to lunch out."

"So that's it," said Chéri. "Well, of all . . . I'm speechless. . . ."

"But if you like I can give you two fried eggs, and half my ham, my salad, my stout and my strawberries. No extra charge for coffee."

Chéri looked at him in impotent fury. "Why?"

"Business," said Desmond, with a deliberately nasal twang. "Champagne! You heard what I was saying a moment ago. Oh! these wine-merchants! If one didn't put on the screw . . . But I'm a match for them."

157

He knotted his fingers and the knuckle-joints cracked with commercial pride.

"Yes or no?"

"Yes, you swine."

Chéri chucked his soft felt hat at his head; but Desmond

picked it up and brushed it with his forearm, to show that this was not the moment for childish jokes. They had eggs in aspic, ham and tongue, and good black stout with coffee-coloured foam on it. They spoke little, and Chéri, gazing out on to the paved courtyard, was politely bored.

'What am I doing here? Nothing, except that I'm not at home, sitting down to cutlets Fulbert-Dumonteil.' He visualised Edmée in white, the baby-faced American Colonel, and Arnaud, the Physician-in-Charge, in whose presence she acted the docile little girl. He thought of Charlotte Peloux's epaulettes, and a sort of fruitless affection for his host was coming over him, when the latter asked him an abrupt question:

"Do you know how much champagne was drunk here last night, between four o'clock yesterday and four o'clock this morning?"

"No," said Chéri.

"And do you know how many bottles were returned empty from those delivered here between May the first and June the fifteenth?"

"No," said Chéri.

"Say a number."

"No idea," Chéri grunted.

"But say something! Say a number! Have a guess, man! Name some figure!"

Chéri scratched the table cloth as he might during an examination. He was suffering from the heat, and from his own inertia.

"Five hundred," he got out at last.

Desmond threw himself back in his chair and, as it swerved through the air, his monocle shot a piercing flash of sunlight into Chéri's eye.

"Five hundred! You make me laugh!"

He was boasting. He did not know how to laugh: his nearest approach was a sort of sob of the shoulders. He drank some coffee, to excite Chéri's curiosity, and then put down his cup again.

"Three thousand, three hundred, and eighty-two, my boy. And do you know how much that puts in my pocket?"

"No," Chéri interrupted, "and I don't give a damn. That's enough. My mother does all that for me if I want it. Besides . . ." He rose, and added in a hesitant voice: "Besides, money doesn't interest me."

"Strange," said Desmond, hurt. "Strange. Amusing."

"If you like. No, can't you understand, money doesn't interest me . . . doesn't interest me any more."

These simple words fell from his lips slowly. Chéri spoke them without looking up, and kicked a biscuit crumb along the carpet; his embarrassment at making this confession, his secretive look, restored for a fleeting instant the full marvel of his youth.

For the first time Desmond stared at him with the critical attention of a doctor examining a patient, 'Am I dealing with a malingerer?' Like a doctor, he had recourse to confused and soothing words.

"We all go through that. Everyone's feeling a little out of sorts. No one knows exactly where he stands. Work is a wonderful way of putting you on your feet again, old boy. Take me, for instance. . . ."

"I know," Chéri interrupted. "You're going to tell me I haven't enough to do."

"Yes, it's your own fault." Desmond's mockery was condescending in the extreme. "For in these wonderful times . . ." He was going on to confess his deep satisfaction with business, but he pulled himself up in time. "It's also a question of upbringing. Obviously, you never learned the first thing about life under Léa's wing. You've no idea how to manage people and things."

159

"So they say." Chéri was put out. "Léa herself wasn't fooled. You mayn't believe me, but though she didn't trust me, she always consulted me before buying or selling."

He thrust out his chest, proud of the days gone by, when distrust was synonymous with respect.

"You've only got to apply yourself to it again—to money matters," Desmond continued, in his advisory capacity. "It's a game that never goes out of fashion."

"Yes," Chéri acquiesced rather vaguely. "Yes, of course. I'm only waiting."

"Waiting for what?"

"I'm waiting. . . . What I mean is . . . I'm waiting for an opportunity . . . a better opportunity. . . ."

"Better than what?"

"What a bore you are. An excuse—if you like—to take up again everything the war deprived me of years ago. My fortune, which is, in fact . . ."

"Quite considerable?" Desmond suggested. Before the war, he would have said "enormous," and in a different tone of voice. A moment's humiliation brought a blush to Chéri's cheek.

"Yes . . . my fortune. Well, the little woman, my wife, now makes that her business."

"Oh, no!" exclaimed Desmond, in shocked disapproval.

"Oh, yes, I promise you. Two hundred and sixteen thousand in a little flare-up on the Bourse the day before yesterday. So, don't you see, the question now arises, 'How am I to interfere?' . . . Where do I stand, in all this? When I suggest taking a hand, they say . . ."

"They? Who are 'they'?"

"What? Oh, my mother and my wife. They start saying: 'Take it easy. You're a warrior. Would you like a glass of orangeade? Run along to your shirt-maker, he's making you look a fool. And while you are going the rounds, you might call in and collect my necklace, if the clasp's been mended . . .' and so on, and so forth."

He was growing excited, hiding his resentment as best he could, though his nostrils were quivering, and his lips as well.

"So must I now tout motor-cars, or breed Angora rabbits, or direct some high-class establishment? Have I got to engage myself as a male nurse or accountant in that bargain-basement, my wife's Hospital?" He walked as far as the window, and came back to Desmond precipitately. "Under the orders of Doctor Arnaud, Physician-in-Charge, and pass the basins round for him? Must I take up this night club business? Can't you *see* the competition!"

He laughed in order to make Desmond laugh; but Desmond, no doubt a little bored, kept a perfectly straight face.

"How long ago did you start thinking of all this? You certainly had no such ideas in the spring, or last winter, or before you were married."

"I had no time for it," Chéri answered quite simply. "We went off on our travels, we began furnishing the house, we bought motors just in time to have them requisitioned. All that led up to the war. Before the war . . . before the war I was . . . a kid from a rich home. I was rich, damn it!"

"You still are."

"I still am," Chéri echoed.

He hesitated once more, searching for words. "But now, it's not at all the same thing. People have got the jitters. And work, and activity, and duty, and women who serve their country—not half they don't—and are crazy about oof . . . they're such thorough-going business-women that they make you disgusted with the word business. They're such hard workers it's enough to make you loathe the sight of work." He looked uncertainly at Desmond, "Is it really wrong to be rich, and take life easy?"

Desmond enjoyed playing his part and making up for past subservience. He put a protective hand on Chéri's shoulder.

"My son, be rich and live your own life! Tell yourself that you're the incarnation of an ancient aristocracy. Model yourself on the feudal barons. You're a warrior."

"*Merde,*" said Chéri.

"Now you're talking like a warrior. Only, you must live and let live, and let those work who like it."

"You, for instance."

"Me, for instance."

"Obviously, you're not the sort to let yourself be messed about by women."

161

"No," said Desmond curtly. He was hiding from the world
a perverse taste for his chief cashier—a gentle creature with
brown hair scraped well back, rather masculine and hairy. She
wore a religious medallion round her neck, and smilingly confessed, "For two pins I'd commit murder: I'm like that."

"No. Emphatically, no! Can't you mention anything without sooner or later dragging in 'my wife, women,' or else 'in
Léa's time'? Is there nothing else to talk about in 1919?"

Beyond the sound of Desmond's voice, Chéri seemed to be
listening to some other, still unintelligible sound. 'Nothing else
to talk about,' he repeated to himself. 'Why should there be?'
He was daydreaming, lulled by the light and the warmth, which
increased as the sun came round into the room. Desmond went
on talking, impervious to the stifling heat, and as white as winter
endive. Chéri caught the words "little birds" and began to pay
attention.

"Yes, I've a whole heap of amusing connections, with
whom, of course, I'll put you in touch. And when I say 'birds',
I'm speaking far too frivolously of what amounts to a unique
collection, you understand, utterly unique. My regulars are tasty
pieces, and all the tastier for the last four years. Just you wait
and see, old boy! When my capital is big enough, what a restaurant I'll show the world! Ten tables, at most, which they'll fall
over each other to book. I'll cover in the courtyard. . . . You
may be sure my lease provides for all additions I make! Cork-
lino in the middle of the dance-floor, spot-lights. . . . That's
the future! It's out there. . . ."

The tango merchant was holding forth like a founder of
cities, pointing towards the window with outstretched arm.
Chéri was struck by the word "future," and turned to face the
spot indicated by Desmond, somewhere high up above the
courtyard. He saw nothing, and felt limp. The reverberations of
the two o'clock sun smote glumly down upon the little slate roof
of the old stables, where the concierge of *Desmond's* had his
lodging. "What a ballroom, eh?" said Desmond with fervour,

pointing to the small courtyard. "And it won't be long now before I get it!"

Chéri stared intently at this man who, each day, expected and received his daily bread. 'And what about me?' he thought, inwardly frustrated.

"Look, here comes my swipes-merchant," Desmond shouted. "Make yourself scarce. I must warm him up like a bottle of Corton."

He shook Chéri's hand with a hand that had changed its character: from being narrow and boneless, it had become broad, purposeful, disguised as the rather firm hand of an honest man. 'The war . . .' thought Chéri, tongue in cheek.

"You're off? Where?" Desmond asked.

He kept Chéri standing on the top of the steps long enough to be able to show off such a decorative client to his wine merchant.

"Over there," said Chéri, with a vague gesture.

"Mystery," murmured Desmond. "Be off to your seraglio!"

"Oh no," said Chéri, "you're quite wrong."

He conjured up the vision of some female—moist flesh, nakedness, a mouth. He shuddered with impersonal disgust, and, repeating 'You're quite wrong' under his breath, got into his runabout.

He carried away with him an all too familiar uneasiness, the embarrassment and irritation of never being able to put into words all that he really wanted to say; of never meeting the person to whom he would have to confide a half-formed admission, a secret that could have changed everything, and which, for instance, this afternoon would have dispersed the ominous atmosphere from the bleached pavements and the asphalt, now beginning to melt under a vertical sun.

'Only two o'clock,' he sighed, 'and, this month, it stays light till well after nine.'

The breath of wind raised by the speed of his motor was like a hot dry towel being flapped in his face, and he yearned for the make-believe night behind his blue curtains, to the accompaniment of the simple drip-drop-drip of the Italian fountain's sing-song in the garden.

'If I slip quickly through the hall, I'll be able to get in again without being seen. *They'll* be having coffee by now.'

He could almost catch a whiff of the excellent luncheon, of the lingering smell of the melon, of the dessert wine which Edmée always had served with the fruit; and, ahead of time, he saw the verdigrised reflection of Chéri closing the door lined with plate glass.

'In we go!'

Two motors were dozing in the shade of the low-hanging branches just inside the gates, one his wife's and the other American, both in the charge of an American chauffeur who was himself taking a nap. Chéri drove on as far as the deserted Rue de Franqueville, and then walked back to his own front door. He let himself in without making a sound, took a good look at his shadowy form in the green-surfaced mirror, and softly went upstairs to the bedroom. It was just as he had longed for it to be —blue, fragrant, made for rest. In it he found everything that his thirsty drive had made so desirable: and more besides, for there was a young woman dressed in white, powdering her face and tidying her hair in front of a long looking-glass. Her back was turned to Chéri, and she did not hear him enter. Thus he had more than a moment to observe in the glass how flushed luncheon and the hot weather had made her, and to note her strange expression of untidiness and triumph and her general air of having won an emotionally outrageous victory. All at once Edmée caught sight of her husband and turned to face him without saying a word. She examined him critically from top to toe, waiting for him to speak first.

Through the half-open window facing the garden, floated up the baritone notes of Doctor Arnaud's voice, singing, "*Oy Marie, Oy Marie.*"

Edmée's whole body seemed to incline towards this voice,

but she restrained herself from turning her head in the direction of the garden.

The slightly drunken courage visible in her eyes might well forebode a serious situation. Out of contempt or cowardice, Chéri, by putting a finger to his lips, enjoined silence upon her. He then pointed to the staircase with the same imperative finger. Edmée obeyed. She went resolutely past him, without being able to repress, at the moment when she came closest to him, a slight twist of the hips and quickening of the step, which kindled in Chéri a sudden impulse to strike her. He leant over the banisters, feeling reassured, like a cat that has reached safety at the top of a tree; and, still thinking of punishing, smashing, and taking flight, he waited there, ready to be wafted away on a flood of jealousy. All that came to him was a mediocre little feeling of shame, all too bearable, as he put his thoughts into words, 'Punish her, smash up the whole place! There's better to do than that. Yes, there's better to do.' But what, he did not know.

Each morning for him, whether he woke early or late, was the start of a long day's vigil. At first he paid but scant attention, believing it to be merely the persistence of an unhealthy habit picked up in the army.

In December, 1918, after putting his knee-cap out of joint, he had eked out in his bed at home a short period of convalescence. He used to stretch himself in the early morning and smile. 'I'm comfortable. I'm waiting for the time when I feel much better. Christmas this year is really going to be worth while.'

Christmas came. When the truffles had been eaten, and the holly twig dipped in brandy set alight on a silver platter, in the presence of an ethereal Edmée, very much the wife, and to the acclamations of Charlotte, of Madame de La Berche, and members of the nursing staff of the Hospital, together with a sprinkling of Rumanian officers and athletic adolescent American colonels, Chéri waited. 'Oh, if only those fellows would go away! I'm waiting to go to sleep, head in the cool air and feet warm, in my own good bed!' Two hours later, he was still waiting for sleep, laid out as flat as a corpse, listening to the mocking call of the little winter owls in the branches—a challenge to the blue light of his unshuttered room. At last he fell asleep; but a prey to his insatiable vigilance from the peep of dawn, he began to wait for his breakfast, and gave utterance to his hearty impatience: "What the hell do they think they're doing with the grub downstairs?" He did not realise that whenever he swore or used "soldiers' slang", it always went with an affected state of mind. His jolliness was a method of escape. Breakfast was brought to him by Edmée; but in his wife's bustling movements he never failed to discern haste and the call of duty, and he would ask for more toast, or for another hot roll which he no longer really wanted, simply from a malicious wish to delay Edmée's departure, to delay the moment when he would once more, inevitably, resume his period of waiting.

A certain Rumanian lieutenant used to be sent off by Edmée to look for concentrated disinfectant and absorbent cotton wool, or again to press a demand upon Ministers—"What the government refuses point-blank to a Frenchman, a foreigner gets every time," she affirmed. He used to bore Chéri stiff by cracking up the duties of a soldier, fit or nearly fit, and the paradisal purity of the Coictier Hospital. Chéri went along there with Edmée, sniffed the smells of antiseptics which relentlessly suggest underlying putrefaction, recognised a comrade among the "Trench Feet" and sat down on the edge of his bed, forcing himself to assume the cordiality prescribed by war novels and patriotic plays. He knew well enough, all the same, that a man in sound health, who had come through unscathed, could find no peer or equal among the crippled. Wherever he looked, he saw the fluttering white wings of the nurses, the red-brick colour of the faces and hands upon the sheets. An odious sense of impotence weighed upon him. He caught himself guiltily stiffening one of his arms as if held in a sling, or dragging one of his legs. But the next moment he could not help taking a deep breath and picking his way between the recumbent mummies with the light step of a dancer. He was forced reluctantly to reverence Edmée, because of her authority as a non-commissioned angel, and her aura of whiteness. She came across the ward, and, in passing, put a hand on Chéri's shoulder; but he knew that the desire behind this gesture of tenderness and delicate possession was to bring a blush of envy and irritation to the cheek of a young dark-haired nurse who was gazing at Chéri with the candour of a cannibal.

He felt bored, and consumed by the feeling of weariness that makes a man jib at the serried ranks of masterpieces before him as he is being dragged round a museum. The plethora of whiteness, thrown off from the ceiling and reflected back from the tiled floor, blotted out all corners, and he felt sorry for the men lying there, to whom shade would have been a charity, though no one offered it. The noonday hour imposes rest and privacy upon the beasts of the field, and the silence of deep woodland undergrowth upon the birds of the air, but civilised men no longer obey the dictates of the sun. Chéri took a few steps towards his wife, with the intention of saying: "Draw the curtains, install a punkah, take away that macaroni from the poor wretch who's blinking his eyes and breathing so heavily, and let him eat his food when the sun goes down. Give them shade, let them have any colour you like, but not always and everywhere this eternal white." With the arrival of Doctor Arnaud, he lost his inclination to give advice and make himself useful.

The Doctor, with his white linen belly and his red gold hair, had taken no more than three steps across the ward, before the hovering non-commissioned angel glided to earth again, to minister as a humble seraph, rosy with faith and zeal. Chéri thereupon turned to Filipesco, who was distributing American cigarettes, shouted "Are you coming?" in contemptuous tones, and bore him away; but not before he had bidden farewell to his wife, to Doctor Arnaud, to nurses male and female, with the

167

haughty affability of an official visitor. He crossed the rough gravel of the little courtyard, got into his car, and allowed himself no more than a dozen words' soliloquy: 'It's the regular thing. The correct move for the Physician-in-Charge.'

Never again did he cross the threshold of the Hospital, and thereafter Edmée invited him on State occasions only, out of official courtesy, much as one might, at a dinner party, politely offer the snipe to a vegetarian guest.

He was now given over to reflection, and a prey to idleness. Before the war his idleness had been so light and varied, with the resonant ring of a flawless empty glass. During the war, too, he had endured periods of inertia under military discipline, inertia modified by cold, mud, risk, patrols, and even, on occasion, a little fighting. Conditioned to indolence by his upbringing and the life of a sensual young man, he had watched, himself untouched, the fresh young vulnerable companions all round him pine away in silence, solitude, and frustration. He had witnessed the ravages inflicted on intelligent people by the lack of newspapers as if they were being deprived of a daily drug. Whereas he had relapsed into contemplative silence—like a cat in a garden at night—content with a short letter, a postcard, or a cunningly packed parcel, other men, so-called superior men, had appeared to him to be showing every symptom of ruinous mental starvation. Thus he had learned to take pride in bolstering up his patience, and had brooded over two or three ideas, over two or three persistent memories, as highly coloured as a child's, and over his inability to imagine his own death.

Time and again, throughout the war, on coming out of a long dreamless sleep or a fitful bout of spasmodically interrupted rest, he would awake to find himself somewhere outside the present time and, his more recent past sloughed off, restored to the days of his boyhood—restored to Léa. Later, Edmée would suddenly rise up from the past, distinct and clear in every detail, and this evocation of her form, no less than its almost immediate disappearance, had always put Chéri in good spirits. "That gives me two of them," he reckoned. Nothing came to him from Léa; he did not write to her. But he received postcards signed by the crabbed fingers of old mother Aldonza, and cigars chosen by the Baroness de La Berche. Sometimes he dreamed of a long soft-wool scarf, as blue as a pair of blue eyes and with a very faint suggestion of the scent associated with it throughout long hours of warmth and slumber. He had loved this scarf and hugged it to him in the dark, until it had lost its fragrance and the freshness of the blue eyes, and he had thought of it no more.

For four years he had not bothered his head about Léa. Her trusty old cronies, had occasion arisen, would have forwarded news of any events in her life. He never imagined anything happening to her. What had Léa in common with sickness, or Léa with change?

In 1918 he could not believe his ears when the Baroness de La Berche casually mentioned "Léa's new flat".

"Has she moved, then?"

"Where have you sprung from?" the Baroness answered. "The whole world knows it. The sale of her house to the Americans was a brilliant deal, you bet! I've seen her new flat. It's small, but it's very cosy. Once you sit down in it, you never want to get up again."

Chéri clung to the words "small, but cosy". Unable to imagine anything different, he supplied an over-all rose-pink background, threw in that huge galleon of gold and steel—the bed with its lace rigging—and hung Chaplin's pearly-breasted nymph from some floating cloud.

When Desmond began looking about for a sleeping partner for his night club, Chéri had spasms of alarm and anxiety. "The blackguard's certain to try and tap Léa, or get her mixed up in some fishy business . . . I'd better tip her off on the telephone." He did nothing of the sort, however. Telephoning to a discarded mistress is riskier far than holding out your hand in the street to a nervous enemy who tries to catch your eye.

169

* * *

He went on biding his time, even after surprising Edmée in front of the looking-glass, after that flagrant exhibition of over-excitement, flushed cheeks, and untidiness. He let the hours slip by, and did not put into words—and so accentuate—his certainty that a still almost chaste understanding existed between his wife and the man who had been singing *"Oy Marie!"* For he felt much lighter in spirit, and for several days stopped uselessly consulting his wrist-watch as soon as daylight began to fade. He developed the habit of sitting out under the trees in a basket-chair, like a newly arrived guest in an hotel garden. There he marvelled to see how the oncoming night blotted out the blue of the monks-hood, producing in its stead a hazier blue into which the shapes of the flowers were fused, while the green of their leaves persisted in distinct clumps. The edging of rose-coloured pinks turned to rank mauve, then the colour ebbed rapidly and the July stars shone yellow between the branches of the weeping ash.

He tasted at home the pleasures enjoyed by a casual passer-by who sits down to rest in a square, and he never noticed how long he remained there, lying back with his hands dangling. Sometimes he gave a fleeting thought to what he called "the looking-glass scene" and the atmosphere in the blue room when it had been secretly troubled by a man's sudden appearance, theatrical behaviour, and flight. He whispered over and over, with foolish mechanical regularity, "That's one point estab-lished. That's what's called a point-t-established", running the two words together into one.

At the beginning of July he bought a new open motor, and called it his Riviera Runabout. He drove Filipesco and Des-mond out along drought-whitened roads, but returned to Paris every evening, cleaving alternate waves of warm and cool air, which began to lose their good smells the nearer the motor drew to Paris.

One day he took out the Baroness de La Berche, a virile companion, who, when they came to the barriers of the Octroi, raised her forefinger to the little felt hat pulled well down on her head. He found her agreeable, sparing of words, interested in wayside inns overgrown with wistaria, and in village wine-shops with their cellar-smell and wine-soaked sand. Rigid and in silence, they covered two hundred miles or more, without ever opening their mouths except to smoke or feed. The following day Chéri again invited Camille de La Berche with a curt "Well, how about it, Baroness?" and whisked her off without further ado.

The trusty motor sped far afield through the green countryside, and came back at nightfall to Paris like a toy at the end of a string. That evening, Chéri, while never taking his eye off the road, could distinguish on his right side the outline of an elderly woman, with a man's profile as noble as that of an old family coachman. It astonished him to find her worthy of respect because she was plain and simple, and when he was alone in her company for the first time and far away from town-life, it began to dawn on him that a woman burdened with some monstrous sexual deformity needs must possess a certain bravura and something of the dignified courage of the condemned.

Since the war this woman had found no further use for her unkindness. The Hospital had put her back in her proper place, that is to say, among males, among men just young enough, just tamed enough by suffering, for her to live serenely in their midst, and forget her frustrated femininity.

On the sly, Chéri studied his companion's large nose, the greying hairy upper lip, and the little peasant eyes which glanced incuriously at ripe cornfields and scythed meadows.

For the first time he felt something very like friendship for old Camille, and was led to make a poignant comparison: "She is alone. When she's no longer with her soldiers or with my mother, she's alone. She too. Despite her pipe and her glass of wine, she's alone."

171

On their way back to Paris, they stopped at a "hostelry" where there was no ice, and where, trained against the plinths of columns and clinging to ancient baptismal fonts dotted about the lawn, the rambler-roses were dying, frizzled by the sun. A neighbouring copse screened this dried-up spot from any breeze, and a small cloud, scorched to a cherry hue, hung motionless, high in the heavens.

The Baroness knocked out her short briar pipe on the ear of a marble fawn.

"It's going to be grilling over Paris to-night."

Chéri nodded in agreement, and looked up at the cloud. The light reflected from it mottled his white cheeks and dimpled chin, like touches of pink powder on an actor's face.

"Yes," he said.

"Well, you know, if the idea tempts you, let's not go back till to-morrow morning. Just give me time to buy a piece of soap and a tooth-brush. . . . And we'll telephone your wife. Then, to-morrow morning we can be up and on our way by four o'clock, while it's fresh."

Chéri sprang to his feet in unthinking haste. "No, no, I can't."

"You can't? Come, come!"

Down near his feet he saw two small mannish eyes, and a pair of broad shoulders shaking with laughter.

"I didn't believe that you were still held on such a tight rein," she said. "But, of course, if you are . . ."

"Are what?"

She had risen to her feet again, robust and hearty, and clapped him vigorously on the shoulder.

"Yes, yes. You run around all day long, but you go back to your kennel every night. Oh, you're kept well in hand."

He looked at her coldly: already he liked her less. "There's no hiding anything from you, Baroness. I'll fetch the car, and in under two hours we'll be back at your front door."

172

Chéri never forgot their nocturnal journey home, the sadness of the lingering crimson in the west, the smell of the grasses, the feathery moths held prisoner in the beam of the headlamps. The Baroness kept watch beside him, a dark form made denser by the night. He drove cautiously; the air, cool at faster speeds, grew hot again when he slowed down to take a corner. He trusted to his keen sight and his alert senses, but he could not help his thoughts running on the queer massive old woman motionless at his right side, and she caused him a sort of terror, a twitching of the nerves, which suddenly landed him within a few inches of a waggon carrying no rear lamp. At that moment a large hand came lightly to rest on his forearm.

"Take care, child!"

He certainly had not expected either the gesture or the gentle tone of the voice. But nothing justified the subsequent emotion, the lump like a hard fruit stone in his throat, 'I'm a fool, I'm a fool,' he kept repeating. He continued at a slower speed, and amused himself by watching the refraction of the beams, the golden zigzags and peacock's feathers, that danced for a moment round the headlamps when seen through the tears that brimmed his eyes.

'She told me that it had a hold on me, that I was held well in hand. If she could see us, Edmée and me. . . . How long is it since we took to sleeping like two brothers?' He tried to count: three weeks, perhaps more? 'And the joke about the whole business is that Edmée makes no demands, and wakes up smiling.' To himself, he always used the word "joke" when he wished to avoid the word "sad". 'Like an old married couple, what! like an old married couple . . . Madame and her Physician-in-Charge, Monsieur . . . and . . . his car. All the same, old Camille said that I was held. Held. Held. Catch me ever taking that old girl out again. . . .'

He did take her out again, for July began to scorch Paris. But neither Edmée nor Chéri complained about the dog-days. Chéri used to come home, polite and absentminded, the backs of his hands and the lower part of his face nut-brown. He walked about naked between the bathroom and Edmée's boudoir.

173

"You must have been roasted to-day, you poor townees!" Chéri jeered.

Looking rather pale and almost melting away, Edmée straightened her pretty odalisque back and denied that she was tired.

"Oh well, not quite as bad as that, you know. There was rather more air than yesterday. My office down there is cool, you know. And then, we've had no time to think about it. My young man in bed twenty-two, who was getting on so well . . ."

"Oh yes!"

"Yes, Doctor Arnaud isn't too pleased about him."

She didn't hesitate to make play with the name of the Physician-in-Charge, much as a player moves up a decisive piece on the chess-board. But Chéri did not bat an eyelid, and Edmée followed his movements, those of a naked male body dappled a delicate green from the reflected light of the blue curtains. He walked to and fro in front of her, ostentatiously pure, trailing his aura of scent, and living in another world. The very self-confidence of this naked body, superior and contemptuous, reduced Edmée to a mildly vindictive immobility. She could not now have claimed this naked body for her own except in a voice altogether lacking the tones and urgency of desire—that is, in the calm voice of a submissive mate. Now she was held back by an arm covered with fine gold hairs, by an ardent mouth behind a golden moustache, and she gazed at Chéri with the jealous and serene security of a lover who covets a virgin inaccessible to all.

They went on to talk about holidays and travelling arrangements, in light-hearted and conventional phrases.

"The war hasn't changed Deauville enough, and what a crowd . . ." Chéri sighed.

"There's simply no place where one can eat a good meal, and it's a huge undertaking to reorganise the hotel business!" Edmée affirmed.

One day, not long before the Quartorze Juillet, Charlotte Peloux was lunching with them. She happened to speak of the success of some business deal in American blankets, and complained loudly that Léa had netted a half share of the profits. Chéri raised his head, in astonishment. "So you still see her?"

Charlotte Peloux enveloped her son in the loving glances induced by old port, and appealed to her daughter-in-law as witness: "He's got an odd way of putting things—as if he'd been gassed—hasn't he? . . . It's disturbing at times. I've never stopped seeing Léa, darling. Why should I have stopped seeing her?"

"Why?" Edmée repeated.

He looked at the two women, finding a strange flavour in their kindly attention.

"Because you never talk to me about her . . ." he began, ingenuously.

"Me!" barked Charlotte. "For goodness sake . . . Edmée, you hear what he says? Well at least it does credit to his feelings for you. He has so completely forgotten about everything that isn't you."

Edmée smiled without answering, bent her head, and adjusted the lace that edged the low-cut neck of her dress by tweaking it between her fingers. The movement drew Chéri's attention to her bodice, and through the yellow lawn he noticed that the points of her breasts and their mauve aureolas looked like twin bruises. He shuddered, and his shudder made him realise that the conventional beauty and all the most secret details of her charming body, that the whole of this young woman, in fact, so close and so disloyal, no longer aroused in him anything but positive repugnance. Nonsense, nonsense; but he was whipping a dead horse. And he listened to Charlotte's ever flowing stream of nasal burblings.

" . . . and then again, the day before yesterday, I was saying in your presence, that motor for motor, well—I'd far rather have a taxi, a taxi, any day, than that prehistoric old Renault of Léa's—and if it wasn't the day before yesterday, it was yesterday, that I said—speaking of Léa—that if you're a woman living on your own and you've got to have a manservant, you might just as well have a good-looking one. And then Camille was saying, only the other day when you were there, how angry she was with herself for having sent a second barrel of Quarts-de-Chaumes round to Léa instead of keeping it for herself. I've complimented you often enough on your fidelity, my darling; I must now scold you for your ingratitude. Léa deserved better of you. Edmée will be the first to admit that!"

"The second," Edmée corrected.

"Never heard a word of it," Chéri said.

He was gorging himself with hard pink July cherries, and flipping them from beneath the lowered blind at the sparrows in the garden, where, after too heavy a watering, the flower beds were steaming like a hot spring. Edmée, motionless, was cogitating on Chéri's comment, "Never heard a word of it." He certainly was not lying, and yet his off-hand assumed school-boyishness, as he squeezed the cherry stones and took aim at a sparrow by closing his left eye, spoke clearly enough to Edmée. 'What can he have been thinking about, if he never heard a word?'

Before the war, she would have looked for the woman in the case. A month earlier, on the day following the looking-glass scene, she would have feared reprisals, some Red Indian act of cruelty, or a bite on the nose. But no . . . nothing . . . he lived and roamed about innocently, as quiet in his freedom as a prisoner in the depths of a gaol, and as chaste as an animal brought from the Antipodes, which does not bother to look for a kindred female in our hemisphere.

Was he ill? He slept well, ate according to his fancy—that is, delicately, sniffing all the meat suspiciously, and preferring fruit and new-laid eggs. No nervous twitch disfigured the lovely balance of his features, and he drank more water than champagne. 'No, he's not ill. And yet he's . . . something. Something that I should guess, perhaps, if I were still in love with him. But . . .' Once again she fingered the lace round the neck of her bodice, inhaled the warmth and fragrance that rose up from between her breasts, and as she bent down her head she saw the precious twin pink and mauve discs through the material of her dress. She blushed with carnal pleasure, and dedicated the scent and the mauve shadows to the skilful, condescending, red-haired man whom she would be meeting again in an hour's time.

'They've spoken of Léa in front of me every day, and I didn't hear. Have I forgotten her, then? Yes, I have forgotten her. But then what does it mean, "to forget"? If I think of Léa, I see her clearly, I remember the sound of her voice, the scent which she sprayed herself with and rubbed so lavishly into her long hands.' He took such a deep breath that his nostrils were indented and his lips curled up to his nose in an expression of exquisite pleasure.

"Fred, you've just made the most horrible face; you were the spit and image of that fox Angot brought back from the trenches."

It was the least trying hour of the day for the pair of them, awake and in bed with breakfast over. After a refreshing shower-bath, they were gratified to hear the drenching rain—three months ahead of the proper season—falling in sheets that stripped the false Parisian autumn of its leaves and flattened the petunias. They did not bother to find an excuse, that morning, for having wilfully remained behind in town. Had not Charlotte Peloux hit upon the proper excuse the previous evening? She had declared, "We're all good Parigots, born and bred, aren't we! True blue one and all! We and the concierges can claim that we've had a real taste of the first post-war summer in Paris!"

"Fred, are you in love with that suit? You never stop wearing it. It doesn't look fresh, you know."

Chéri raised a finger in the direction of Edmée's voice, a gesture which enjoined silence and begged that nothing should divert his attention while he was in the throes of exceptional mental labours.

'I should like to know if I have forgotten her. But what is the real meaning of "forgotten"! A whole year's gone by without my seeing her.' He felt a sudden little shock of awakening, a

177

tremor, when he found that his memory had failed to account for the war years. Then he totted up the years and, for an instant, everything inside him stopped functioning.

"Fred, shall I never get you to leave your razor in the bathroom, instead of bringing it in here!"

Almost naked and still damp, he took his time in turning round, and his back was silver-flecked with dabs of talcum powder.

"What?"

The voice, which seemed to come from afar, broke into a laugh.

"Fred, you look like a cake that's been badly sugared. An unhealthy looking cake. Next year, we won't be as stupid as we have been this. We'll take a place in the country."

"Do you want a place in the country?"

"Yes. Not this morning, of course."

She was pinning up her hair. She pointed with her chin to the curtain of rain, streaming down in a grey torrent, without any sign of thunder or wind.

"But next year, perhaps . . . Don't you think?"

"It's an idea. Yes, it's an idea."

He was putting her politely at arm's length, in order to return to his surprising discovery. 'I really did think that it was only one year since I'd seen her. I never took the war into reckoning. I haven't seen her for one, two, three, four, five years. One, two, three, four. . . . But, in that case, have I really forgotten her? No! Because these women have spoken of her in front of me, and I've never jumped up and shouted, "Hold on! If that's true—then what about Léa?" Five years . . . How old was she in 1914?'

He counted once more, and ran up against an unbelievable total. 'That would make her just about sixty to-day, wouldn't it? . . . How absurd!'

"And the important thing," Edmée went on, "is to choose it carefully. Let's see, a nice part of the world would be . . ."

"Normandy," Chéri finished for her, absent-mindedly.

"Yes, Normandy. Do you know Normandy?"

"No . . . Not at all well. . . . It's green. There are lime trees, ponds . . ."

He shut his eyes, as though dazed.

"Where do you mean? In what part of Normandy?"

"Ponds, cream, strawberries and peacocks. . . ."

"You seem to know a lot about Normandy! What grand country it must be! What else d'you find there?"

He appeared to be reading out a description as he leaned over the round mirror in which he made sure of the smoothness of chin and cheeks after shaving. He went on, unmoved, but hesitatingly. "There are peacocks. . . . Moonlight on parquet floors, and a great big red carpet spread on the gravel in front of . . ."

He did not finish. He swayed gently, and slithered on to the carpet. His fall was checked halfway by the side of the bed. As his head lay against the rumpled sheets, the overlying tan of his pallid cheeks had the greenish tinge of an old ivory.

Hardly had he reached the floor when Edmée, without uttering a sound, threw herself down beside him. With one hand she supported his drooping head, and with the other held a bottle of smelling-salts to his nostrils, from which the colour was visibly ebbing. But two enfeebled arms pushed her away.

"Leave me alone. . . . Can't you see I'm dying?"

He was not dying, however, and under Edmée's fingers his pulse retained its rhythm. He had spoken in a subdued whisper, with the glib, emphatic sincerity of very young would-be suicides who, at one and the same moment, both court death and fight shy of it.

His lips were parted over gleaming teeth and his breathing was regular; but he was in no haste to come right back to life. Safely ensconced behind his tightly shut eyes, he sought refuge in the heart of that green domain, so vivid in his imagination at the instant of his fainting fit—a flat domain, rich in strawberry-beds and bees, in pools of moonbeams fringed with warm stones. . . . After he regained his strength, he still kept his eyes shut, thinking 'If I open my eyes, Edmée will then see the picture in my mind.'

She remained on one knee, bending over him. She was looking after him efficiently, professionally. She reached out with her free hand, picked up a newspaper and used it to fan his forehead. She whispered insignificant but appropriate words, "It's the storm. . . . Relax. . . . No, don't try to move. . . . Wait till I slip this pillow under you. . . ."

He sat up again, smiling, and pressed her hand in thanks. His parched mouth longed for lemons or vinegar. The ringing of the telephone snatched Edmée away from him.

"Yes, yes. . . . What? Yes, of course I know it's ten. Yes. What?"

From the imperious brevity of her replies, Chéri knew that it was someone telephoning from the Hospital.

"Yes, of course I'm coming. What? In . . ." With a rapid glance she estimated Chéri's term of recovery. "In twenty-five minutes. Thanks. See you presently."

She opened the two glass doors of the french windows to their fullest extent, and a few peaceful drops of rain dripped into the room, bringing with them an insipid river smell.

"Are you better, Fred? What exactly did you feel? Nothing wrong with your heart, is there? You must be short of phosphates. It's the result of this ridiculous summer we're having. But what can you expect?"

She glanced at the telephone furtively, as she might at an onlooker.

Chéri stood up on his feet again without apparent effort. "Run along, child. You'll be late at your shop. I'm quite all right."

"A mild grog? A little hot tea?"

"Don't bother about me. . . . You've been very sweet. Yes, a little cup of tea—ask for it on your way out. And some lemon."

Five minutes later she was gone, after giving him a look, which she believed expressed solicitude only. She had searched in vain for a true sign, for some explanation of so inexplicable a state of affairs. As though the sound of the door shutting had severed his bonds, Chéri stretched himself and found that he felt light, cold, and empty. He hurried to the window and saw his wife crossing the small strip of garden, her head bowed under the rain. 'She's got a guilty back,' he pronounced, 'she's always had a guilty back. From the front, she looks a charming little lady. But her back gives the show away. She's lost a good half-hour by my having fainted. But "back to our muttons", as my mother would say. When I got married, Léa was fifty-one—at the very least—so Madame Peloux assures me. That would make her fifty-eight now, sixty perhaps. . . . The same age as General Courbat? No! That's too rich a joke!'

He tried his hardest to associate the picture of Léa at sixty with the white bristling moustache and crannied cheeks of General Courbat and his ancient cab-horse stance. 'It's the best joke out!'

The arrival of Madame Peloux found Chéri still given over to his latest pastime, pale, staring out at the drenched garden, and chewing a cigarette that had gone out. He showed no surprise at his mother's entrance, "You're certainly up with the lark, my dear mother."

"And you've got out of bed the wrong side, it would seem," was her rejoinder.

"Pure imagination. There are, at least, extenuating circumstances to account for your activity, I presume?"

She raised both eyes and shoulders in the direction of the ceiling. A cheeky little leather sports hat was pulled down like a vizor over her forehead.

"My poor child," she sighed, "if you only knew what I'm engaged on at this moment! If you knew what a gigantic task . . ."

He took careful stock of the wrinkles on his mother's face, the inverted commas round her mouth. He contemplated the small flabby wavelet of a double chin, the ebb and flow of which now covered, now uncovered, the collar of her mackintosh. He

181

started to weight up the fluctuating pouches under her eyes, repeating to himself: 'Fifty-eight . . . Sixty . . .'

"Do you know the task I've set myself? Do you know?" She waited a moment, opening wider her large eyes outlined by black pencil. "I'm going to revive the hot springs at Passy! *Les Thermes de Passy!* Yes, that means nothing to you, of course. The springs are there under the Rue Raynouard, only a few yards away. They're dormant; all they need is to be revived. Very active waters. If we go the right way about it, it will mean the ruination of Uriage, the collapse of Mont Dore, perhaps—but that would be too wonderful! Already I've made certain of the co-operation of twenty-seven Swiss doctors. Edmée and I have been getting to work on the Paris Municipal Council. . . . And that's exactly why I've come—I missed your wife by five minutes. . . . What's wrong with you? You're not listening to me. . . ."

He persisted in trying to relight his damp cigarette. He gave it up, threw the stub out upon the balcony, where large drops of rain were rebounding like grasshoppers; then he gravely looked his mother up and down.

"I am listening to you," he said. "Even before you speak I know what you're going to say. I know all about this business of yours. It goes by the varying names of company promotion, wheezes, commissions, founders' shares, American blankets, bully-beef, etcetera. . . . You don't suppose I've been deaf or blind for the last year, do you? You are nasty, wicked women, that's all there is to it. I bear you no ill will."

He stopped talking and sat down, by force of habit rubbing his fingers almost viciously over the little twin scars beneath his right breast. He looked out at the green, rain-battered garden, and on his relaxed features weariness battled with youth—weariness, hollowing his cheeks and darkening his eye-sockets, youth perfectly preserved in the ravishing curve and full ripeness of his lips, the downiness of his nostrils, and the raven-black abundance of his hair.

"Very well, then," said Charlotte Peloux at length. "That's a nice thing to hear, I must say. The devil turned preacher! I seem to have given birth to a Censor of Public Morals."

He showed no intention of breaking the silence, or of making any movement whatever.

"And by what high standards do you presume to judge this poor corrupt world? By your own honesty, I don't doubt!"

Buckled into a leather jerkin, like a yeoman of old, she was at the top of her form and ready for the fray. But Chéri appeared to be through with all fighting, now and for ever.

"By my honesty? . . . Perhaps. Had I been hunting for the right word, I should never have hit upon that. You yourself said it. Honesty will pass."

She did not deign to reply, postponing her offensive until a later moment. She held her tongue that she might give her full attention to her son's peculiar new aspect. He was sitting with his legs very wide apart, elbows on knees, his hands firmly locked together. He continued to stare out at the garden laid flat by the lashing rain, and after a moment he sighed without turning his head: "Do you really call this a life?"

As might be expected, she asked: "What life?"

He raised one arm, only to let it fall again. "Mine. Yours. Everything. All that's going on under our eyes."

Madame Peloux hesitated a moment. Then she threw off her leather coat, lit a cigarette, and she too sat down.

"Are you bored?"

Coaxed by the unusual sweetness of a voice that sounded ethereally solicitous, he became natural and almost confidential.

"Bored? No, I'm not bored. What makes you think I'm bored? I'm a trifle . . . what shall I say? . . . a trifle worried, that's all."

183

"About what?"

"About everything. Myself. . . . Even about you."

"I'm surprised at that."

"So am I. These fellows . . . this year . . . this peace."

He stretched his fingers apart as though they were sticky or tangled in overlong hair.

"You say that as we used to say 'This war' . . ." She put a hand on his shoulder and tactfully lowered her voice. "What is the matter with you?"

He could not bear the questioning weight of this hand; he stood up, and began moving about in a haphazard way. "The matter is that everyone's rotten. No!" he begged, seeing an artificial look of indignation on the maternal countenance, "No, don't start all over again. No, present company *not* excluded. No, I do *not* accept the fact that we are living in splendid times, with a dawn of this, a resurrection of that. No, I am *not* angry, don't love you any less than before, and there is nothing wrong with my liver. But I do seriously think that I'm nearly at the end of my tether."

He cracked his fingers as he walked about the room, sniffing the sweet-smelling spray of the heavy rain as it splashed off the balcony. Charlotte Peloux threw down her hat and her red gloves, a gesture intended as a peace-offering.

"Do tell me exactly what you mean, child. We're alone." She smoothed back her sparse hennaed hair, cut boyishly short. Her mushroom-coloured garb held in her body as an iron hoop clamps a cask. 'A woman. . . . She has been a woman. . . . Fifty-eight. . . . Sixty. . . .' Chéri was thinking. She turned on him her lovely velvety eyes, brimming with maternal co-quetry, the feminine power of which he had long forgotten. This sudden charm of his mother's warned him of the danger lying ahead, and the difficulty of the confession towards which she was leading him. But he felt empty and listless, tormented by what he lacked. The hope of shocking her drove him on still further.

"Yes," he said, in answer to his own question. "You have your blankets, your macaroni and spaghetti, your légions d'honneur. You joke about the meetings of the Chambre des Députés and the accident to young Lenoir. You are thrilled by

Madame Caillaux, and by the hot springs at Passy. Edmée's got her shopful of wounded and her Physician-in-Charge. Desmond dabbles in dancehalls, wines and spirits, and white slavery. Filipesco bags cigars from Americans and hospitals, to hawk them round night clubs. Jean de Touzac . . . is in the surplus store racket. What a set! What . . ."

"You're forgetting Landru," Charlotte put in edgeways.

His eyes twinkled as he gave the slyest of winks, in silent tribute to the malicious humour that rejuvenated his old pugilist of a mother.

"Landru? That doesn't count, there's a pre-war flavour about that. There's nothing odd about Landru. But as for the rest—well . . . well, to cut it short, there's not one who's not a rotter and . . . and I don't like it. That's all."

"That's certainly short, but not very clear," Charlotte said, after a moment. "You've a nice opinion of us. Mind you, I don't say you're wrong. Myself, I've got the qualities of my defects, and nothing frightens me. Only, it doesn't give me an inkling of what you're really after."

Chéri swayed awkwardly on his chair. He frowned so furiously that the skin on his forehead contracted in deep wrinkles between his eyes, as though trying to keep a hat on his head in a gusty wind.

"What I'm really after . . . I simply don't know. I only wish people weren't such rotters. I mean to say, weren't *only* rotten. . . . Or, quite simply, I should like to be able not to notice it."

He showed such hesitancy, such a need of coming to terms with himself, that Charlotte made fun of it. "Why notice it, then?"

185

"Ah, well. . . . That's just the point, you see."

He gave her a helpless smile, and she noticed how much her son's face aged as he smiled. 'Someone ought constantly to be telling him hard-luck stories,' she said to herself, 'or else making him really angry. Gaiety doesn't improve his looks . . .' She blew out a cloud of smoke and in her turn allowed an ambiguous commonplace to escape her. "You didn't notice anything of that before."

He raised his head sharply. "Before? Before what?"

"Before the war, of course."

"Ah, yes . . ." he murmured, disappointed. "No, before the war, obviously. . . . But before the war I didn't look at things in the same way."

"Why?"

The simple word struck him dumb.

"I'll tell you what it is," Charlotte chid him, "you've turned honest."

"You wouldn't think of admitting, by any chance, that I've simply remained so?"

"No, no, don't let's get that wrong." She was arguing, a flush on her cheeks, with the fervour of a prophetess. "Your way of life before the war, after all—I'm putting myself in the position of people who are not exactly broad-minded and who take a superficial view of things, understand!—such a way of life, after all, has a name!"

"If you like," Chéri agreed. "What of it?"

"Well then, that implies a . . . a way of looking at things. Your point of view was a gigolo's."

"Quite possibly," said Chéri, unmoved. "Do you see any harm in that?"

"Certainly not," Charlotte protested, with the simplicity of a child. "But, you know, there's a right time for everything."

"Yes . . ." He sighed deeply, looking out towards a sky masked by cloud and rain. "There's a time to be young, and there's a time to be less young. There's a time to be happy . . . d'you think it needed you to make me aware of that?"

She seemed suddenly to be upset, and walked up and down the room, her round behind tightly moulded by her dress, as plump and brisk as a little fat bitch. She came back and planted herself in front of her son.

"Well, darling, I'm afraid you're heading for some act of madness."

"What?"

"Oh! there aren't so many. A monastery. Or a desert island. Or love."

Chéri smiled in astonishment. "Love? You want me . . . in love with . . ." He jerked his chin in the direction of Edmée's boudoir, and Charlotte's eyes sparkled.

"Who mentioned her?"

He laughed, and from an instinct of self-preservation became offensive again.

"*You* did, and in a moment you'll be offering me one of your American pieces."

She gave a theatrical start. "An American piece? Really? And why not a rubber substitute as provided for sailors into the bargain?"

He was pleased with her jingoistic and expert disdain. Since childhood he had had it dinned into him that a French woman demeans herself by living with a foreigner, unless, of course, she exploits him, or he ruins her. And he could reel off a list of outrageous epithets with which a native Parisian courtesan would brand a dissolute foreign woman. But he refused the offer, without irony. Charlotte threw out her short arms and protruded her lower lip, like a doctor confessing his helplessness.

"I don't suggest that you should work . . ." she risked shamefacedly.

Chéri dismissed this importunate suggestion with a shrug of the shoulders.

"Work," he repeated . . . "work, what you mean by that is hobnobbing with fellows. You can't work alone, short of painting picture post-cards or taking in sewing. My poor mother, you fail to realise that, if fellows get my goat, women can hardly be said to inspire me either. The truth is, that I have no further use for women at all," he finished courageously.

187

"Good heavens!" Charlotte caterwauled. She wrung her hands as though a horse had slipped and fallen at her feet; but harshly her son enjoined silence with a single gesture, and she was forced to admire the virile authority of this handsome young man, who had just owned up to his own particular brand of impotence.

"Chéri! . . . my little boy! . . ."

He turned to her with a gentle, empty, and vaguely pleading look in his eyes.

She gazed into the large eyes that shone with an exaggerated brilliance, due, perhaps, to their unblemished white, their long lashes and the secret emotion behind them. She longed to enter through these magnificent portals and reach down to the shadowed heart which had first started to beat so close to her own. Chéri appeared to be putting up no defence and to enjoy being balked, as if under hypnosis. Charlotte had, in the past, known her son to be ill, irritable, sly; she had never known him unhappy. She felt, therefore, a strange kind of excitement, the ecstasy that casts a woman at a man's feet at the moment when she dreams of changing a despairing stranger into an inferior stranger—that is to say, of making him rid himself of his despair.

"Listen, Chéri," she murmured very softly. "Listen. . . . You must . . . No, no, wait! At least let me speak. . . ."

He interrupted her with a furious shake of the head, and she saw it was useless to insist. It was she who broke their long exchange of looks, by putting on her coat again and her little leather hat, making towards the door. But as she passed the table, she stopped, and casually put her hand out towards the telephone.

188

"Do you mind, Chéri?"

He nodded his consent, and she began in a high-pitched nasal shrill like a clarinet. "Hullo . . . Hullo . . . Hullo . . . Passy, two nine, two nine. Hullo . . . Is that you, Léa? But of course it's me. What weather, eh! . . . Don't speak of it. Yes, very well. Everyone's very well. What are you doing to-day?

Not budging an inch! Ah, that's so like you, you self-indulgent creature! Oh, you know, I'm no longer my own mistress. . . . Oh no, not on that account. Something altogether different. A vast undertaking. . . . Oh, no, not on the telephone. . . . You'll be in all day then? Good. That's very convenient. Thank you. Goodbye, Lea darling!"

She put back the receiver, showing nothing but the curve of her back. As she moved away, she inhaled and exhaled puffs of blue smoke, and vanished in the midst of her cloud like a magician whose task is accomplished.

Without hurrying, he climbed the single flight of stairs up to Léa's flat. At six in the evening, after the rain, the Rue Raynouard re-echoed, like the garden of a boarding-school, with the chirrup of birds and the cries of small children. He glanced quickly, coldly, at everything, refusing to be surprised at the heavy looking-glasses in the entrance-hall, the polished steps, the blue carpet, or the lift-cage lavishly splashed with as much lacquer and gold as a sedan-chair. On the landing he experienced, for a moment, the deceptive sense of detachment and freedom from pain felt by a sufferer on the dentist's doorstep. He nearly turned away, but, guessing that he might feel compelled to return later, he pressed the bell with a determined finger. The maid, who had taken her time in coming to the door, was young and dark, with a butterfly cap of fine lawn on her bobbed hair: her unfamiliar face took from Chéri his last chance of feeling moved.

"Is Madame at home?"

The young servant, apparently lost in admiration of him, could not make up her mind.

"I do not know, Monsieur. Is Monsieur expected?"

"Of course," he said, with a return of his old harshness.

She left him standing there, and disappeared. In the half-light, he was quick to take in his surroundings, with eyes blurred by the gloom, and alert sensitive nostrils. There was nowhere a vestige of that light golden scent, and some ordinary pine essence sputtered in an electric scent-burner. Chéri felt put out, like someone who discovers that he is on the wrong floor. But a great peal of girlish laughter rang out, its notes running down a deep descending scale. It was muffled by some curtain or other, but at once the intruder was cast into a whirlpool of memories.

"Will Monsieur please come to the drawing-room."

He followed the white butterfly, saying over to himself as he went: "Léa's not alone. She's laughing. She can't be alone. So long as it's not my mother." Beyond an open door, he was being welcomed by rosy pink daylight and he waited, standing there, for the rebirth of the world heralded by this dawn.

A woman was writing at a small table, facing away from him. Chéri was able to distinguish a broad back and the padded cushion of a fat neck beneath a head of thick grey vigorous hair, cut short like his mother's. 'So I was right, she's not alone. But who on earth can this good woman be?'

"And, at the same time, write down your masseur's address for me, Léa, and his name. You know what I'm like about names. . . ."

These words came from a woman dressed in black, also seated, and Chéri felt a preliminary tremor of expectation running through him: 'Then . . . where is Léa?'

The grey-haired lady turned round, and Chéri received the full impact of her blue eyes.

"Oh, good heavens, child—it's you!"

He went forward as in a dream, and kissed an outstretched hand.

"Monsieur Frédéric Peloux—Princess Cheniaguine."

Chéri bent over and kissed another hand, then took a seat.

"Is he your . . . ?" queried the lady in black, referring to him with as much freedom as if he had been a deaf-mute.

Once again the great peal of girlish laughter rang out, and Chéri sought for the source of this laugh here, there, and everywhere—anywhere but in the throat of the grey-haired woman.

"No, no, he isn't! Or rather, he isn't any longer, I should say. Valérie, come now, what are you thinking of?"

She was not monstrous, but huge, and loaded with

exuberant buttresses of fat in every part of her body. Her arms, like rounded thighs, stood out from her hips on plump cushions of flesh just below her armpits. The plain skirt and the nondescript long jacket, opening on a linen blouse with a jabot, proclaimed that the wearer had abdicated, was no longer concerned to be a woman, and had acquired a kind of sexless dignity.

Léa was now standing between Chéri and the window, and he was not horrified at first by her firm, massive, almost cubic, bulk. When she moved to reach a chair, her features were revealed, and he began to implore her with silent entreaties, as though faced with an armed lunatic. Her cheeks were red and looked over-ripe, for she now disdained the use of powder, and when she laughed her mouth was packed with gold. A healthy old woman, in short, with sagging cheeks and a double chin, well able to carry her burden of flesh and freed from restraining stays.

"Tell me, child, where have you sprung from? I can't say I think you're looking particularly well."

She held out a box of cigarettes to Chéri, smiling at him from blue eyes which had grown smaller, and he was frightened to find her so direct in her approach, and as jovial as an old gentleman. She called him "child", and he turned away his eyes, as though she had let slip an indecent word. But he exhorted himself to be patient, in the vague hope that this first picture would give place to a shining transfiguration.

The two women looked him over calmly, sparing him neither goodwill nor curiosity.

"He's got rather a look of Hernandez . . ." said Valérie Cheniaguine.

"Oh, I don't see that at all," Léa protested. "Ten years ago perhaps . . . and, anyhow, Hernandez had a much more pronounced jaw!"

"Who's that?" Chéri asked, with something of an effort.

"A Peruvian who was killed in a motor accident about six months ago," said Léa. "He was living with Maximilienne. It made her very unhappy."

"Didn't prevent her finding consolation," said Valérie.

"Like anyone else," Léa said. "You wouldn't have wished her to die of it, surely?"

She laughed afresh, and her merry blue eyes disappeared, lost behind wide cheeks bulging with laughter. Chéri turned away his head and looked at the woman in black. She had brown hair and an ample figure, vulgar and feline like thousands and thousands of women from the south. She seemed in disguise, so very carefully was she dressed as a woman in good society. Valérie was wearing what had long been the uniform of foreign princesses and their ladies—a black tailor-made of undistinguished cut, tight in the sleeve, with a blouse of extremely fine white batiste, showing signs of strain at the breast. The pearl buttons, the famous necklace, the high stiff whalebone collar, everything about Valérie was as royal as the name she legitimately bore. Like royalty, too, she wore stockings of medium quality, flat-heeled walking shoes and expensive gloves, embroidered in black and white.

From the cold and calculating way she looked him over, Chéri might have been a piece of furniture. She went on with her criticisms and comparisons at the top of her voice.

"Yes, yes, there is something of Hernandez, I promise you. But, to hear Maximilienne to-day, Hernandez might never have existed . . . now that she has made quite certain of her famous Amerigo. And yet! And yet! I know what I'm talking about. I've seen him, her precious Amerigo. I'm just back from Deauville. I saw the pair of them!"

"No! Do tell us!"

Léa sat down, overflowing the whole armchair. She had acquired a new trick of tossing back her thick grey hair; and at each shake of the head, Chéri saw a quivering of the lower part of her face, which looked like Louis XVI's. Ostensibly, she was giving Valérie her full attention, but several times Chéri noticed a mischievous faltering in one of the little shrunk blue eyes, as they sought to catch those of the unexpected visitor.

"Well, then," Valerie started on her story, "she had hidden

him in a villa miles outside Deauville, at the back of beyond. But that did not suit Amerigo at all—as you will readily understand, Monsieur!—and he grumbled at Maximilienne. She was cross, and said: 'Ah! that's what the matter is—you want to be on view to the world and his wife, and so you shall be!' So she telephoned to reserve a table at the Normandy for the following evening. Everyone knew this an hour later, and so I booked a table as well, with Becq d'Ambez and Zahita. And we said to ourselves: 'We're going to be allowed to see this marvel at last!' On the stroke of nine there was Maximilienne, all in white and pearls, and Amerigo. . . . Oh, my dear, what a disappointment! Tall, yes, that goes without saying . . . in point of fact, rather too tall. You know what I always say about men who are too tall. I'm still waiting to be shown one, just one, who is well put together. Eyes, yes, eyes, I've got nothing to say against his eyes. But—from here to there, don't you see (she was pointing to her own face), from here to there, something about the cheeks which is too rounded, too soft, and the ears set too low. . . . Oh, a very great disappointment. And holding himself as stiff as a poker."

"You're exaggerating," said Léa. "The cheeks—well what about cheeks?—they aren't so very important. And, from here to there, well really it's beautiful, it's noble; the eyelashes, the bridge of the nose, the eyes, the whole thing is really too beautiful! I'll grant you the chin: that will quickly run to flesh. And the feet are too small, which is ridiculous in a boy of that height."

"No, there I don't agree with you. But I certainly noticed that the thigh was far too long in proportion to the leg, from here to there."

They went on to thrash out the question, weighing up, with a wealth of detail and point by point, every portion of the fore and hind quarters of this expensive animal.

'Judges of pedigree fat cattle,' Chéri thought. 'The right place for them is the Commisariats.'

"Speaking of proportions," Léa continued, "you'll never come across anything to touch Chéri. . . . You see, Chéri,

194

you've come at just the right moment. You ought to blush. Valérie, if you can remember what Chéri was like only six, or say seven years ago . . ."

"But certainly, of course, I remember clearly. And Monsieur has not changed so very much, after all. . . . And you were so proud of him!"

"No," said Léa.

"You weren't proud of him?"

"No," said Léa with perfect calm, "I was in love with him." She manoeuvred the whole of her considerable body in his direction, and let her gay glance rest upon Chéri, quite innocently. "It's true I was in love with you, very much in love, too."

He lowered his eyes, stupidly abashed before these two women, the stouter of whom had just proclaimed so serenely that she and he had been lovers. Yet at the same time the voluptuous and almost masculine tone of Léa's voice besieged his memory, torturing him unbearably.

"You see, Valérie, how foolish a man can look when reminded of a love which no longer exists? Silly boy, it doesn't upset me in the least to think about it. I love my past. I love my present. I'm not ashamed of what I've had, and I'm not sad because I have it no longer. Am I wrong, child?"

He uttered a cry, almost as if someone had trodden on his big toe. "No, no, of course not! The very reverse!"

"It's charming to think you have remained such good friends," said Valérie.

Chéri waited for Léa to explain that this was his first visit to her for five years, but she just gave a good-humoured laugh and winked with a knowing air. He felt more and more upset. He did not know how to protest, how to shout out loud that he laid no claim to the friendship of this colossal woman, with the cropped hair of an elderly 'cellist—that, had he but known, he would never have come upstairs, never crossed her threshold, set foot on her carpet, never collapsed in the cushioned armchair, in the depths of which he now lay defenceless and dumb.

195

"Well, I must be going," Valérie said. "I don't mean to wait for crush-hour in the Métro, I can tell you."

She rose to face the strong light, and it was kind to her Roman features. They were so solidly constructed that the approach of her sixtieth year had left them unharmed: the cheeks were touched up in the old-fashioned way, with an even layer of white powder, and the lips with a red that was almost black and looked oily.

"Are you going home?" Léa asked.

"Of course I am. What d'you suppose my little skivvy would get up to if left to herself!"

"Are you still pleased with your new flat?"

"It's a dream! Especially since the iron bars were put across the windows. And I've had a steel grid fixed over the pantry fanlight, which I had forgotten about. With my electric bells and my burglar-alarms . . . Ouf! It's been long enough before I could feel at all safe!"

"And your old house?"

"Bolted and barred. Up for sale. And the pictures in store. My little entresol flat is a gem for the eighteen hundred francs it costs me. And no more servants looking like hired assassins. You remember those two footmen? The thought of them still gives me the creeps!"

"You took much too black a view, my dear."

"You can't realise, my poor friend, without having been through it all. Monsieur, delighted to have met you. . . . No, don't you move, Léa."

She enfolded them both in her velvety barbaric gaze, and was gone. Chéri followed her with his eyes until she reached the door, yet he lacked the courage to follow her example. He remained where he was, all but snuffed out by the conversation of these two women who had been speaking of him in the past tense, as though he were dead. But now Léa was coming back into the room, bursting with laughter. "Princess Cheniaguine! Sixty millions! and a widow!—and she's not in the least bit happy. If that can be called enjoying life, it's not my idea of it, you know!"

She clapped her hand on her thigh as if it were a horse's crupper.

"What's the matter with her?"

"Funk. Blue funk, that's all. She's not the sort of woman who knows how to carry such wealth. Cheniaguine left her everything. But one might say that it would have done her less harm if he'd taken her money instead of leaving her his. You heard what she said?"

She subsided into the depths of a well upholstered armchair, and Chéri hated to hear the gentle sigh of its cushions as they took the weight of her vast bulk. She ran the tip of her finger along the grooved moulding of the chair, blew away the few specks of dust, and her face fell.

"Ah! things are not at all what they were, not even servants. Eh?"

He felt that he had lost colour, and that the skin round his mouth was growing tighter, as during a severe frost. He fought back an overwhelming impulse to burst out in rancour mingled with entreaties. He longed to cry out loud: 'Stop! Show me your real self! Throw off your disguise! You must be somewhere behind it, since it's your voice I hear. Appear in your true colours! Arise as a creature reborn, with your hair newly hennaed this morning, your face freshly powdered: put on your long stays again, the blue dress with its delicate jabot, the scent like a meadow that was so much a part of you. In these new surroundings I search for it in vain! Leave all this behind, and come away to Passy—never mind the showers—Passy with its dogs and its birds, and in the Avenue Bugeaud we'll be sure to find Ernest polishing the brass bars on your front door.' He shut his eyes, utterly worn out.

197

"And now, my child, I'm going to tell you something for your own good. What you need is to have your urine tested. Your colour's shocking and you've got that pinched look round your lips—sure signs, both of them: you're not taking proper care of your kidneys."

Chéri opened his eyes again, and they took their fill of this placid epitome of disaster seated in front of him. Heroically he said: "D'you really think so? It's quite possible."

"You mean, it's certain. And then, you've not got enough flesh on you. . . . It's no use telling me that the best fighting cocks are scraggy. You could do with a good ten pounds more on you."

"Give them to me," he said with a smile. But he found his cheeks singularly recalcitrant and opposed to smiling, almost as though his skin had stiffened with age.

Léa burst into a peal of happy laughter, and Chéri tasted a pleasure which he could not have borne for long; he listened again to its full and rounded tones, the very laugh which in the old days used to greet some outrageous impertinence on the part of the "naughty little boy".

"That I could well afford! I've certainly been putting on weight, haven't I? Eh? Look . . . here . . . would you believe it? . . . and again here!"

She lit a cigarette, exhaled a double jet of smoke through her nostrils, and shrugged her shoulders. "It's age!"

The word flew out of her mouth so lightly that it gave Chéri a sort of extravagant hope. 'Yes: she's only joking. In a flash she'll reappear as her real self.' For an instant she seemed to take in the meaning of the look he gave her.

"I've changed a lot, haven't I, child? Fortunately, it doesn't much matter. As for you, I don't like the look of you at all. . . . You've been fluttering your wings too much, as we used to say in the old days. Eh?"

He detested this new "Eh?" with which she peppered her sentences so freely. But he stiffened at each interrogation, and each time mastered his rising excitement, preferring to remain in ignorance of both its reason and its aim.

"I don't ask whether you have any troubles at home. In the

first place, it's none of my business; and besides, I know your wife as if I were her mother."

He listened to the sound of her voice without paying much attention. He noticed, above all, that when she stopped smiling or laughing, she ceased to belong to any assignable sex. Despite her enormous breasts and crushing backside, she seemed by virtue of age altogether virile and happy in that state.

"And I know your wife to be thoroughly capable of making a man happy."

He was powerless to hide his inward laughter, and Léa quickly went on to say.

"What I said was 'a man,' and not 'any man'. Here you are in my house, without a word of warning. You've not come, I take it, just to gaze into my beautiful eyes, eh?"

She turned on Chéri those once "beautiful blue eyes", now so diminished, marbled with tiny red veins, quizzical, neither kind nor unkind, alert and bright certainly, but . . . but where was now the limpid freshness that had laved their whites with palest blue? Where the contour of their orbs, with the round-ness of fruit, breast, or hemisphere, and blue as a land watered by many a river?

Jestingly, he said, "Pooh! aren't you sharp! A real detective!" And it amazed him to find that he had fallen into such a carefree posture, with his legs crossed, like a handsome young man with bad manners. For inwardly he was watching his other self, hopelessly distracted and on his knees, waving his arms, baring his breast, and shrieking incoherently.

"I'm not a particularly stupid woman. But you must admit that you don't present me to-day with a very difficult problem!"

She drew in her chin and its lower folds spread over her neck: the kneeling ghost of his other self bowed its head like a man who has received a death-blow.

"You show every known sign of suffering from the disease of your generation. No, no, let me go on. Like all your soldier friends, you're looking everywhere for your paradise, eh! the paradise they owe you as a war hero: your own special Victory Parade, *your* youth, *your* lovely women. . . . They owe you all that and more, for they promised you everything, and, dear God, you deserved it. And what do you find? A decent ordinary life. So you go in for nostalgia, listlessness, disillusion and neurasthenia. Am I wrong?"

"No," said Chéri, for he was thinking that he would give his little finger to stop her talking.

Léa clapped him on the shoulder, letting her hand with its large rings rest there. As he bent his head down towards it, he could feel on his cheek the heat of this heavy hand.

"Oh!" Léa continued, raising her voice. "You're not the only one! I've come across dozens of boys, since the war ended, exactly in your state of . . ."

"Where?" Chéri interrupted.

The suddenness of the interruption and its aggressive character put an end to Léa's parsonic eloquence. She withdrew her hand.

"They're to be met with everywhere, my child. Is it possible to be so vain? You seem to think you're unique because you find the post-war world insipid. Don't flatter yourself to that extent!"

She gave a low chuckle, and a toss to her sportive grey hair, and then a self-important smile like a judge who has a nice taste in wine. "And you do flatter yourself, you know, always imagining that you're the only one of your kind."

She took a step back and narrowed her gaze, adding, perhaps a little vindictively: "You were unique only for . . . for a time."

Behind this veiled but carefully chosen insult, Chéri discovered something of her femininity at last. He sat bolt upright, delighted to find himself suffering less acutely. But by this time Léa had reverted to her milk and honey.

"But you didn't come here to have that said about you. Did you make up your mind on the spur of the moment?"

"Yes," said Chéri.

He could have wished that this monosyllable might have been the last word between the two of them. Shyly, he let his gaze wander to all the things that surrounded Léa. From the nearest plate he took a dry cake shaped like a curved tile, and then put it back, convinced that it would turn to brick-red grit in his mouth were he to take a bite out of it. Léa noticed this action, and the painful way he swallowed his saliva.

"Tut, tut, so we're suffering from nerves, are we? Peeky chin, and dark lines under the eyes. That's a pretty state of affairs!"

He closed his eyes, and like a coward decided to listen and not look.

"Listen to me, child, I know a little restaurant in the Avenue des Gobelins. . . ."

He looked up at her, in the full hope that she was going mad, that in this way he would be able to forgive her for both looking and behaving like an old woman.

"Yes, I know a little restaurant . . . Let me speak! Only, you must be quick, before the smart set and the newspapers take it into their heads to make it fashionable, and the good woman herself is replaced by a chef. She does all the cooking at present, and, my dear . . ." She brought thumb and forefinger together on the tip of her lips, and blew an imitation kiss. Chéri turned away to look out of the window, where the shadow thrown by a branch flicked at the steady shaft of sunlight, impatiently but at regular intervals, much as a bent reed or river-plant appears to strike at the ripples of a regularly flowing current.

"What an odd sort of conversation . . ." he ventured in strained tones.

"No more odd than your presence in my house," Léa snapped back at him.

With a wave of the hand he made it clear that he wanted peace, only peace, with as few words spoken as possible, and preferably none at all. He felt defeated in face of this elderly woman's boundless reserves of energy and appetite. Léa's quick blood was now rising and turning her bulging neck and her ears to purple. 'She's got a crop like an old hen,' he thought, with something of his old enjoyment of cruelty.

"And that's the truth!" she hurled at him excitedly. "You drag yourself round here, for all the world like an apparition, and when I do my best to find some way of putting things to rights, I who, when all's said and done, do happen to know you rather well . . .'

He smiled at her despondently, 'And how in the world should she know me? When far shrewder people than she, and even than I myself . . .'

"A certain kind of sickness of the soul, my child, of disillusion, is just a question of stomach. Yes, yes, you may laugh!" He was not laughing, but she might well think he was. "Romanticism, nerves, distaste for life: stomach. The whole lot, simply stomach. Love itself! If one wished to be perfectly sincere, one would have to admit there are two kinds of love—well-fed and ill-fed. The rest is pure fiction. If only I knew how to write, or to make speeches, my child, what things I could say about that! Oh, of course, it wouldn't be anything new, but I should know what I was talking about, and that would be a change from our present-day writers."

Something worse than this obsession with the kitchen was upsetting Chéri: the affectation, the false tone of voice, the almost studied joviality. He suspected Léa of putting on an act of hearty and sybaritic geniality, just as a fat actor, on the stage, plays "jovial" characters because he has developed a paunch.

As though defiantly, she rubbed her shiny, almost blotchy red nose with the back of her first finger, and fanned the upper part of her body with the aid of the two revers of her long jacket. In so doing, she was altogether too cheerfully inviting Chéri to sit in judgment on her appearance, and she even ran her hand through her thick grey locks as she shook them free of her head.

"Do you like my hair short?"

He deigned to reply only by a silent shake of the head, just like someone brushing aside an idle argument.

"Weren't you saying something just now about a little restaurant in the Avenue des Gobelins . . . ?"

It was now her turn to brush aside an irrelevance. She was beginning to understand, and he could see from the quivering of her nostrils that at last she was piqued. His animal instincts, which had been shocked into dullness, were now on the alert and it was as though a weight had been lifted from his mind. He intended somehow to find a way past this shameless flesh, the greying curls and "merry friar" joviality, and reach the being concealed behind them, to whom he was coming back, as to the scene of a crime. He remained close to this buried treasure, burrowing towards it spontaneously. 'How in the world did old age come upon her? All of a sudden, on waking up one morning? or little by little? And this surplus fat, this extra avoirdupois, under the weight of which armchairs groan? Was it some sudden shock that brought about this change and unsexed her? Could it, perhaps, have been grief on my account?' But he asked these questions of no one but himself, and without voicing them. 'She is piqued. She's on the way to understanding me. She's just going to tell me. . . .'

He watched her rise to her feet, walk over to the bureau, and start to tidy the papers lying on the open hinged flap. He noticed that she was holding herself more upright than when he had first entered the room, and that, under his following eye, she straightened her back still more. He accepted the fact that she was really colossal, her body seeming to run absolutely straight from armpit to hip. Before turning round again to face Chéri, she arranged a white silk scarf tightly round her neck, despite the heat of the room. He heard her take a deep breath, before she came towards him with the slow rolling gait of a ponderous animal.

She smiled at him. "I am not doing my duty as a hostess, it would seem. It's not very polite to welcome someone by giving them advice, especially useless advice."

203

From under a fold of her white scarf peeped insinuatingly a twisting, coiling, resplendent string of pearls, which Chéri at once recognised.

Held captive beneath the translucent skin, the seven colours of the rainbow flickered with some secret fire of their own all over the surface of each precious sphere. Chéri recognised the pearl with a dimple, the slightly egg-shaped pearl, and the biggest pearl of the string, distinguishable by its unique pink. 'These pearls, these at least, are unchanged! They and I remain unchanged.'

"So you've still got your pearls," he said.

She was astonished by the foolish phrase, and looked as though she wanted to interpret it.

"Yes, in spite of the war. Are you thinking that I could, or should, have sold them? Why should I have sold them?"

"Or 'for whom'?" he answered jokingly, in a tired voice.

She could not restrain a rapid glance towards the bureau and its scattered papers; and Chéri, in his turn, felt he knew the thought behind it, guessing that it was aimed at some yellowish postcard-photograph, probably the frightened features of a beardless boy in uniform. Disdainfully, he considered this imaginary face and said to himself, 'That's none of my concern,' adding a moment later, 'But what is there here that does concern me?'

The agitation which he had brought in his heart was now excited by everything around him; everything added to it—the setting sun, the cries of insect-chasing swallows, and the ember-glowing shafts of light stabbing through the curtains. He remembered that Léa carried with her wherever she went this incandescent rose-pink, as the sea, on its ebb-tide, carries with it far out from shore the earthy smells of pastures and new-mown hay.

No word passed between them for a while, and they were kept in countenance by pretending to listen to the clear fresh notes of a child singing. Léa had not sat down again. Standing massively in front of him, she carried her irretrievable chin higher than before, and betrayed some vague distress by the frequent fluttering of her eyelids.

"Am I making you late? Have you to go out this evening? Do you want to dress?" The questions were abrupt, and forced Léa to look at Chéri.

"Dress? Good Lord, and in what do you wish me to dress? I *am* dressed—irrevocably—once and for all."

She laughed her incomparable laugh, starting on a high note and descending the scale by leaps of equal interval till she got to the deep musical reaches reserved for sobs and amorous moans. Chéri unconsciously raised a hand in supplication.

"Dressed for life, I tell you! And how convenient that is! Blouses, fine linen, and this uniform on top, and here I am in full fig. Equally ready for dinner either at Montagné's or somewhere modest, ready for the cinema, for bridge, or for a stroll in the Bois."

"And what about love—which you're forgetting to mention?"

"Oh, child!"

She blushed: and, though her face was dark with the chronic red of sufferers from arthritis, the blush could not be concealed. Chéri, after the first caddish satisfaction of having said something outrageous, was seized with shame and remorse at the sight of this maidenly reaction.

"I was only joking," he said, in some confusion. "Have I gone too far?"

"Of course not. But you know very well I have never cared for certain kinds of impropriety or for jokes that are not really funny."

She strove to control her voice, but her face revealed that she was hurt, and every coarsened feature gave signs of a distress that could perhaps be outraged modesty.

'Dear God, if she takes it into her head to cry!' and he imagined the catastrophic effect of tears coursing down each cheek into the single deep ravine near the mouth, and of her eyelids reddened by the salt of tears.

205

He hastened to intercept: "No, no, you mustn't think that! How could you! I never meant . . . Please, Léa. . . ."

From her quick reaction he realised suddenly that this was the first time he had spoken her name. Proud, as in the old days, of her self-control, she gently stopped him.

"Don't worry, child. I'm not offended. But I've only got you here for a few minutes, so don't spoil them by saying anything I shouldn't care to remember."

Her gentle tone left him cold, and her actual words seemed offensively tactful to him. 'Either she's lying, or she really has become the sort of person she pretends. Peace, purity, and the Lord knows what! She might as well wear a ring in her nose! Peace of heart, guzzling, and the cinema. . . . Lies, lies, all lies! She wants to make me think that women find growing old comfortable, positively enjoyable. How can she expect *me* to swallow that? Let her bore anyone else she likes with her fine talk about how cosy life is, and the little restaurants with the most delicious country dishes. I'm not having any! Before I could toddle, I knew all there is to know about reducing. I was *born* among ageing beauties! All my life I've watched them, my painted pixies, squabbling about their wrinkles, and, well into their fifties, scratching each other's eyes out over some wretched gigolo!'

"You sit there saying nothing, and I'm not used to it any more. I keep on thinking that there's something you want to say to me."

On her feet, separated from Chéri by an occasional table with a decanter and port glasses, she made no effort to defend herself against the severe inspection to which she was being subjected; but from the almost invisible tremors that passed over her body, Chéri noted the muscular effort required to keep in her spreading stomach. 'How many times must she have put on her full-length corset again, left it off, then valiantly put it on again, before abandoning it for ever? . . . How often of a morning must she have varied the shades of her face powder, rubbed a new rouge on her cheeks, massaged her neck with cold-cream and a small lump of ice tied up in a handkerchief, before becoming resigned to the varnished hide that now shines on her cheeks!' Impatience alone, perhaps, had made her tremble, yet this faint tremor led him to expect—so stubbornly blind was he to reality—some miraculous new blossoming, some complete metamorphosis.

"Why don't you say something?" Léa persisted.

Little by little she was losing her poise, though she was careful not to move. She was playing with her rope of large pearls, knotting and unknotting, round her big well-manicured and wrinkled fingers, their luminous, indescribably bedewed and everlasting lustre.

'Perhaps it's simply because she's frightened of me,' Chéri mused. 'A man who says nothing must always seem a bit cranky. She's thinking of Valérie Cheniaguine's terrors. If I put my hand out, would she scream for help? My poor Nounoune!' He lacked the courage to pronounce this name out loud, and, to protect himself from even a moment's sincerity, he spoke:

"What are you going to think of me?"

"It all depends," Léa answered guardedly. "At the moment you remind me of people who bring along a little box of cakes and leave it in the hall, saying to themselves: 'There'll be plenty of time to produce these later,' and then pick them up again when they go."

Reassured by the sound of their voices, she had begun to reason like the Léa of old, quick on the uptake, and as wily as a sharp-witted peasant. Chéri rose to his feet, walked round the table which separated him from Léa, and the daylight streaming through the pink curtains struck him full in the face. This made it easy for her to compute the passage of days and years from his features, which were all of them in danger, though still intact. There was something about so secret a falling away to tempt her pity and trouble her memory, and perhaps extract from her the word or gesture that would precipitate Chéri into a frenzy of humiliation. As he stood there, a sacrifice to the light, with eyes lowered as if he were asleep, it seemed to him this was his last

207

chance of extorting from her one last affront, one last prayer, one final act of homage.

Nothing happened, so he opened his eyes. Once more he had to accept the true picture—in the shape of his stalwart old friend, who, prudently keeping her distance, was bestowing on him a certain degree of benevolence from small and slightly suspicious blue eyes.

Disillusioned and bewildered, he looked all over the room for her, except in the very spot where she stood. 'Where is she? Where is she? This old woman is hiding her from me. She's bored by me, and she's waiting for me to go, thinking it all an infernal nuisance, these crowding memories and this returning ghost. . . . But if by any chance I did ask for her help, if I beg her to give me back Léa . . .' Deep inside him, his kneeling double was still palpitating, like a body from which the lifeblood is being drained. With an effort of which he would never have deemed himself capable, Chéri tore himself away from this tortured image.

"I must be going," he said out loud, and he added on a note of rather cheap wit, "and I'm taking my box of cakes with me."

Léa's exuberant bosom heaved with a sigh of relief. "As you like, my child. But I'm always here, you know, if you're in any little trouble."

Though she seemed so obliging, Chéri could sense an underlying resentment. Within that vast edifice of flesh crowned with silvery thatch, femininity had for a moment reasserted itself in tones resounding with an intelligent harmony. But Chéri could not respond: like a ghost he had come, and with the shyness of a ghost he must vanish, in his own despite.

"Of course," Chéri replied, "and I thank you."

From that moment on, he knew, unerringly and spontaneously, exactly how to manage his exit. All the right words sprang to his lips, fluently, mechanically.

"You do understand, don't you, I came here to-day . . . why not sooner, you may ask? I know I ought to have come a long while ago. . . . But you will forgive me. . . ."

"Of course," Léa said.

"I'm even more hare-brained than before the war, you know, so that . . ."

"I understand, I understand."

And because of this interruption, he thought that she must be impatient to see the last of him. A few words were exchanged during Chéri's retreat, in the intervals of bumping into some piece of furniture, crossing a strip of sunshine from the court-yard window—after the pink light in the drawing-room it seemed by comparison almost blue—kissing a puffy hand bulging with rings when it was raised to his lips. Another of Léa's laughs, which broke off abruptly half way down its usual scale, just like a fountain when the jet is turned off and the crest of the plume, suddenly bereft of its stem, falls back to earth in a myriad separate pearls. . . . The staircase seemed to glide away under Chéri's feet like a bridge connecting two dreams, and once more he was in the Rue Raynouard. Even the street was unfamiliar.

He noticed that the rosy tints of the sky were wonderfully reflected in the rain-filled gutters and on the blue backs of the low-skimming swallows. And now, because the evening was fresh, and because all the impressions he was bringing away with him were slipping back perfidiously into the recesses of his mind —there to assume their final shape and intensity—he came to believe that he had forgotten all about them, and he felt happy.

Only the sound of an old woman's bronchial cough, as she sat over her glass of crème-de-menthe, disturbed the peace of the bar room where the murmur of the Place de l'Opéra died away, as though muffled in an atmosphere too thick to carry any eddies of sound. Chéri ordered a long drink and mopped his brow: this precaution was a carry-over from the days when he had been a little boy and sat listening to the babble of female voices, as, with Biblical gravity, they bandied such golden rules as: "If you want your milk of cucumber with real cucumber in it, you must make it yourself . . .", or "Never rub the perspiration into your face when you're overheated, or the perspiration will get under your skin and ruin it."

The silence, and the emptiness of the bar, created an illusion of coolness, and at first Chéri was not conscious of the couple who, with heads bent close together across a narrow table, were lost in inaudible whisperings. After a few moments his attention was drawn to this unknown man and woman by an occasional hissing sibilant which rose above the main stream of their chatter, and by the exaggerated expressions on their faces. They looked like servants, underpaid, overworked, and patient.

He took a mouthful or two of the fizzy iced drink, leaned his head back against the yellow plush of the banquette, and was delighted to feel a slackening of the mental strain which, for the last fortnight, had been sapping his strength. The dead weight of the present had not accompanied him across the threshold of the bar, which was old-fashioned, with red walls, gilt festoons, plaster roses, and a large open hearth. The cloakroom attendant could be half-seen in her tiled kingdom, counting every stitch as she mended the linen, her white hair bowed beneath a green lamp.

A passer-by dropped in. He did not trespass upon the yellow room, but took his drink standing at the bar as though to be discreet, and left without a word. The Odol odour of the crème-de-menthe was the only thing distasteful to Chéri, and he frowned in the direction of the dim old woman. Under a black and battered soft hat, he could distinguish an old face, accentuated here and there by rouge, wrinkles, kohl, and puffiness—all jumbled together—rather like a pocket into which have been popped, higgledly-piggledy, handkerchief, keys, and loose change. A vulgar old face, in short—and commonplace in its vulgarity, characterised, if at all, only by the indifference natural to a savage or a prisoner. She coughed, opened her bag, blew her nose vaguely, and replaced the seedy black reticule on the marble-topped table. It had an affinity with the hat, for it was made of the same black cracked taffeta, and equally out of fashion.

Chéri followed her every movement with an exaggerated repugnance; during the last two weeks he had been suffering, more than he could reasonably be expected to bear, from everything that was at once feminine and old. That reticule sprawling over the table almost drove him from the spot. He wanted to avert his eyes, but did nothing of the sort: they were riveted by a small sparkling arabesque, an unexpected brilliance fastened to the folds of the bag. His curiosity surprised him, but half a minute later he was still staring at the point of sparkling light, and his mind became an absolute blank. He was roused from his trance by a subconscious flash of triumphant certainty, and this gave him back the freedom to think and breathe. 'I know! It's the two capital L's interlaced!'

He enjoyed a moment of calm satisfaction, not unlike the sense of security on reaching a journey's end. He actually forgot the cropped hair on the nape of that neck, the vigorous grey locks, the big nondescript coat buttoned over a bulging stomach; he forgot the contralto notes of the peal of youthful laughter—everything that had dogged him so persistently for the past fortnight, that had deprived him of any appetite for food, any ability to feel that he was alone.

'It's too good to last!' he thought. So, with a brave effort, he returned to reality. He looked more carefully at the offending object, and was able to reel off: 'The two initials, set in little brilliants, which Léa had designed first for her suède bag, then for her dressing-table set of light tortoise-shell, and later for her writing-paper!' Not for a moment would he admit that the monogram on the bag might represent some other name.

He smiled ironically. 'Coincidence be blowed! I wasn't born yesterday! I came upon this bag by chance this evening, and to-morrow my wife will go and engage one of Léa's old footmen—again by chance. After that I shan't be able to go into a single restaurant, cinema, or tobacconist's without running up against Léa at every turn. It's my own fault. I can't complain. I ought to have left her alone.'

He put some small change beside his glass, and got up before summoning the barman. He faced away from the old woman as he slipped between the two tables, holding himself in under his waistcoat, like a tomcat squeezing under a gate. This he managed so adroitly that the edge of his coat only just brushed against the glass of green crème-de-menthe. Murmuring an apology, he made a dash for the glass door, to escape into the fresh air beyond. Horrified, but not really in the least surprised, he heard a voice call out after him, "Chéri!"

He had feared—known indeed—that this was coming. He turned to find that there was nothing about the raddled old ruin to help him recall her name; but he made no second attempt to escape, realising that everything would be explained.

"Don't you recognise me? You don't? But how could you? More women were aged by the war than men were killed by it and that's a fact. All the same, it's not for me to complain; I didn't risk losing anyone in the war. . . . Eh! Chéri! . . ."

She laughed; and recognition was complete, for he saw that what he had taken for decrepitude was only poverty and natural indifference. Now that she was holding herself upright and laughing, she did not look more than her age—sixty or there-abouts—and the hand with which she sought Chéri's was certainly not that of a doddering old grandmother.

"The Pal!" Chéri murmured, almost in tones of admiration.

"Are you really pleased to see me?"

"Oh, yes. . . ."

He was not telling a lie. He was gaining assurance step by step and thinking, 'It's only her . . . Poor Old Pal . . . I'd begun to fear . . .'

"Will you have a glass of something, Pal?"

"Just a whisky and soda, my pretty. My! haven't you kept your looks!"

He swallowed the bitter compliment which she tossed to him from the peaceful fringes of old age.

"And decorated, too," she added out of pure politeness. "Oh! I knew all about it, you may be sure! We all knew about it."

The ambiguous plural failed to wrest a smile from Chéri, and the Pal thought she had shocked him.

"When I say 'we', I'm speaking of those of us who were your real friends—Camille de La Berche, Léa, Rita, and me. You may be sure Charlotte would never have told me a word about it. As far as she's concerned, I don't exist. But—and I may as well say so—she doesn't exist for me, either." She stretched out across the table a pale hand that had long forgotten the light of day. "You must understand that Charlotte will never again be anything to me but the woman who contrived to get poor little Rita arrested and detained for twenty-four hours. . . . Poor Rita, who had never known a word of German. Was it Rita's fault, I ask you, if she happened to be Swiss?"

"I know, I know. I know the whole story," Chéri broke in precipitately.

213

The Pal raised her huge dark watery eyes towards him, full of inveterate complicity and a compassion that was always misplaced. "Poor kid," she sighed. "I understand you. Forgive me. Ah! you've certainly had your cross to bear!"

He questioned her with a look, no longer accustomed to the overstatements that added a rich funereal tone to the Pal's vocabulary, and he feared she might be going to talk to him about the war. But she was not thinking of the war. Perhaps she never had, for it is the concern of two generations only.

She went on to explain. "Yes, I was saying that to have such a mother must have been a heavy cross to bear for a son like you —for a boy, that's to say, with a blameless life, both before marriage and after! A nice, quiet boy and all that; not one to sow his wild oats all over the place, or to squander his inheritance."

She wagged her head, and bit by bit he began to piece together the past. He rediscovered her, though she had the mask of a ravaged tragedy queen. Her old age was without nobility, yet bore no signs of illness, no tell-tale trace that betrayed her addiction to opium. The drug is merciful to those unworthy of it.

"Have you quite given up the pipe?" asked Chéri sharply.

She raised a white untended hand. "What do you suppose? That kind of foolishness is all very well when you're not all on your own. In the days when I used to shock you young men, yes. . . . You remember when you used to come back at nights? Ah! you were very fond of that. . . . 'Dear old Pal,' you used to say to me, 'just let me have another little pipeful, and pack it well!'"

Without turning a hair, he accepted this humble flattery, as he might from an old retainer, who fibs in order to fawn. He smiled knowingly, and scrutinised the folds of black tulle round her neck, looking in the shadows under the faded hat for a necklace of large fake pearls.

Almost mechanically and sip by sip, he drank the whisky which had been put in front of him by mistake. He did not care for spirits as a rule, but this evening he enjoyed the whisky, for it helped him to smile easily and softened to his touch unpolished surfaces and rough materials; it enabled him to listen kindly to an old woman for whom the present did not exist. They met again on the further side of the superfluous war-years and the young, importunate dead: the Pal spanned the gap by throwing across to Chéri a bridge of names—names of old men who bore charmed lives, of old women revitalised for the struggle or turned to stone in their ultimate shape, never to alter again. She recounted in detail a hard-luck story of 1913, some unhappiness that had taken place before August, 1914, and something trembled in her voice when she spoke of La Loupiote—a woman now dead—"The very week of your wedding, dear boy! you see what a coincidence it was? the hand of Fate was upon us, indeed"—dead after four years of a pure and peaceful friendship.

"We slanged each other day in, day out, dear boy, but only in front of other people. Because, don't you see, it gave them the impression that we were 'a couple'. Who would have believed it, if we hadn't gone for each other hammer and tongs? So we called each other the most diabolical names, and the onlookers chuckled: 'Have you ever seen such a devoted pair?' Dear boy, I'll tell you something else that will knock you flat—surely you must have heard about the will Massau was supposed to have made. . . ."

"What Massau?" Chéri asked, languidly.

"Oh, come. You knew him as well as you know yourself! The story of the will—so called—that he handed to Louise MacMillar. It was in 1909, and at the time I am speaking of, I was one of the Gérault pack, his pack of 'faithful hounds'—and there were five of us he fed every evening at *La Belle Meunière* down at Nice; but on the Promenade des Anglais, you must remember, we only had eyes for you—dolled up in white like an English baby, and Léa all in white as well. . . . Ah! what a pair you made! You were the sensation—a miracle, straight from the hands of the Creator! Gérault used to tease Léa: 'You're far too *young*, girlie, and what's worse you're too proud. I shan't take you on for fifteen or twenty years at least. . . .' And to think that such a man had to be taken from us! Not a tear at his funeral that wasn't genuine, the whole nation was in mourning. And now let me get on with the story of the will. . . ."

Chéri was deluged with a perfect flood of incidents, a tide of bygone regrets and harmless resurrections, all declaimed with the ease and rapidity of a professional mourner. The two of them formed a symmetrical pattern as they leaned towards each other. The Pal lowered her voice when she came to the dramatic passages, giving out a sudden laugh or exclamation; and he saw in one of the looking-glasses how closely they seemed to resemble the whispering couple whose place they had taken. He got up, finding it imperative to put an end to this resemblance. The barman imitated his movement, but from afar, like a discreet dog when its master comes to the end of a visit. "Ah! well . . . yes . . ." said the Pal, "well, I'll finish the rest another time."

"After the next war," said Chéri, jokingly. "Tell me, those two capital letters. . . . Yes, the monogram in little brilliants. . . . It's not yours, Pal?"

He pointed at the black bag with the tip of his forefinger, extending it slowly while withdrawing his body, as though the bag were alive.

"Nothing escapes you," the Pal said in admiration. "You're quite right. She gave it to me, of course. She said to me: 'Such bits of finery are far too frivolous for me nowadays!' She said: 'What the devil do you suppose I'd be doing with those mirrors and powder and things, when I've a great face like a country policeman's?' She made me laugh. . . ."

To stem the flood, Chéri pushed the change from his hundred-franc note towards the Pal. "For your taxi, Pal."

They went out on to the pavement by the tradesman's entrance, and Chéri saw from the fainter lamp-light that night was coming on.

"Have you not got your motor?"

"My motor? No. I walked; it does me good."

216

"Is your wife in the country?"

"No. Her Hospital keeps her in Paris."

The Pal nodded her invertebrate hat. "I know. She's a big-hearted woman. Her name's been put forward for a decoration, I understand from the Baroness."

"What?"

"Here, stop that taxi for me, dear boy, the closed one. . . . And Charlotte's going big guns in her support; she knows people round Clemenceau. It will make up a little for the story about Rita . . . a little, not very much. She's as black as Sin itself, is Charlotte, my boy."

He pushed her into the oven of the taxi, where she sank back and became enveloped in the shadow. She ceased to exist. It was as though he had never met her, now that he heard her voice no longer. He took stock of the night, filling his lungs with the dust-laden air that foretold another scorching day. He pictured, as in a dream, that he would wake up at home, among gardens watered every evening, among the scent of Spanish honeysuckle and the call of birds, resting alongside his wife's straight hips. . . . But the Pal's voice rose up from the depths of the taxi: "Two hundred and fourteen, Avenue de Villiers! Remember my address, Chéri! And you know that I often dine at the *Giraffe*, Avenue de Wagram, don't you, if ever you should want me. . . . You know, if ever you should be looking for me."

'That's really the limit,' thought Chéri, lengthening his step. ' "If I should ever be looking for her." I ask you! Next time I come across her, I'll turn round and walk the other way.'

Cooled off and calmer, he strode without effort along the *quais* as far as the Place de l'Alma, and from there took a taxi back to the Avenue Henri-Martin. The eastern sky was already burnished with dull copper-coloured tints, which seemed rather to betoken the setting of some planet than the dawn of a summer day. No clouds streaked the vault of the heavens, but a haze of particles hung heavy and motionless over Paris, and would presently flare up and smoulder with the sombre glow of

217

red-hot metal. As dawn breaks, the dog-days drain great cities and their suburbs of the moist pinks, floral mauves and dewy blues that suffuse the sky above open country where plant life flourishes in profusion.

Nothing was stirring in the house when Chéri came to turn the tiny key in the lock. The flagged hall still smelt of the previous evening's dinner, and the cut branches of syringa, arranged by the armful in white vases tall enough to hide a man, filled the air with unbreathable poison. A stray grey cat slipped past him, stopped dead in the middle of the passage, and coldly inspected the intruder.

"Come here, little clerk of the Courts," Chéri called in a low voice. The cat glared at him almost insultingly and did not budge. Chéri remembered that no animal—no dog, horse or cat —had ever shown him any signs of affection. He could hear, across a span of fifteen years, Aldonza's raucous voice prophesying: 'A curse lies on those from whom animals turn away.' But when the cat, now wide awake, began to play with a small green chestnut, bowling it along with its front paw, Chéri smiled and went on up to his room.

He found it as dark and blue as a stage night. The dawn penetrated no further than the balcony, bedecked with well trained roses and pelargoniums fastened with raffia. Edmée was asleep, her bare arms and toes peeping out from under a light blanket. She was lying on her side, her head inclined, one finger hooked through her pearls. In the half-light she seemed to be immersed in thought rather than sleep. Her wavy hair strayed over her cheek, and Chéri could hear no sound of her breathing.

'She's enjoying a peaceful sleep,' thought Chéri. 'She's dreaming of Doctor Arnaud, or the Legion of Honour, or Royal Dutch shares. She's pretty. How pretty she is! . . . "Don't you worry, only another two or three hours, and you'll go to find your Doctor Arnaud. That's not so bad, is it? You'll meet again in the Avenue de l'Italie, in your beloved joint with its stink of carbolic. You'll answer 'Yes, Doctor; No, Doctor,' like a good little girl. You'll both of you put on really serious expressions;

you'll jiggle with thermometers—ninety-nine point six, a hundred and two point four—and he'll take your small carbolicky paw in his great coal-tarry mitt. You're lucky, my girl, to have a romance in your life! Don't worry. I shan't deprive you of it. . . ." I wouldn't mind, myself. . . .'

All of a sudden Edmée woke up with such a start that Chéri caught his breath, as though rudely interrupted in the middle of a sentence.

"It's you! It's you! Why, it *is* you after all."

"If you were expecting someone else, I offer my apologies," said Chéri, smiling at her.

"That's very clever. . . ." She sat up in bed and tossed back her hair. "What time is it? Are you getting up? Oh no, I see you've not been to bed yet. . . . You've just come in. . . . Oh, Fred! What have you been up to this time?"

" 'This time' is a compliment. . . . If you only knew what I've been doing. . . ."

She was no longer at the stage where, hands over her ears, she besought him, "No, no! say nothing! Don't tell me!" But, faster than his wife, Chéri was leaving behind that childishly malicious period when, amidst floods of tears and stormy scenes which ended by her throwing herself into his arms in the early hours of the morning, he would draw her down with him into the deep sleep of reconciled antagonists. No more little games of that sort. . . . No more betrayals. . . . Nothing, now, but this enforced and unavowable chastity.

He chucked his dusty shoes to the other end of the room, and sat down on the soft lace-frilled sheets, offering his wife a pallid face accustomed to dissemble everything except his will to dissemble. "Smell me!" he said. "Come on! I've been drinking whisky."

She brought her charming mouth to his, putting a hand on her husband's shoulder. "Whisky . . ." she repeated wonderingly. "Whisky . . . why?"

A less sophisticated woman would have asked "With whom?" and her cunning did not pass unnoticed. Chéri showed that two could play at that game by answering, "With an old pal. Do you want to hear the whole truth?"

She smiled, now caught in the dawning light which, with growing boldness, touched the edge of the bed, the looking-glass, a picture-frame, and then the golden scales of a fish swimming round and round in a crystal bowl.

"No, Fred, not the whole truth. Only a half-veiled truth, suitable for the small hours." At the same time, her thoughts were busy. She was certain—or nearly so—that Chéri had not been drawn away from her either by love or by lust. She let her acquiescent body fall helplessly into his arms, yet he felt on his shoulder a thin, hard hand, unrelaxed in its guarded prudence.

"The truth is," he went on, "that I don't know her name. But I gave her . . . wait a moment . . . I gave her eighty-three francs."

"Just like that, all at once! The first time you met her? It's princely!"

She pretended to yawn, and slipped softly back into the depths of the bed, as though not expecting an answer. He gave her a moment's pity; then a brilliant horizontal ray brought into sharper relief the almost naked body lying beside him, and his pity vanished.

'She's . . . she has kept her good looks. It's not fair.'

She lay back, her lips parted, looking at him through half-closed eyes. He saw a gleam of the candid, calculating, uncharacteristically feminine expression that a woman bestows on the man who is going to pleasure her, and it shocked his unavowable chastity. From his superior position he returned this look with another—the uncommunicative, enigmatic look of the man who prefers to abstain. Not wishing to move away, he simply looked towards the golden daylight, the freshness of the watered garden, and the blackbirds, weaving liquid sequences of sound round the dry incessant chirps of the sparrows. Edmée could see signs of emaciation and prolonged fatigue on his features. His cheeks were blue with a day's growth of beard. She noticed that his fine hands were not clean, that his finger-nails had not been near soap and water since the previous evening, and that the dark lines which accentuated the hollows under his eyes were now spreading, in the shape of crow's feet, towards his nose. This handsome young man—she decided—without collar or shoes, looked ravaged, as if he had had to spend a night in prison. Without losing his looks, he had shrunk in accordance with some mysterious scaling down, and this enabled her to regain the upper hand. She no longer invited him to join her, sat up in bed, and put a hand on his forehead.

"Ill?"

Slowly he let his attention wander back from the garden to his wife.

"What? . . . No, no, nothing's wrong with me, except I'm sleepy. So sleepy that I can hardly bring myself to go to bed—if you know what I mean. . . ."

He smiled, showing dry gums and lips colourless on the insides. But, above all, this smile betrayed a sadness that sought no remedy, modest as a poor man's suffering. Edmée was on the point of questioning him categorically, but then thought better of it.

"Get into bed," she ordered, making room for him.

"Bed? It's water I need. I feel so filthy, I can't tell you."

He just had the strength to lift up a water bottle, take a gulp from the neck, then throw off his coat, before he fell back like a log on the bed, and lay there without moving again, drained by sleep.

For some little time Edmée gazed at the half-stripped stranger lying like a drugged man beside her. Her watchful eye wandered from bluish lips to hollowed eyes, from outflung hand to forehead sealed upon a single secret. She summoned her self-control and composed her features, as though afraid the sleeper might take her by surprise. She got out of bed softly, and, before shutting out the dazzling sunlight, drew a silk counterpane to hide the outstretched untidy body looking like a burglar who had been knocked out. She arranged this so as to give the beautiful rigid features their full splendour, carefully pulling it down over the drooping hand with a slight qualm of pious disgust, as though hiding a weapon that perhaps had killed.

He never twitched a muscle—having retired for a few moments within an impregnable fastness. In any case, Edmée's hospital training had given her fingers a professional touch, which, if not exactly gentle, was competent to go straight to the required spot without touching or in any way affecting the surrounding area. She did not get back into bed; but, sitting half-naked, enjoyed the unexpected freshness of the hour when the sun rouses the winds. The long curtains stirred, as if breathing and, dependent on the breeze, stippled Chéri's sleep with fitful flecks of dark blue.

As she gazed at him, Edmée was not thinking of the wounded, or of the dead, whose peasant hands she had joined together upon coarse cotton sheets. No invalid in the grip of a nightmare, not one among the dead, had ever resembled Chéri: sleep, silence, and repose made him magnificently inhuman.

Extreme beauty arouses no sympathy. It is not the prerogative of any one country. Time's finger had touched Chéri only to make him more austere. The mind—whose task it is to curb the splendour of mankind while degrading it piecemeal—respected Chéri as an admirable temple dedicated to instinct. What could avail the Machiavellian deceit, the ardour and the cunning self-sacrifice imposed by love, against this inviolable standard-bearer of light and his untutored majesty?

Patient and, on occasion, subtle as she was, it never occurred to Edmée that the feminine appetite for possession tends to emasculate every living conquest, and can reduce a magnificent but inferior male to the status of a courtesan. Her lower-middle-class wisdom made her determined not to relinquish the gains—money, ease, domestic tyranny, marriage—acquired in so few years and rendered doubly attractive by the war.

She gazed at the limp, worn-out, almost empty-looking body. 'That's Chéri,' she said to herself; 'yes, that's Chéri all right . . . That's how small a thing he is!' She shrugged a shoulder and added: 'That's what he's reduced to, this wonderful Chéri of theirs . . .' doing her best to induce contempt for the man lying thus supine. She called up memories of rapturous nights, of languid early mornings bathed in sunlight and pleasure, and, as a result—since he had progressively grown to disdain her—she saw fit to pay but coldly vindictive homage to this body so sumptuously laid out under the pall of flowered silk and the refreshing wing of the curtains. She put one hand on the small, pointed breast set low on her slender body, and squeezed it like a pulpy fruit, as if calling this most tempting allurement of her young body to witness the injustice of his desertion. 'What Chéri himself needs is doubtless something else. What he needs is . . .'

But vain were her attempts to put her scorn into words. Even a woman loses the desire and the ability to despise a man who suffers in silence and alone.

All of a sudden, Edmée felt satiated with the spectacle: the shadows thrown by the curtains, the pallor of the sleeper, and the white bed helped to invest it with the romantic colouring of death and the nether world. She jumped to her feet, strong and ready to face this world, but determined to avoid any emotional attack upon the traitor lying on the disordered bed, the absentee seeking refuge in sleep, silent, ailing and repulsive. She was neither irritated nor unhappy. Her heart would beat more feverishly in her breast, the blood mount more quickly to her pearl-pale cheeks, only at the thought of the healthy red-haired man whom she called "dear master" or "chief" in tones of serious playfulness. Arnaud's thick gentle hands; his laugh; the points of light that sunshine or the lamp in the operating-theatre caused to twinkle on his red moustache; his very coat—the white surgery-coat he wore and even took off in the hospital, just like an intimate garment that never passes beyond the bedroom door. . . . Edmée sprang up as though for a dance.

'That, oh yes, *that's* my life!' She gave a toss of the head that sent her hair flying out like a horse's mane, and went into the bathroom without turning round.

Unimaginative in style, and in its very ordinary proportions, the dining-room made no pretence to luxury except in the panels of yellow stuff starred with purple and green. The grey and white stucco of the surrounding walls deflected too much light on the guests, deprived already of all shade by the merciless glare of the top lighting.

A galaxy of crystal sequins shimmered with every movement of Edmée's dress. For the family dinner, Madame Peloux was still wearing her tailor-made with leather buttons, and Camille de La Berche her nurse's veil, under the cowl of which she bore a striking resemblance to Dante, only far hairier. Because it was so hot, the women spoke little: so did Chéri, because it was his habit. A warm bath followed by a cold shower had triumphed over his fatigue; but the powerful light, ricocheting upon his cheeks, accentuated their cavities, and he kept his eyes lowered, to allow the shadow from his eyebrows to fall directly over the lids.

"To-night, Chéri doesn't look a day over sixteen," boomed the deep bass of the Baroness out of the blue.

No one took up her remark, and Chéri acknowledged it with a slight bow.

"Not for a long time," the Baroness continued, "have I seen the oval of his face so slender."

Edmée frowned imperceptibly. "I have. During the war, of course."

"That's true, that's true," piped Charlotte Peloux in shrill agreement. "Heavens! how worn out he looked in 1916, at Vésoul! Edmée, my dear child," she went on in the same breath, "I've seen you-know-who to-day, and *everything* is going along very nicely. . . ."

Edmée blushed in a docile, unbecoming manner, and Chéri raised his eyes. "You've seen who? And what's going along nicely?"

"Troussellier's pension—my little soldier who's had his right arm off. He left the Hospital on June the twentieth. Your mother's taking up his case at the War Office."

She had not hesitated for words, and she let her calm golden gaze rest on Chéri: yet he knew she was lying.

"It's a question of whether he'll get his red riband. After all, poor boy, it's certainly his turn. . . ."

She was lying to him in front of two friends who knew that she was lying. 'Why don't I pick up the water-bottle and crash it down in the middle of them?' But he made no movement. What strength of feeling would have given him the impetus to brace his body and direct his hand?

"Abzac is leaving us in a week's time," began Madame de La Berche.

"That's not certain," Edmée took her up with an air of knowing better. "Doctor Arnaud isn't at all satisfied that he should be allowed to go off like that on his new leg. You can just see the man, liable to do any sort of silly thing, and always with the possibility of gangrene. Doctor Arnaud knows only too well that it was exactly that sort of thing, all through the war. . . ."

Chéri looked at her, and she stopped abruptly in the middle of her pointless sentence. She was fanning herself with a rose on a leafy stalk. She waved away a dish which she was offered, and put her elbows on the table. In her white dress and bare shoulders, even when sitting still, she was not exempt from a secret contentment, a self-satisfaction, which revealed her true nature. Something outrageous radiated from her soft outlines. Some tell-tale glow betrayed the woman bent on "arriving", who up till the present had met only with success.

'Edmée,' Chéri concluded, 'is a woman who should never grow older than twenty. How like her mother she's getting!'

The next moment the resemblance had vanished. Nothing obvious about Edmée recalled Marie-Laure: only in one respect did her daughter exhibit something of the poisonous, pink and white, impudent beauty exploited by the red-haired Marie-Laure to ensnare her victims during her palmy days—and that was in her shamelessness. Careful as she was not to shock anyone, those who still retained their native shrewdness, by instinct or from lack of education, were shocked by her all the same, as if by a second-rate race-horse, or a jewel that looked too new. The servants, as well as Chéri, were frightened of something in Edmée, whom they guessed to be more vulgar than themselves.

Authorised by Edmée, who was lighting a cigarette, the Baroness de La Berche slowly grilled the tip of her cigar before inhaling the first rapturous puff. Her white Red Cross veil fell over her manly shoulders and she looked like one of those grave-faced men who, at Christmas parties, adorn their heads with tissue paper Phrygian caps, programme-sellers' kerchiefs, or shakos. Charlotte undid the plaited leather buttons of her jacket and drew towards her a box of Abdullas; while the butler, mindful of the customs of the house, pushed within easy reach of Chéri a small conjuror's table on wheels—full of secret drawers, sliding double-bottomed compartments, and liqueurs in silver phials. Then he left the room; and there was no longer against the yellow panels the tall silhouette of an elderly Italian with a face carved out of box-wood, and crowned with white hair.

"Old Giacomo really does look an aristocrat," said the Baroness de La Berche, "and I know what I'm talking about."

Madame Peloux shrugged her shoulders, a movement that had long since ceased to lift her breasts. Her white silk blouse with a jabot sagged under the weight of her bosom, and her short, dyed, but still abundant hair glowed a livid red above large disastrous eyes and high forehead, suggesting a leader of the French Revolution.

"He's got the distinguished looks of all elderly Italians with white hair. They're all Papal Chamberlains, by the look of them, and they can write out the menu for you in Latin; but you've only to open a door and you'll find them raping a little girl of seven."

Chéri welcomed this outburst of virulence as a timely shower. His mother's malice had parted the clouds again, bringing back an atmosphere in which he could breathe. Not so long ago he had begun to enjoy discovering traces of the old Charlotte, who, from the safety of her balcony, would refer to a pretty woman passing below as "a tuppeny-ha'penny tart," and who, to Chéri's "Do you know her, then?" would reply, "No! Whatever next! Do you expect me to know that slut?" Only recently had he begun to take a confused pleasure in Charlotte's superior vitality, and, confusedly, he now preferred her to the other two creatures present; but he was unaware that this preference, this partiality, could perhaps be termed filial affection. He laughed, and applauded Madame Peloux for still being—and quite startlingly so—the woman he had known, detested, feared, and insulted. For an instant, Madame Peloux took on her authentic character in her son's eyes; that is to say, he estimated her at her proper value, a woman high-spirited, all-consuming, calculating and at the same time rash, like a high financier; a woman capable of taking a humorist's delight in spiteful cruelty. "She's a scourge, certainly," he said to himself, "and no more. A scourge, but not a stranger." Looking at the way the points of her hair impinged upon her Jacobin forehead, he recognised a similarity to the blue-black jutting points on his own forehead, which emphasised the whiteness of his skin and the blackbird sheen of his hair.

'She's my mother all right,' he thought. 'No one's ever told me I'm like her, but I am.' The "stranger" was sitting opposite, glimmering with the milky, veiled brilliance of a pearl. Chéri heard the name of the Duchess of Camastra thrown out by the deep voice of the Baroness, and on the stranger's face he saw a fleeting rapacity flicker and die, like the serpent of flame that suddenly flares up along a burnt vine-twig before it is consumed among the embers. But she did not open her mouth, and took no part in the volley of military curses which the Baroness was firing at a hospital-rival.

"They're properly in the soup, it appears, over some new-fangled injection or other. Two men died within two days of being given the needle. That needs some explaining!" said Madame de La Berche with a hearty laugh.

"You've got it wrong," corrected Edmée dryly. "That's an old story of Janson-de-Sailly resuscitated."

"No smoke without fire," sighed Charlotte charitably. "Chéri, are you sleepy?"

He was dropping with fatigue, but he admired the powers of resistance of these three women: neither hard work, the Parisian summer, nor perpetual movement and jabber could put them out of action.

"The heat," he murmured laconically. He caught Edmée's eye, but she made no comment and refrained from contradicting him.

"Pooh, pooh, pooh," chanted Charlotte. "The heat! But, of course. . . . Pooh, pooh, pooh."

Her eyes, which remained fixed on Chéri's, overflowed with blackmailing tenderness and complicity. As usual, she knew everything there was to be known: back-stairs gossip, concierges' chatter. Perhaps Léa herself, for the pleasure of a feminine fib, of winning one last trick, had told Charlotte. The Baroness de La Berche emitted a little neigh, and the shadow of her large clerical nose covered the lower part of her face.

228

"God in Heaven!" swore Chéri.

His chair fell to the floor behind him, and Edmée, alert and on the watch, promptly jumped to her feet. She showed not the slightest astonishment. Charlotte Peloux and the Baroness de La Berche at once put themselves on the defensive, but in the old-fashioned way—hands clutching skirts, ready to gather them up and fly. Chéri, leaning forward with his fists on the table, was panting and turning his head to right and left, like a wild animal caught in a net.

"You, to start with, you . . ." he stammered. He pointed at Charlotte; used as she was to such scenes, she was galvanised by this filial threat in the presence of witnesses.

"What? What? What?" she barked in sharp little yelps. "You dare to insult me? a little whippersnapper like you, a wretched little whippersnapper who, were I to open my mouth . . ."

The wine-glasses quivered at the sound of her piercing voice, but her words were cut short by a shriller voice: "Leave him alone!"

After three such abrupt explosions the silence seemed deafening, and Chéri, his physical dignity restored, shook himself, and a smile spread over his green face.

"I beg your pardon, Madame Peloux," he said mischievously.

She was already conferring blessings on him with eye and hand, like a champion in the ring, pacified at the end of a round.

"You're hot-blooded and no mistake!"

"He's a soldier all right," said the Baroness, as she shook hands with Edmée. "I must say goodbye, Chéri; they'll be missing me in my dug-out."

She refused a lift in Charlotte's motor, and insisted on going home on foot. The tall figure, the white nurse's veil, and the glow of her cigar would strike terror at night into the heart of the fiercest footpad. Edmée accompanied the two old women as far as the front door, an exceptional act of courtesy, which allowed Chéri time to draw what conclusions he could from his wife's wary action and her diplomatic peacemaking.

He drank a glass of cold water very slowly, as he stood beneath the cataract of light, thinking the matter over and savouring his terrible loneliness.

'She defended me,' he kept repeating to himself. 'She defended me with no love in her heart. She protected me as she protects the garden against blackbirds, her store of sugar against thieving nurses, or her cellar against the footmen. Little doubt she knows that I went to the Rue Reynouard, and came back here, never to go there again. She's not said a word about it to me, in any case—perhaps because she doesn't care. She protected me, because it wouldn't have done for my mother to talk. She defended me with no love in her heart.'

He heard Edmée's voice in the garden. She was testing his mood from afar. "You don't feel ill, Fred, do you? Would you like to go straight to bed?"

She put her head through the half-open door, and he laughed bitterly to himself: 'How cautious she's being.'

She saw his smile and grew bolder. "Come along, Fred. I believe I'm just as tired as you, or I wouldn't have let myself go just now. I've been apologising to your mother."

She switched off some of the cruel light, and gathered the roses from the table-cloth to put them into water. Her body, her hands, her head bending over the roses and set off by a haze of fair hair from which the heat had taken most of the crimp—everything about her might have charmed a man.

"I said *a man*—I didn't say *any man*," Léa's insidious voice kept ringing in Chéri's ears.

'I can behave as I like to her,' he thought, as he followed Edmée with his eyes. 'She'll never complain, she'll never divorce me; I've nothing to fear from her, not even love. I should be happy enough, if I chose.'

But, at the same time, he recoiled with unspeakable repugnance from the idea of the two of them living together in a home where love no longer held sway. His childhood as a bastard, his long adolescence as a ward, had taught him that his world, though people thought of it as reckless, was governed by a code almost as narrow-minded as middle-class prejudice. In it, Chéri had learned that love is a question of money, infidelity, betrayals, and cowardly resignation. But now he was well on the way to forgetting the rules he had been taught, and to be re-pelled by acts of silent condescension.

He therefore ignored the gentle hand on his sleeve. And, as he walked with Edmée towards the room whence would issue no sound of endearment or reproach, he was overcome with shame, and blushed at the horror of their unspoken agreement.

He found himself out of doors, dressed for the street and hardly conscious of having put on his soft hat and light raincoat. Behind him lay the drawing-room, misty with tobacco smoke; the overpowering scent of women and flowers; the cyanide smell of cherry brandy. There he had left Edmée, Doctor Arnaud, Filipesco, Atkins, and the two Kelekian girls, well-connected young women who, having done a little mild lorry-driving during the war, had no use now for anything but cigars, motors, and their garage-hand friends. He had left Desmond sitting between a real estate merchant and an Under-Secretary in the Ministry of Commerce, together with an invalided poet and Charlotte Peloux. Also a fashionable young married couple, who had obviously been put wise. Throughout dinner they had looked greedy but prudish, with a knowing expression and a simple-minded eagerness to be shocked—as though expecting Chéri to dance stark naked, or Charlotte and the Under-Secretary to make violent love to one another in the middle of the carpet.

232 Chéri had made off, aware that his behaviour had been stoical, with no other lapse than a sudden loss of interest in the present: an awkward thing to lose in the middle of a meal. Even so, his trance could have lasted little more than a moment, had been instantaneous, like a dream. But now he was putting a distance between himself and the strangers who thronged his house, and the sound of his footfall on the sand was as light as

the soft padding of an animal. His light silver-grey coat shaded into the mist that had fallen over the Bois; and a few nocturnal loiterers must have envied a young man who was in such a hurry to go nowhere in particular.

He was haunted by the vision of his crowded house. He could still hear the sound of voices, and carried with him the memory of faces, of smiles, and especially of the shape of mouths. An elderly man had talked about the war; a woman about politics. He remembered, too, the new understanding between Desmond and Edmée, and the interest his wife had taken in some building scheme. 'Desmond! . . . Just the husband for my wife!' And then, dancing . . . the strange effect of the tango on Charlotte Peloux. Chéri quickened his step.

The night was filled with the damp mist of a too early autumn and the full moon was shrouded. A great milky halo, ringed with a pallid iridescence, had replaced the planet, and was sometimes itself hidden by fitful puffs of scudding cloud. The smell of September was already in the leaves that had fallen during the dog days.

'How mild it is,' Chéri thought.

He rested his weary limbs on a bench, but not for long. He was rejoined by an invisible companion, to whom he refused his seat on the bench—a woman with grey hair, wearing a long coat, who poured forth a relentless gaiety. Chéri turned his head towards the gardens of La Muette, as though he could hear, even at that distance, the cymbals of the jazz-band.

The time had not yet come for him to go back to the blue room, where perhaps the two society girls were still smoking good cigars, as they sat side-saddle on the blue velvet of the bed, keeping the real estate merchant amused with mess-room tales.

233

'Oh! for a nice hotel bedroom, a jolly pink room, very ordinary and very pink . . .' But would it not lose its very ordinariness the moment the light was turned out and total darkness gave the right of entry—a ponderous, mocking entry—to a figure with vigorous grey hair, dressed in a long, nondescript coat?

He smiled at the intruder, for he was past the stage of fear. 'There, or in any other place, *she* will be just as faithful. But I simply can't go on living with those people.'

Day by day, hour by hour, he was becoming more scornful, more exacting. Already he was severely critical of the Agony Column heroes, and young war widows who clamoured for new husbands, like the parched for cold water. His uncompromising intolerance extended to the world of finance, without his realising how grave was the change. 'That Company for transporting raw hides they talked about at dinner. . . . How disgusting it was! And they don't mind discussing it at the top of their voices. . . .' But nothing in the world would have induced him to protest, to reveal that he was fast becoming a man utterly out of sympathy with his surroundings. Prudently, he kept quiet about that, as about everything else. When he had taken Charlotte Peloux to task for having disposed of several tons of sugar in rather a dubious fashion, had she not reminded him—and in no uncertain terms—of the time when he had shouted, without a trace of embarrassment, "Hand over five louis, Léa, so that I can go and buy some cigarettes"?

'Ah!' he sighed, 'they'll never understand anything, these women. It wasn't at all the same thing.'

Thus he let his thoughts run on, as he stood, bareheaded, his hair glistening, barely distinguishable in the mist. The shadowy form of a female passed close beside him, running. The rhythm of her steps and the crunch as each foot bit into the gravel betrayed anxiety and haste. Then the shadowy woman fell into the arms of a shadowy man who came to meet her, and down they fell together, breast to breast, as though struck by the same bullet.

'Those two are trying to hide,' Chéri thought. 'They're deceiving someone somewhere. The whole world's busy deceiving and being deceived. But I . . .' He did not finish the sentence, but a repugnance made him jump to his feet, an action that meant, 'But I am chaste.' A faint ray of light, flickering uncertainly over stagnant, hitherto unfeeling regions of his

inmost being, was enough to suggest that chastity and loneliness
are one and the same misfortune.

As night advanced, he began to feel the cold. From his
prolonged, aimless vigils, he had learned that, at night, tastes,
smells, and temperatures vary according to the hour, and that
midnight is warm in comparison with the hour which immediately precedes the dawn.

'The winter will soon be on us,' he thought, as he lengthened his stride, 'and none too soon, putting an end to this inter-
minable summer. Next winter, I should like . . . let me see
. . . next winter . . .' His attempts at anticipation collapsed
almost at once; and he came to a halt, head lowered, like a horse
at the prospect of a long steep climb ahead.

'Next winter, there'll still be my wife, my mother, old gam-
mer La Berche, Thingummy, What's-his-name, and the rest of
them. There'll be the same old gang. . . . And for me there'll
never again be . . .'

He paused once more, to watch a procession of low clouds
advancing over the Bois, clouds of an indescribable pink, set
upon by a gusty wind which buried its fingers in their misty
tresses, twisting and dragging them across the lawns of heaven,
to carry them off to the moon. Chéri gazed with eyes well used
to the translucent magic of the night, which those who sleep
regard as pitch-dark.

The apparition of the large, flat, half-veiled moon among
the scurrying vaporous clouds, which she seemed to be pursuing
and tearing asunder, did not divert him from working out an
arithmetical fantasy: he was computing—in years, months,
hours and days—the amount of precious time that had been lost
to him for ever.

'Had I never let her go when I went to see her again that
day before the war—then it would have meant three or four
years to the good; hundreds and hundreds of days and nights
gained and garnered for love.' He did not fight shy of so big a
word.

'Hundreds of days—a lifetime—life itself. Life as it was in

the old days, life with my "worst enemy", as she used to call herself. My worst enemy! who forgave me all, and never let me off a single thing.' He seized hold of his past, to squeeze out every remaining drop upon his empty, arid present; bringing back to life, and inventing where necessary, the princely days of his youth, his adolescence shaped and guided by a woman's strong capable hands—loving hands, ever ready to chastise. A prolonged, sheltered, oriental adolescence, in which the pleasures of the flesh had their passing place, like silent pauses in a song. A life of luxury, passing whims, childish cruelty, with fidelity a yet unspoken word.

He threw back his head to look up at the nacreous halo which irradiated the whole sky, and he gave a low cry, 'It's all gone to hell! I'm thirty years old!'

He hurried on his way back home, heaping curses on himself to the rhythm of his quickened steps. 'Fool! The tragedy is not her age, but mine. Everything may be over for her, but, for me . . .'

He let himself in without making a sound, to find the house in silence at last; to be nauseated by the lingering stale smell of those who had dined, wined, and danced there. In the looking-glass fitted to the door in the hall he met face to face the young man who had grown so thin, whose cheeks had hardened, whose sad beautifully moulded upper lip was unshaven and blue, whose large eyes were reticent and tragic. The young man, in effect, who had ceased, inexplicably, to be twenty-four years old.

'For me,' Chéri completed his thought, 'I really do believe that the last word has been said.'

"What I need is somewhere quiet, you understand. . . . Any little place would do. . . . A bachelor flat, a room, a corner. . . ."

"I wasn't born yesterday," said the Pal, reproachfully.

She raised disconsolate eyes towards the festoons on the ceiling: "A little love, of course, of course, a little kiss—something to warm a poor lonely heart. . . . You bet I understand! Any special fancy?"

Chéri frowned. "Fancy? For whom?"

"You don't understand, my pretty. . . . Fancy for any particular district?"

"Ah! . . . No, nothing special. Just a quiet corner."

The Pal nodded her large head in collusion. "I see, I see. Something after my style—like my flat. You know where I rest my bones?"

"Yes."

"No, you don't know at all. I was certain you wouldn't write it down. Two hundred and fourteen Rue de Villiers. It's not big, and it's not beautiful. But you don't want the sort of place where the whole street knows your business."

"No."

"I got mine, of course, through a little deal with my landlady. A jewel of a woman, by the way, married, or as good as. Periwinkle blue eyes, and a head like a bird; but she bears the mark of Fate on her forehead, and I already know from her cards that she can't say no to anything, and that—"

"Yes, yes. You were saying just now that you knew of a flat. . . ."

"Yes, but not good enough for you."

"You don't think so?"

"Not for you . . . not for the two of you!"

The Pal hid a suggestive smile in her whisky, and Chéri turned from its smell—like wet harness. He put up with her quips about his imaginary conquests, for he saw, round her scraggy neck, a string of large faked pearls which he thought he recognised. Every visual reminder of his past halted him on his downward path, and, during such respites, he felt at peace.

"Ah!" sighed the Pal, "How I'd love to catch a glimpse of her! What a pair! . . . I don't know her, of course, but I can just see you two together! . . . Of course you'll provide everything yourself?"

"For whom?"

"Why, the furniture in your love-nest, of course!"

He looked at the Pal in bewilderment. Furniture . . . What furniture? He had been thinking only of one thing: a refuge of his own, with a door that opened and closed for him and no one else, safe from Edmée, Charlotte, all of them. . . .

"Will you furnish it in period or in modern style? La belle Serrano arranged her entire ground floor with nothing but Spanish shawls, but that was a bit eccentric. You're old enough, of course, to know your own mind. . . ."

He hardly heard her, far away in his dreams of a future home that would be secret, small, warm and dark. At the same time, he was drinking red currant syrup, like any young "miss", in the red-and-gold, out-of-date, unchanging bar, just as it used to be when, a small boy, Chéri had come there to sip his first fizzy drink through a straw. . . . Even the barman himself had not changed, and if the woman sitting opposite Chéri was now a withered specimen, at least he had never known her beautiful, or young.

'They all change, the whole of that set—my mother, my wife, all the people they see—and they live for change. My

mother may change into a banker, Edmée into a town council-
lor. But I . . .'

In imagination, he quickly returned to that refuge, existing
at some unknown point in space, but secret, small, warm,
and . . .

"Mine's done up in Algerian style," the Pal persisted. "It's
no longer in the fashion, but I don't mind—especially as the
furniture is hired. You'll be sure to recognise many of the
photos I've put up: and then there's the portrait of La Loupiote.
. . . Come and have a look at it. Please do."

"I'd like to. Let's go!"

On the threshold he hailed a taxi.

"But d'you never have your motor? Why haven't you got
your motor? It's really quite extraordinary how people with motors never have their motor!"

She gathered up her faded black skirts, caught the string of
her lorgnette in the clasp of her bag, dropped a glove, and
submitted to the stares of the passers-by with the lack of embarrassment of a Negro. Chéri, standing at her side, received
several insulting smiles and the admiring condolences of a
young woman, who called out: "Lord, what a waste of good
material!"

In the taxi, patiently and half asleep, he endured the old
thing's tattle. And then some of her stories were soothing: the
one about the ridiculous little dog which had held up the return
from the races in 1897, and then Mère La Berche eloping with a
young bride on the day of her wedding in 1893.

"That's it over there. This door's stuck, Chéri, I can't get
out. I warn you, there's not much light in the passage, nor, for
that matter, is there much out here. . . . It's only a ground-
floor flat, when all's said and done! . . . Wait where you are a
second."

He waited, standing in the semi-darkness. He heard the
jingle of keys, the wheezy old creature's gasps for breath and
then her fussy servant's voice, "I'm lighting up. . . . Then
you'll find yourself in a familiar landscape. I've got electricity, of

course. . . . There, let me introduce you to my little morning-room, which is also my large drawing-room!"

He went in, and, from kindness—hardly bothering to glance at it—praised the room; it had a low ceiling and reddish walls, kippered by the smoke of innumerable cigars and cigarettes. Instinctively, he looked all round for the window, barricaded by shutters and curtains.

"You can't see in here? You're not an old night-bird like your Pal. Wait, I'll switch on the top light."

"Don't bother. . . . I'll just come in and—" He broke off, staring at the most brightly lit wall, covered with small frames and photographs pinned through the four corners. The Pal began to laugh.

"What did I say about a familiar landscape! I was quite sure you'd enjoy looking at them. You haven't got that one, have you?"

'That one' was a very large photographic portrait-study, touched up with water colours now quite faded. Blue eyes, a laughing mouth, a chignon of fair hair, and a look of calm yet exultant triumph. . . . High-breasted—in a First Empire corselet, legs showing through gauze skirts, legs that never finished, rounded out at the thigh, slender at the knee, legs that. . . . And a fetching hat, a hat that turned up on one side only, trimmed like a single sail to the wind.

"She never gave you that one, not that one, I bet! It makes her a goddess, a fairy walking on clouds! And yet it's absolutely her, of course. This big photo is the loveliest, to my way of thinking, but I'm still every bit as fond of the others. Here, for instance, look at this little one here—much more recent, of course—isn't it a sight for sore eyes?"

A snapshot, clinging to the wall with the help of a rusty pin, showed a woman standing in the shade against a sunlit garden.

'It's the navy-blue dress and the hat with the seagulls,' Chéri said to himself.

"I'm all for flattering portraits, myself," the Pal went on. "A portrait like this one. Come now—you must confess—isn't it enough to make you join your hands and believe in God?"

A degraded and smarmy art, to lend glamour to the "portrait photograph," had lengthened the neck line and modified those around the sitter's mouth. But the nose, just sufficiently aquiline, the delicious nose with its ravishing nostrils, and the chaste little dimple, the velvety cleft that indented the upper lip under the nose—these were untouched, authentic, respected by even the photographer.

"Would you believe it? She wanted to burn the lot, pretending that nobody to-day is the least interested in what she used to be like. My blood boiled, I shrieked like a soul in torment, and she gave me the whole collection the very same day that she made me a present of the bag with her monogram. . . ."

"Who's this fellow with her . . . here . . . in this one underneath?"

"What were you saying? What's that? Wait till I take off my hat."

"I'm asking you who this is—this fellow—here. Get a move on, can't you?"

"Heavens, don't bustle me about so. . . . That? It's Bacciocchi, come! Naturally, you can hardly be expected to recognise him, he dates from two turns before you."

"Two what?"

"After Bacciocchi, she had Septfons—and yet no—wait . . . Septfons was earlier than that. . . . Septfons, Bacciocchi, Spéleïeff, and you. Oh! do look at those check trousers! . . . How ridiculous men's fashions used to be!"

"And that photo over there; when was that taken?"

241
....

He drew back a step, for at his elbow the Pal's head was craning forward, and its magpie's nest of felted hair smelt like a wig.

"That? That's her costume for Auteuil in . . . in 1888, or '89. Yes, the year of the Exhibition. In front of that one, dear boy, you should raise your hat. They don't turn out beauties like that any more."

"Pooh! . . . I don't think it so stunning."

The Pal folded her hands. Hatless, she looked older, and her high forehead was a buttery yellow under hair dyed greenish black.

"Not so stunning! That waist you could encircle with your ten fingers! That lily neck! And be good enough to let your eyes rest on that dress! All in frilled sky-blue chiffon, dear boy, and looped up with little pink moss-roses sewn on to the frills, and the hat to match! And the little bag to match as well—we called them alms-bags at that time. Oh! the beauty she was then! There's been nothing since to compare with her first appearances: she was the dawn, the very sun of love."

"First appearances where?"

She gave Chéri a gentle dig in the ribs. "Get along with you. . . . How you make me laugh! Ah! the trials of life must melt into thin air when you're about the house!"

His rigid features passed unobserved. He was still facing the wall, seemingly riveted by several Léas—one smelling an artificial rose, another bending over a book with medieval hasps, her swan neck rising from a pleatless collar, a white and rounded neck like the bole of a birch-tree.

"Well, I must be going," he said, like Valérie Cheniaguine.

"What d'you mean—you must be going? What about my dining-room? And my bedroom? just glance at them, my pretty! Take a note of them for your little love-nest."

"Ah! yes. . . . Listen; not to-day, because . . ." He glanced distrustfully towards the rampart of portraits, and lowered his voice. "I've an appointment. But I'll come back . . . to-morrow. Probably to-morrow, before dinner."

"Good. Then I can go ahead?"

"Go ahead?"

"With the flat."

"Yes, that's right. See about it. And thanks."

* * *

'I really begin to wonder what the world's coming to. . . .
Young or old—it's hard to tell which are the most disgusting.
. . . Two "turns" before me! . . . and "the first appearances",
said the old spider, "the dazzling first appearances". . . . And
all quite openly. No, really, what a world!'

He found that he had been keeping up the pace of a professional walker in training, and that he was out of breath. And all
the more because the distant storm—which would not burst
over Paris—had walled off what breeze there was behind a vio-
let bastion, now towering straight up against the sky. Alongside
the fortifications of the Boulevard Berthier, under trees stripped
bare by the summer drought, a sparse crowd of Parisians in
rope-soled sandals and a few half-naked children in red jerseys
seemed to be waiting for a tidal wave to come rolling up from
Levallois-Perret. Chéri sat down on a bench, forgetting that his
strength was apt to play him tricks. He was unaware that his
strength was being sapped in some mysterious manner ever
since he had started to fritter it away on night vigils, and had
neglected to exercise or nourish his body.

' "Two turns!" Really! Two turns before me! And after me,
how many? Add the whole lot together, myself included, and
how many turns d'you get?'

Beside a blue-clad, seagull-hatted Léa, he could see a tall,
broad Spéleïeff, smiling expansively. He remembered a sad Léa,
red-eyed with weeping, stroking his head when he was a small
boy and calling him a "horrid little man in the making".

"Léa's lover" . . . "Léa's new pet" . . . Traditional and
meaningless words—as common on everyone's lips as talk about
the weather, the latest odds at Auteuil, or the dishonesty of
servants. "Are you coming, kid?" Spéleïeff would say to Chéri.
"We'll go out and have a porto at Armenonville, while we wait
for Léa to join us. Nothing would drag her out of bed this
morning."

"She's got a ravishing new little Bacciocchi," Madame
Peloux had informed her son, aged fourteen or fifteen at the
time.

But, a bundle of sophistication and innocence, brought up in the midst of love, yet blinded by its proximity, Chéri, at that tender age, had talked love, as children learn a language by ear, picking up words, pleasant or filthy, merely as sounds without meaning. No vivid or voluptuous vision arose behind the shadow of this huge Spéleïeff so recently risen from Léa's bed. And was there really very much difference between this "ravishing little Bacciocchi" and a "prize Pekingese"?

No photograph or letter, no story from the only lips that might have told him the truth, had blighted the enclosed Paradise in which Léa and Chéri had dwelt for so many years. Next to nothing in Chéri existed which dated back beyond Léa: why, then, should he bother about a man who, before his day, had brought warmth or sadness or riches to his mistress?

A fair-haired little boy with fat knees came and planted his crossed arms on the bench beside Chéri. They glared at each other with identical expressions of offended reserve, for Chéri treated all children as strangers. For some time this boy let his pale blue eyes rest on Chéri, who watched some sort of indescribable smile, full of scorn, mount up from the small anaemic mouth to the flax-blue pupils of the eyes. Then the child turned away, and, picking up his dirty toys from the dust, began to play at the foot of the bench, blotting Chéri out of existence. Then Chéri got up and walked away.

Half an hour later, he was lying in a warm, scented bath, clouded by some milky bath essence. He lay revelling in its luxury and comfort, in the soft lather of the soap, and in the remote faint sounds about the house, as though they were the rewards of an act of great courage, or else blessings he was tasting for the last time.

His wife came into the room humming, broke off at the sight of him, and narrowly failed to disguise her speechless astonishment at finding Chéri at home and in his bath.

"Am I in your way?" he asked, with no irony.

"Not in the least, Fred."

She began to take off her day clothes with youthful abandon, with total disregard for modesty or immodesty, and Chéri was amused by her haste to be undressed and in a bath.

'How completely I'd forgotten her,' he thought, as he looked at the odalisque back, supple but well-covered, of the woman bending down to untie her shoelaces.

She did not speak to him, but went about her business like a woman who believes she is safely by herself, and in front of his eyes rose the figure of the child who, not long since, had been playing in the dust at his feet, resolutely ignoring his presence.

"Tell me . . ."

Edmée raised a surprised forehead, a soft half-naked body.

"What would you say to our having a child?"

"Fred! . . . What are you thinking of?"

It was almost a cry of terror, and already Edmée was clutching a wisp of lawn close to her bosom with one hand, while with the other she groped, fumbling, for the first kimono within reach. Chéri could not hold back his laughter.

"Would you like my revolver? I'm not going to assault you."

"Why are you laughing?" she asked, almost in a whisper. "You should never laugh."

"I seldom laugh. But do tell me . . . now that all is quiet and peaceful between us . . . do tell me why. Are you really so terrified at the thought that we could have had, could still have, a child?"

"Yes," she said cruelly, and her unexpected frankness shocked even herself.

She never took her eyes off her husband, lying full length in a low armchair, and she murmured distinctly enough for him to hear, "A child . . . who'd be sure to take after you. You twice over, you twice over in the single lifetime of one woman? No. . . . Oh, no."

He began a gesture which she misinterpreted.

"No, I beg of you. . . . There's nothing more to be said. I

245

won't even discuss it. Let's leave things as they are. We've only to be a little cautious, and go on . . . I ask nothing of you . . ."

"That suits you?"

Her only answer was to put on a look, insulting in its misery and plaintive helplessness, a seraglio look that well suited her nakedness. Her freshly powdered cheeks, the touch of colour on her youthful lips, the light brown halo round her hazel eyes, the care bestowed on every feature of her face, were in striking contrast to the confusion of her body, bare except for the crumpled silk shift she was clasping to her breasts.

'I can no longer make her happy,' thought Chéri, 'but I can still make her suffer. She is not altogether unfaithful to me. Whereas I am not untrue to her . . . I have deserted her.'

Turning away from him, she began to dress. She had regained her freedom of movement and her disingenuous tolerance. The palest of pink frocks now hid from view the woman who, a moment since, had pressed her last stitch of clothing to her bosom, as though to a wound.

She had recovered, too, her buoyant determination, her desire to live and hold sway, her prodigious and feminine aptitude for happiness. Chéri despised her afresh; but a moment came when the rays of the evening sun, shining through her transparent pink dress, outlined the shape of a young woman who no longer bore any semblance to the wounded Circassian: a heaven-aspiring form, as supple and vigorous as a serpent about to strike.

'I can still hurt her, but how quickly she recovers! In this house, too, I am no longer needed, no longer expected. She has gone far beyond me, and is going further: I am, the old creature would say, her "first turn". It's now for me to follow her example, if only I could. But I can't. And then would I, if I could? Unlike some of us, Edmee has never come up against what one meets only once in a lifetime and is floored by completely. Spéleïeff was fond of saying that, after a really bad crash—which, however, involved no broken bones—some horses would let themselves be killed rather than take the fence again. I am just the same.'

He cast about for further sporting, and rather brutal, metaphors that would make his own fall and misfortunes seem an accident. But he had started his night too early, and, dog-tired, his dreams were haunted by sweet ghosts in sky-blue flounces, and half-remembered figures from the pages of the imperishable literature which finds its way into tawdry love-nests, from tales and poems dedicated to constancy and to lovers undivided in death: writings irresistible to adolescents and time-worn courtesans, who are akin in their credulity and passion for romance.

"Then she said to me: 'I know who's at the back of all this: it's Charlotte again, making mischief about me. . . .' 'It's no more than you deserve,' I told her, 'you've only to stop going to see Charlotte as much as you do, and trusting her with all your secrets.' She retorted: 'I'm a much closer friend of Charlotte's than of Spéleïeff's and I've known her far longer. I assure you Charlotte, Neuilly, bezique and the child would be a far greater loss to me than Spéleïeff—you can't change the habits of a lifetime.' 'That doesn't prevent your faith in Charlotte costing you a pretty penny,' I said. 'Oh! well,' was her answer, 'what's good is worth paying for.' That's her all over, you'll agree: big-hearted and generous but no fool. And with that she went off to dress for the Races—she told me she was going to the Races with a gigolo. . . ."

"With me!" Chéri exclaimed bitterly. "Am I right? It was me?"

"I don't deny it. I simply tell you things as they took place. A white dress—of white crêpe-de-chine—Oriental-looking, edged with blue Chinese embroidery, the very dress you see her in here, in this snapshot, taken at the Races. And nothing will get it out of my head that this man's shoulder you can see behind her is you."

"Fetch it me!" Chéri ordered.

The old woman got up, pulled out the rusty drawing-pins tacking the photograph to the wall, and brought it back to Chéri. Lolling on the Algerian divan, he raised a tousled head, and, barely running his eyes over it, flung the snapshot across the room.

"When have you seen me wearing a collar that gapes at the back, and a short coat to go to the Races? Come, think again! I don't find that sort of thing at all funny."

She ventured a tut-tut of timid censure, bent her stiff knees to pick up the photograph, and went on to open the door into the passage.

"Where are you going?"

"I can hear the water for my coffee boiling. I'm going to pour it out."

"Good. But come back here again."

She disappeared in a shuffle of rustling taffeta and heelless slippers. Left to himself, Chéri settled his neck against the mo-quette cushion stamped with Tunisian designs. A new and star-tlingly bright Japanese kimono, embellished with pink wistaria on a ground of amethyst, had replaced his coat and waistcoat. The fag-end of a too-far-smoked cigarette was almost burning his lips, and his hair, falling fanwise down to the level of his eyebrows, half covered his forehead.

Wearing so feminine and flowered a garment did not make his appearance in any way ambiguous: he merely acquired an ignominious majesty that stamped every feature with its proper value. He seemed bent on death and destruction, and the photo-graph had flashed like a blade from his hand as he hurled it from him. Hard, delicate bones in his cheeks moved to the rhythm of his working jaws. The whites of his eyes flickered in the dark-ness round him like the crest of a wave, with the moonbeams interruptedly following its course.

Left alone, however, he let his head sink back against the cushion, and closed his eyes.

249

"Lord!" exclaimed the Pal coming back into the room, "you'll not look more handsome when laid out on your death-bed! I've brought in the coffee. Would you care for some? Such an aroma! It will waft you to the Isles of the Blest."

"Yes. Two lumps."

His words were curt, and she obeyed with a humility that suggested, perhaps, a deep subservient pleasure.

"You didn't eat anything for dinner?"

"I had enough."

He drank his coffee, without moving, supporting himself on one elbow. An Oriental curtain, draped like a canopy, hung from the ceiling directly above the divan, and in its shade lay an ivory and enamel Chéri, robed in exquisite silks, reclining upon an old worn dust-bedraggled rug.

The Pal set out, piece by piece upon a brass-topped table, the coffee-set, an opium lamp capped with a glass cowl, two pipes, the pot of paste, the silver snuff-box used for cocaine, and a flask, which, tight-stoppered as it was, failed to control the cold and treacherously volatile expansion of the ether. To these she added a pack of tarot cards, a case of poker chips, and a pair of spectacles, before settling herself down with the apologetic air of a trained hospital nurse.

"I've already told you," grunted Chéri, "all that paraphernalia means nothing to me."

Once again she stretched out her sickly white hands in pro-testation. In her own home she adopted what she called her "Charlotte Corday style": hair flowing loose, and wide white linen fichus crossed over her dusty mourning, looking a mixture of decorum and fallen virtue—like a heroine of the Salpêtrière Prison.

"No matter, Chéri. They're just in case. And it does make me so happy to see the whole of my little armoury set out in its proper order under my eyes. The arsenal of dreams! the munitions of ecstasy! the gateway to illusion!"

She nodded her long head and looked up to the ceiling, with the compassionate eyes of a grandmother who ruins herself on toys. Her guest partook of none of her potions. Some sort of physical sense of honour still survived in him, and his disdain for drugs was akin to his distaste for brothels.

For a number of days—he had kept no count of them—he had found his way to this black hole, presided over by an attendant Norn. Ungraciously, and in terms that brooked no argument, he had paid her for food, coffee and her own liqueurs, and for his personal requirements in the way of cigarettes, fruit, ice and soft drinks. He had commanded his slave to buy the sumptuous Japanese robe, scents and expensive soaps. She was moved less by desire for money than by the pleasure of acting as an accomplice. She devoted herself to Chéri with enthusiasm, a revival of her old zeal as a missionary of vice who, with garrulous and culpable alacrity, would divest and bathe a virgin, cook an opium pellet, and pour out intoxicating spirits or ether. This apostolate was fruitless, for her singular guest brought back no paramour, drank soft drinks only, stretched himself on the dusty divan and delivered only one word of command: "Talk."

She did talk, following, she believed, her own fancies; but, now brutally, now subtly, he would direct the muddied meanderings of her reminiscences. She talked like a sewing-woman who comes in by the day, with the continuous, stupefying monotony of creatures whose days are given over to long and sedentary tasks. But she never did any sewing, for she had the aristocratic unpracticalness of a former prostitute. While talking, she would pin a pleat over a hole or stain, and take up again the business of tarot cards and patience. She would put on gloves to grind coffee bought by the charwoman, and then handle greasy cards without turning a hair.

She talked, and Chéri listened to her soporific voice and the shuffle of her felted slippers. He reclined at ease, magnificently robed, in the ill-kempt lodging. His guardian dared ask no questions. She knew enough: he was a monomaniac, as his abstemiousness proved. The illness for which she was ministering was mysterious; but it was an illness. She took the risk of inviting, as from a sense of duty, a very pretty young woman, childish and professionally gay. Chéri paid her neither more nor less attention than he would a puppy, and said to the Pal, "Are we going to have any more of your fashionable parties?"

She did not require snubbing a second time, and he never

251
....

had cause to bind her to secrecy. One day she almost hit upon the simple truth, when she proposed asking in two or three of her friends of the good old days; Léa, for instance. He never batted an eyelid.

"Not a soul. Or I'll have to hunt out some better hole."

A fortnight went by, as funereal in its routine as life in a monastery; but it did not pall on either recluse. During the daytime, the Pal set forth on her old woman's junketings; poker parties, nips of whisky, and poisonous gossip, hole-and-corner gambling-dens, lunches of "regional dishes" in the stuffy darkness of a Norman or Limousin restaurant. Chéri would arrive with the first shadow of evening, sometimes drenched to the skin. She would recognise the slam of his taxi-door and no longer asked: "But why do you never come in your motor?"

He would leave after midnight, and usually before day-break. During his prolonged sessions on the Algerian divan, the Pal sometimes saw him drop off to sleep and remain for an instant or two with his neck twisted against his shoulder, as though caught in a snare. She never slept herself till after his departure, having forgotten the need for repose. Only once, in the small hours of the morning, while he was putting back, meticulously and one by one, the contents of his pockets—key on its chain, note-case, little flat revolver, handkerchief, ciga-rette-case of green gold—did she dare to ask: "Doesn't your wife begin to wonder, when you come in so late?"

Chéri raised long eyebrows above eyes grown larger from lack of sleep: "No. Why? She knows perfectly well I've been up to no harm."

"No child, of course, is easier to manage than you are. . . . Shall you be coming again this evening?"

"I don't know. I'll see. Carry on as if I were coming for certain."

Once more he gazed long at all the lily necks, all the blue eyes, that flowered on one wall of his sanctuary, before he went his way, only to return again, faithfully, some twelve hours later.

* * *

By roundabout ways he considered cunning, he would lead the Pal to talk of Léa, then he would clear the narrative of all bawdy asides that might retard it. "Skip it. Skip it!" Barely bothering to enunciate the words, he relied on the initial sibilants to speed up or curtail the monologue. He would listen only to stories without malice in them, and glorifications of a purely descriptive nature. He insisted upon strict respect for documentary truth and checked his chronicler peevishly. He stocked his mind with dates, colours, materials, and places, and the names of dressmakers.

"What's poplin?" he fired at her pointblank.

"Poplin's a mixture of silk and wool, a dry material . . . if you know what I mean; one that doesn't stick to the skin."

"Yes. And mohair? You said 'of white mohair.' "

"Mohair is a kind of alpaca, but it hangs better, of course. Léa was afraid to wear lawn in the summer: she maintained that it was best for underwear and handkerchiefs. Her own lingerie was fit for a queen, you'll remember, and in the days when that photograph was taken—yes, that beauty over there with the long legs—they didn't wear the plain underclothes of to-day. It was frill upon frill, a foam, a flurry of snow; and the drawers, dear boy! they'd have sent your head whirling. . . . White Chantilly lace at the sides and black Chantilly in between. Can't you just see the effect? But *can* you imagine it?"

'Revolting,' thought Chéri, 'revolting. Black Chantilly in between. A woman doesn't wear black Chantilly in between simply to please herself. In front of whose eyes did she wear them? For whom?'

He could see Léa's gesture as he entered her bathroom or boudoir—the furtive gesture as she drew her wrap across her body. He could see the chaste self-confidence of her rosy body as she lay naked in the bath, with the water turned to milk by some essence or other. . . . 'But, for others, she wore drawers of Chantilly lace. . . .'

253

He kicked one of the hay-stuffed moquette cushions to the floor.

"Are you too warm, Chéri?"

"No. Let me have another look at that photo . . . the large framed one. Tilt the what's-its name of your lamp up a bit . . . a bit more . . . that's it!"

Abandoning his usual circumspection, he applied a searching eye to the study of every detail that was new to him, and almost refreshing. 'A high-waisted belt with cameos! . . . Never saw that about the place. And boots like buskins! Was she wearing tights? No, of course not, her toes are bare. Revolting. . . .'

"At whose house did she wear that costume?"

"I don't rightly remember. . . . A reception at the club, I believe . . . or at Molier's."

He handed back the frame at arm's length, to all appearances disdainful and bored. He left shortly afterwards, under an overcast sky, towards the close of a night that smelt of wood smoke and dankness.

He was deteriorating physically and took no account of it. He was losing weight through eating and sleeping too little, walking and smoking too much, thus bartering his obvious vigour for a lightness, an apparent return to youth, which the light of day repudiated. At home, he lived as he pleased, welcoming or running away from guests and callers. All that they knew of him was his name, his almost petrified good looks fined down little by little under an accusing chisel, and the inconceivable ease with which he would ignore them.

So he eked out his peaceful and carefully regimented despair until the last days of October. Then, one afternoon, he was seized by a fit of hilarity, because he caught a glimpse of his wife's unsuspected terror. His whole face lit up with the merriment of a man impervious to all feeling. 'She thinks I'm mad. What luck!'

His merriment was short-lived: for, on thinking it over, he came to the conclusion that, where the brute and the madman are concerned, the brute wins every time. She was frightened of the madman; otherwise would she not have stood her ground, biting her lips and forcing back her tears, in order to worst the brute?

'I am no longer even considered wicked,' he thought bitterly. 'And that's because I am no longer wicked. Oh! the harm the woman I left has done to me! Yet others left her, and she left others. . . . How, I wonder, does Bacciocchi exist at the present time? or Septfons, Spéleïeff, and all the rest of them? But what have we got in common, I and the rest of them? She called me "little bourgeois" because I counted the bottles in the cellar. "Little bourgeois", "faithful heart", "great lover"—those were her names for me—those were my real names: and, though she watched my departure with tears glistening in her eyes, she is still herself, Léa, who prefers old age to me, who sits in the corner by the fire counting over on her fingers: "I've had What's-his-name, and Thingummy-bob, and Chéri, and So-and-so . . ." I thought she belonged to me alone, and never perceived that I was only one among her lovers. Is there anyone left, now, that I am not ashamed of?'

Hardened by now to the exercise of impassivity, he sought to endure the capricious hauntings of such thoughts with resignation, and to be worthy of the devil by which he was possessed. Proud and dry-eyed, with a lighted match held between steady fingers, he looked sideways at his mother, well aware of her watchful eye. Once his cigarette was alight, with a little encouragement he would have strutted like a peacock in front of an invisible public, and taunted his tormentors with a "Good, isn't it?" In a confused way, the strength born of his dissimulation and resistance was gathering in his inmost self. He was beginning now to enjoy his extreme state of detachment, and dimly perceived that an emotional storm could be just as valuable and refreshing as a lull, and that in it he might discover the wisdom which never came to him in calmer moods. As a child, Chéri frequently had taken advantage of a genuine fit of temper, by changing it into a peevishness that would bring him what he wanted. To-day he was fast approaching the point at which, having attained to a definite state of unhappiness, he could rely on it to settle everything.

One gusty, wind-swept, September afternoon, with leaves sailing straight across the sky—an afternoon of blue rifts in the clouds and scattered raindrops—Chéri felt an urge to visit his dark retreat and its attendant, garbed in black, with a touch of white on the chest like a scavenging cat. He was feeling buoyant, and avid for confidences, though these would be sickly, like the fruit of the arbutus and as prickly leaved. Words and phrases of special though ill-defined significance kept running in his head: "Her monogram embroidered in hair on all her lingerie; dear boy, in golden hairs from her own head . . . faery handicraft! And, did I tell you, her masseuse used to pluck the hairs from the calves of her leg, one by one. . . ."

He turned round and left the window. He found Charlotte on a chair looking thoughtfully up at him; and in the restless waters of her great eyes he saw the formation of a prodigious, rounded, crystalline, glistening sphere which detached itself from the bronzed pupil, and then vanished, evaporating in the heat of her flushed cheek. Chéri felt flattered and cheered. 'How kind of her! She's weeping for me.'

An hour later, he found his ancient accomplice at her post. But she was wearing some sort of parson's hat, bunched up with shiny black ribbon, and she held out to him a sheet of blue paper, which he waved aside.

"What's that? . . . I haven't the time. Tell me what's written on it."

The Pal lifted puzzled eyes to his: "It's my mother."

"Your mother? You're joking."

She did her best to appear offended. "I'm not joking at all. Please respect the departed! She is dead." And she added, by way of an excuse, "She was eighty-three!"

"Congratulations. Are you going out?"

"No; I'm going away."

"Where to?"

"To Tarascon, and from there I take a little branch line train that puts me down at . . ."

"For how long?"

"Four or five days . . . at least. There's the solicitor to be seen about the will, because my younger sister . . ."

He burst out, hands to heaven: "A sister now! Why not four children into the bargain?" He was conscious of the unexpectedly high-pitched tone of his voice and controlled it. "Good, very well. What d'you expect me to do about it? Be off, be off. . . ."

"I was going to leave word for you. I'm catching the 7.30."

"Catch the 7.30."

"The time of the funeral service is not mentioned in the telegram: my sister speaks only of the laying out, the climate down there is very hot, they'll have to get through it very quickly, only the business side can keep me there, and over that one has no control."

"Of course, of course."

He was walking to and fro, from the door to the wall with the photographs and back to the door again, and in doing so he knocked against a squashed old travelling-bag. The coffee-pot and cups were steaming on the table.

"I made you your coffee, come what might. . . ."

"Thanks."

They drank standing up, as at a station, and the chill of departure gripped Chéri by the throat and made his teeth chatter secretly.

"Goodbye, then, dear boy," said the Pal. "You may be sure that I'll hurry things as much as I can."

"Goodbye—pleasant journey."

They shook hands, and she did not dare to kiss him. "Won't you stay here for a little while?"

He looked all round in great agitation. "No. No."

"Take the key, then?"

"Why should I?"

"You're at home here. You've fallen into the habit of it. I've told Maria to come every day at five and light a good fire and get the coffee ready. . . . So take my key, won't you? . . ."

With a limp hand he took the key, and it struck him as enormous. Once outside, he longed to throw it away or take it back to the concierge.

The old woman took courage on her way between her own door and the street, loading him with instructions as she might a child of twelve.

"The electric-light switch is on your left as you go in. The kettle is always on the gas-stove in the kitchen, and all you have to do is put a match to it. And your Japanese robe—Maria has her instructions to leave it folded at the head of the divan and the cigarettes in their usual place."

Chéri nodded affirmation once or twice, with the look of courageous unconcern of a schoolboy on the last morning of the holidays. And, when he was alone, it did not occur to him to make fun of his old retainer with the dyed hair, who had placed the proper value both on the last prerogatives of the dead and on the little pleasures of one whom all had now deserted.

The following morning, he awoke from an indecipherable dream, in which a crush of people were all running in the same direction. Though he saw only their backs, each was known to him. As they hurried by, he identified his mother, Léa—unaccountably naked, and out of breath—Desmond, the Pal, and young Maudru . . . Edmée was the only one to turn and smile at him, with the grating little smile of a marten. "But it's the marten Ragut caught in the Vosges!" Chéri cried out in his dream, and this discovery pleased him immeasurably. Then he checked and recounted all the one-way runners, saying over to himself: 'There's one missing. . . . There's one missing. . . .' Once out of his dream, on this side of awakening, it came to him that the one missing was none other than himself: 'I must get back into it. . . .' But the efforts of exerting every limb, like an insect caught on flypaper, served only to widen the bar of blue between his eyelids, and he emerged into that real world in which he was frittering away his time and his strength. He stretched out his legs, and bathed them in a fresh, cool part of the sheets. 'Edmée must have got up some time ago.'

He was surprised to see beneath the window a new garden of marguerites and heliotrope, for in his memory there was only a summer garden of blue and pink. He rang, and the sound of the bell brought to life a maid whose face was unfamiliar.

"Where is Henriette?"

"I've taken her place, sir."

"Since when?"

"Why—for the last month, sir."

He ejaculated an "Ah!", as much as to say, "That explains everything."

"Where's your mistress?"

"Madame is just coming, sir. Madame is ready to go out."

Edmée, indeed, did appear, as large as life, but stopped just inside the door in so marked a manner that Chéri was secretly amused. He allowed himself the pleasure of upsetting his wife a little by exclaiming, "But it's Ragut's marten!" and watching her pretty eyes waver under his gaze.

"Fred, I . . ."

"Yes, you're going out. I never heard you get up."

She coloured slightly. "There's nothing extraordinary in that. I've been sleeping so badly these last few nights, that I've had a bed made up on the divan in the boudoir. You're not doing anything special to-day, are you?"

"But I am," he replied darkly.

"Is it important?"

"Very important." He took his time, and finished on a lighter note: "I'm going to have my hair cut."

"But will you be back for luncheon?"

"No; I'll have a cutlet in Paris. I've made an appointment at Gustave's for a quarter past two. The man who usually comes to cut my hair is ill."

He was childishly courteous, the lie flowering effortlessly

259

on his lips. Because he was lying, his mouth took on its boyhood mould—poutingly provocative and rounded for a kiss. Edmée looked at him with an almost masculine satisfaction.

"You're looking well this morning, Fred. . . . I must fly."

"Are you catching the 7.30?"

She stared at him, struck dumb, and fled so precipitately that he was still laughing when the front door slammed behind her.

'Ah! that does me good,' he sighed. 'How easy it is to laugh when you no longer expect anything from anyone. . . .' Thus, while he was dressing, did he discover for himself the nature of asceticism, and the tuneless little song he hummed through pursed lips kept him company like a silly young nun.

He went down to a Paris he had forgotten. The crowd upset his dubious emotional balance, now so dependent on a crystalline vacuity and the daily routine of suffering.

In the Rue Royale he came face to face with his own full-length reflection at the moment when the brightness of noon broke through the rain-clouds. Chéri wasted no thoughts on this crude new self-portrait, which stood out sharply against a background of newsvendors and shopgirls, flanked by jade necklaces and silver fox furs. The fluid feeling in his stomach, which he compared to a speck of lead bobbing about inside a celluloid ball, must come, he thought, from lack of sustenance, and he took refuge in a restaurant.

With his back to a glass partition, screened from the light of day, he lunched off selected oysters, fish and fruit. Some young women sitting not far away had no eyes for him, and this gave him a pleasant feeling, like that of a chilly bunch of violets laid on closed eyelids. But the smell of his coffee suddenly brought home the need to rise and keep the appointment of which this smell was an urgent reminder. Before obeying the summons, he went to his hairdresser's, held out his hands to be manicured, and slipped off into a few moments' inestimable repose, while expert fingers substituted their will for his.

The enormous key obstructed his pocket. 'I won't go, I won't go! . . .' To the cadence of some such insistent, meaningless refrain, he found his way without mishap to the Avenue de Villiers. His clumsy fumbling round the lock and the rasp of the key made his heart beat momentarily faster, but the cheerful warmth in the passage calmed his nerves.

He went forward cautiously, lord of this empire of a few square feet, which he now owned but did not know. The useless daily arrangement of the armoury had been laid out on the table by the well-trained charwoman, and an earthenware coffee-pot stood in the midst of charcoal embers already dying under the velvet of warm ashes. Methodically, Chéri emptied his pockets and set out one by one his cigarette case, the huge key, his own small key, the flat revolver, his note-case, handkerchief, and watch; but when he had put on his Japanese robe, he did not lie down on the divan. With the silent curiosity of a cat he opened doors and peered into cupboards. His peculiar prudishness shrank back before a primitive but distinctively feminine lavatory. The bedroom, all bed and little else, also was decorated in the mournful shade of red that seems to settle in on those of declining years; it smelt of old bachelors and eau-de-Cologne. Chéri returned to the drawing-room. He switched on the two wall lamps and the beribboned chandelier. He listened to faint far away sounds and, now that he was alone for the first time in this poor lodging, began trying out on himself the influence of its previous inmates—birds of passage or else dead. He thought he heard and recognised a familiar footstep, a slipshod, shambling old animal pad-pad, then shook his head: 'It can't be hers. She won't be back for a week, and when she does come back, what will there be left for me in this world? I'll have . . .'

Inwardly he listened to the Pal's voice, the worn-out voice of a tramp. "But wait till I finish the story of the famous slanging-match between Léa and old Mortier at the Races. Old Mortier thought that with the aid of a little publicity in *Gil Blas* he would get all he wanted out of Léa. Oh! la la, my pretties, what a donkey he made of himself! She drove out to Longchamp—a dream of blue—as statuesque as a goddess, in her victoria drawn by a pair of piebalds. . . ."

He raised his hand towards the wall in front of him, where so many blue eyes were smiling, where so many swan-necks were preening themselves above imperturbable bosoms. '. . . I'll have all this. All this, and nothing more. It's true, perhaps, that this is a good deal. I've found her again, by a happy chance, found her here on this wall. But I've found her, only to lose her again for ever. I am still held up, like her, by these few rusty nails, by these pins stuck in slantwise. How much longer can this go on? Not very long. And then, knowing myself as I do, I'm afraid I shall demand more than this. I may suddenly cry out: "I want her! I must have her! Now! at this very moment!" Then what will become of me?'

He pushed the divan closer to the illustrated wall and there lay down. And as he lay there, all the Léas, with their downward gazing eyes, seemed to be showing concern for him: 'But they only *seem* to be looking down at me, I know perfectly well. When you sent me away, my Nounoune, what did you think there was left for me after you? Your noble action cost you little —you knew the worth of a Chéri—your risk was negligible. But we've been well punished, you and I: you, because you were born so long before me, and I, because I loved you above all other women. You're finished now, you have found your consolation—and what a disgrace that is!—whereas I . . . As long as people say, "There was the War," I can say "There was Léa." 'Léa, the War . . . I never imagined I'd dream of either of them again, yet the two together have driven me outside the times I live in. Henceforth, there is nowhere in the world where I can occupy more than half a place. . . .'

He pulled the table nearer to consult his watch. 'Half-past five. The old creature won't be back here for another week. And this is the first day. Supposing she were to die on the way?'

He fidgeted on his divan, smoked, poured himself out a cup of luke-warm coffee. 'A week. All the same, I mustn't ask too much of myself. In a week's time . . . which story will she be telling me? I know them off by heart—the one about the Four-in-Hand Meet, the one about the slanging-match at Longchamp, the one about the final rupture—and when I've heard every one, every twist and turn of them, what will there be left? Nothing, absolutely nothing. In a week's time, this old woman—and I'm already so impatient for her, she might be going to give me an injection—this old woman will be here, and . . . and she'll bring me nothing at all.'

He lifted beseeching eyes to his favourite photograph. Already this speaking likeness filled him with less resentment, less ecstasy, less heartbreak. He turned from side to side on the hard mattress, unable to prevent his muscles from contracting, like a man who aches to jump from a height, but lacks the courage.

He worked himself up till he groaned aloud, repeating over and over again "Nounoune", to make himself believe he was frantic. But he fell silent, ashamed, for he knew very well that he did not need to be frantic to pick up the little flat revolver from the table. Without rising, he experimented in finding a convenient position. Finally he lay down with his right arm doubled up under him. Holding the weapon in his right hand, he pressed his ear against the muzzle, which was buried in the cushions. At once his arm began to grow numb, and he realised that if he did not make haste his tingling fingers would refuse to obey him. So he made haste, whimpering muffled complaints as he completed his task, because his forearm was hurting, crushed under the weight of his body. He knew nothing more, beyond the pressure of his forefinger on a little lever of tempered steel.

263

FINIS

About the Author

Sidonie Gabrielle Colette (1873–1954) was one of the most famous and honored French writers of this century. The first woman member of The Academie Goncourt, a holder of the Grand Cross of the Legion of Honor, she was also the first woman in French history to be granted a state funeral.

Colette began her writing career in collaboration with Willy, her husband. In 1900, when she was twenty-seven, Colette's first novel, *Claudine at School*, was published and became a sensational success. During the next few years, several *Claudine* books followed. After divorcing Willy, Colette earned her living as a music-hall mime, and in 1907, her first independent novel appeared, *Retreat from Love*.

With the outbreak of World War I, Colette began a career as a special correspondent in Rome and Venice and as a contributor to *Le Matin*, a leading Paris daily. Her journalism included dramatic criticism, law-court reporting, and sketches of contemporary life. During this time, Colette continued to write novels.

During her last years, Colette, crippled by arthritis and confined to her Paris apartment, wrote reminiscences and descriptive works that gained her new renown. Before her death in 1954, at the age of eighty-one, Colette had written more than fifty books and was best known as the creator of *Gigi*, *Chéri* and *The Last of Chéri*, and the *Claudine* novels. Her place in twentieth-century fiction is comparable among her countrymen only with that of Proust.